THE
HOUDINI
SPECTER

TITAN BOOKS BY DANIEL STASHOWER

THE HARRY HOUDINI MYSTERIES

The Dime Museum Murders
The Floating Lady Murder
The Houdini Specter

THE FURTHER ADVENTURES OF SHERLOCK HOLMES

The Ectoplasmic Man

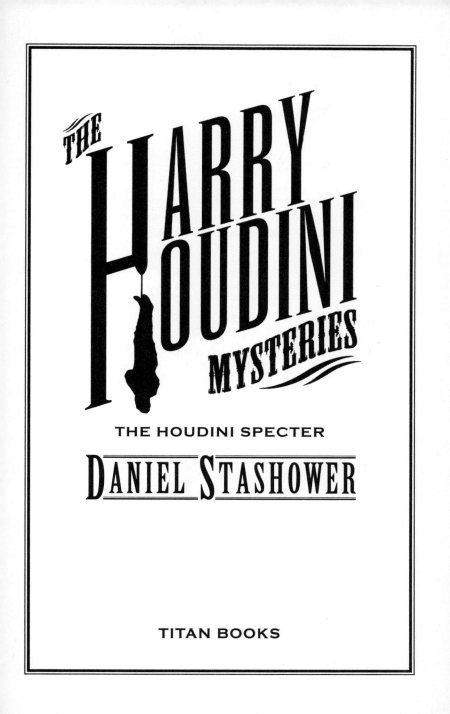

THE HARRY HOUDINI MYSTERIES

THE HOUDINI SPECTER

DANIEL STASHOWER

TITAN BOOKS

THE HARRY HOUDINI MYSTERIES: THE HOUDINI SPECTER

PRINT EDITION ISBN: 9780857682932

E-BOOK ISBN: 9780857686213

Published by Titan Books
A division of Titan Publishing Group Ltd
144 Southwark St, London SE1 0UP

First edition: June 2012

2 4 6 8 10 9 7 5 3 1

Names, places and incidents are either products of the author's imagination or used fictitiously. Any resemblance to actual persons, living or dead (except for satirical purposes), is entirely coincidental.

Visit our website: www.titanbooks.com

A CIP catalogue record for this title is available from the British Library

Printed and bound in the USA.

What did you think of this book? We love to hear from our readers. Please email us at: readerfeedback@titanemail.com, or write to us at the above address.

To receive advance information, news, competitions, and exclusive offers online, please sign up for the Titan newsletter on our website: www.titanbooks.com

THE
HOUDINI
SPECTER

~~≈ 1 ≈~~

THE MAN WITH THE CAST-IRON STOMACH

MONSTROUS.

The old man shifted on his walking stick and gazed sadly at the vast expanse of stone before him. It was not only vulgar but also profane, a bizarre collision of ego and some misplaced sense of piety. It offended every notion of taste and decency. The sheer ostentation might have brought a blush to the cheek of Croesus. Naturally, Harry had thought it was lovely.

Why couldn't he have allowed himself to be buried like a normal person? With a small, tasteful marker of some sort? No, not Harry. He had to go out with a flourish. A thousand tons of granite had been spoiled to create this eyesore, along with a considerable amount of Italian marble. What had they called it at the time? A Greek exedra? That presumably described the curved stone bench that invited silent contemplation. But how to explain the stone figure of the kneeling woman sobbing at the graveside? Over the years, the old man had given her the name Beulah. "Hello, Beulah," he would say, patting her fondly on the shoulder as he passed. "How are the pigeons treating you today?"

His feet were tired from the long walk, and the old man gave out a soft groan as he lowered himself onto the bench, gazing up at the solemn bust of his brother. Here was the crowning touch, he thought to himself. Harry in all his glory, stone-faced in death as he so often was in life, gazing magisterially over the other, presumably lesser, inhabitants of the Machpelah Cemetery. What would Rabbi Samuel Weiss have made of this display? Thou shalt not worship graven images.

With his eyes fixed on the marble bust, the old man reached into the pocket of his brown tick-weave jacket and withdrew a silver flask. *Well*, he thought, lifting the flask in a brisk salute, *another year gone, Harry. Here's to you, you pompous old goat.*

I miss you.

Mrs. Doggett was waiting on the porch when the old man returned to the house in Flatbush. "Those men are here," she said in a voice heavy with exasperation. "Again."

"Those men?" he asked.

"The reporters. From the city."

"Ah."

"It's the same two men," she continued. "One of them is a photographer. They're in the parlor, smoking like wet coal. I don't know why you speak to them every year. It only encourages them."

"You know why I speak to them," he answered, tugging at his French cuffs. "He would have wanted it that way."

"Him," she answered. "Always him."

Mrs. Doggett continued to give voice to her displeasure as she led him into the front room. Newspaper reporters ranked just below potted meat and Estes Kefauver in her esteem. Newspaper reporters who smoked were to be especially despised, more so if they also made slurping noises when they drank their tea.

The old man was no longer listening. He had come to expect this annual visitation from Matthews of the *Herald*, and he had passed a quiet hour at his brother's exedra preparing himself. This year, he had decided, he would try something different. At the start of the interview, he would allow Matthews to believe that he had gone senile. *What's a man to do, Mr. Matthews? You just can't get good fish paste any more. That's what's wrong with this country, my lad. And you can tell that to Mr. Estes Kefauver when you see him.*

Nothing more than a reverse bait and switch; a little something to keep himself entertained. He would wait until Matthews began stealing glances at his watch and then spring the trap. *What's that, Mr. Matthews? You need to be getting back to the city? What a shame. I was just about to tell you what happened to Lucius Craig. You remember him, do you? Yes, his disappearance was something of a scandal at the time. Left half the society matrons in New York brokenhearted, as I recall. I read an article just the other day speculating as to what might have become of him. Should have asked me. I've known for years.*

Interesting man, Mr. Craig. There were some who believed he could speak with the dead. I saw him do some amazing things myself. Spirit messages. Disembodied voices. That sort of thing. I always wondered if—pardon? You want to know what happened to him? Well, Mr. Matthews, I guess there's no easy way to say this.

And here the Great Hardeen would pause and gaze sadly into the distance. *You see, Mr. Matthews, I'm afraid my brother and I made him disappear.*

Permanently.

The old man smiled to himself, then pushed open the parlor door to face his interviewer.

What's that, Mr. Matthews? You'd like to hear the story? But I thought you and Mr. Parker had to be getting back—? No? Well, I can't blame you for wanting to know the truth of the matter. It was front page news at the time and one of the many secrets that the Great Houdini vowed to take to the grave. Me, I'll be content to go to my grave unburdened. Let me see if I can remember how it began. Ah, yes. Biggs. It all started with Biggs.

I seem to recall that the newspapers were filled with accounts of Commodore Dewey destroying the Spanish fleet, which I suppose places things in the late spring of 1898. Harry would have just turned twenty-four at the time; I was two years younger. As always, our finances were at a low ebb. We had recently been fortunate enough to pull a couple of months as touring assistants with Mr. Harry Kellar's illusion show, but at the close of the season we were once again at liberty. We came back to New York, where Harry had been forced to sign on as a platform magician at Huber's Fourteenth Street Museum. It was steady work but strictly small-time, and Harry considered it beneath him. I spent my days making the rounds with his leather-bound press book under my arm, trying to scare up suitable opportunities among the more reputable music halls and variety theaters. I was not wildly successful in this regard, and more than once I abandoned my duties in favor of Ganson's Billiards Hall on Houston.

My recollection is that it was raining heavily on that particular day. Bess was working the chorus at Ravelsen's Review on Thompson Street, and it was a source of some consternation for Harry that her position brought a slightly higher wage than he was earning at the dime museum. I caught up with him backstage at Huber's, where he was pulling a double shift in the Hall of Curiosities.

"Intolerable, Dash!" Harry cried as he came off between shows. He was wearing a feather headdress and a leather singlet for his role as the laconic Running Deer, Last of the Comanche Wizards. His skin was slathered with copperish paste, and there were heavy streaks of lip polish on his cheeks, meant to suggest war paint. "You will have to find something better!" he continued, tossing aside a wooden tomahawk. "I am required to do a degradingly simple rope trick and spout ridiculous noises! 'Hoonga-boonga!' Have you ever heard of an Indian saying 'Hoonga-boonga'?"

"I never heard of an Indian doing the Cut and Restored Rope, now that you mention it."

"At the very least they could have employed Bess as well. She could have played my squaw."

"Bess seems quite content," I answered. "She prefers a singing engagement to working as your assistant. She says she's tired of jumping in and out of boxes."

"She said that?" He leaned into a dressing table mirror to dab at his war paint. "I suppose she is trying to put a brave face on the situation. Yes, that must be it. But at heart I am quite certain that she finds these circumstances as unacceptable as I do. It simply won't do for the wife of the Great Houdini to be seen cavorting in some music hall chorus. I have my reputation to consider!"

"Reputation? Harry, you're lucky to be working back at Huber's. Albert only took you on because he needed someone who could double as a Fire-Proof Man."

"Fire-Proof Man! Of all the indignities! Clutching at a piece of hot coal to show that one is impervious to pain! Thrusting one's hand into a flaming brazier! Ludicrous! The Great Houdini is now reduced to a mere sideshow attraction!"

"How's the arm, by the way?"

"Fine," he answered, wincing slightly. "I just need a bit more practice, that's all." He pushed a feather out of his eyes and adjusted the headdress. "Dash, you must get me out of this booking. Find something where I can do the escape act. It is the only way I will ever break out of the small time. If you do not"—he paused and drew in a deep breath—"I shall be forced to seek other representation."

"Other representation?" I ran a hand through my hair. "Harry, you're welcome to seek other representation, but you'll find that there's a crucial difference between me and the other business managers you may run across."

"Such as?"

"The others expect to be paid."

Harry folded his arms, the very picture of a stoic Comanche. "I'm just asking you to show a bit more initiative, Dash."

"Harry, I'm doing all I can. I have an appointment with Hector Platt at the end of the afternoon."

"Hector Platt?"

"He runs a talent agency near Bleeker Street. He's about the only one in New York who hasn't turned me down flat in the past three weeks. You're welcome to tag along if you think I should be showing more initiative."

I regretted the words as soon as they were out of my mouth. For the rest of the afternoon, Harry could talk of nothing but his "rendezvous with destiny" in the offices of Hector Platt. On stage he appeared newly invigorated, and even the expression "Hoonga-boonga" was given an enthusiastic spin. Between performances he drew me aside to speak in hushed tones of the "celebrated and distinguished Mr. Platt," who would surely be the one to propel the Great Houdini into the front rank of vaudeville. "Mine is a talent that cannot easily be confined to a single venue," Harry told me after the final performance. "The celebrated and distinguished Mr. Platt may have some difficulty in choosing the proper method of highlighting my abilities." He whistled happily as he scrubbed away the last traces of copper body paint.

In truth, Hector Platt was neither celebrated nor distinguished. He was what used to be called a blue barnacle in the show business parlance of the day, a man who tenaciously attached himself to the lower edges of the scene while serving no clear purpose. Very occasionally he would throw a week or two of work my way with one of the lesser circus tours or carnival pitches, but on the whole I considered him a last resort in desperate circumstances. I tried to explain this to Harry as we made our way across town in a covered omnibus, but he would not hear of it.

"Mr. Platt has simply not had the opportunity to avail himself of a truly top-drawer performer," Harry insisted as we alighted on lower Broadway. "We shall both benefit from this fateful association." He rubbed his hands together. "Lead on. Dash! Destiny awaits!"

I shrugged and led Harry down a narrow, winding alley off

Bleecker Street. Beneath a yellow boot-maker's lamp we came upon a door with the words "Platt Theatricals" etched on a pane of cracked glass. I pushed open the door and climbed a dark flight of stairs with Harry at my heels. At the first landing we found a door hanging open on broken hinges. I rapped twice. Hearing a gruff summons from inside, I entered the office.

Hector Platt sat in a high-backed wooden swivel chair, regarding us through the lenses of a brass pince-nez. He liked to think of himself as a country squire in the European fashion, and to that end he wore leather riding boots and silken cravats. An untidy scattering of papers littered the surface of his oblong desk, with a brown clay pipe smouldering in an ashtray within easy reach.

"Hardeen," said Platt in his booming bass drum of a voice. "Haven't seen you in a good four months. Where've you been? You can't possibly have been working all that time!"

"As a matter of fact, my brother and I have been touring with the company of Mr. Harry Kellar," I said primly. "We've only just returned and have elected to rejoin the New York season. You are undoubtedly familiar with the recent successes of my brother, Mr. Harry Houdini." I gestured to Harry, who stepped forward to shake Platt's hand. "Although the stresses of the recent tour have been considerable, my brother has decided that he is willing to entertain suitable offers at this time."

Platt's lips curled as he reached for his clay pipe. "I am gratified to hear it," he said, tamping the pipe bowl with the end of a letter opener. "However, I am obliged to report that news of your brother's triumphs has not yet reached our offices."

"Indeed?" I stroked my chin at this strange lapse. "Well, if you would care to examine our press book, you will find ample testimony to the drawing power of the Great Houdini. No less a journal than the *Milwaukee Sentinel* was inspired to remark that—"

Platt waved the book aside. "I've seen your cuttings more

than once, Hardeen. It might be more profitable to learn of your recent attainments. Tell me, what was it that you and your brother were doing during your time with Mr. Kellar?"

It was a sore point, as Platt undoubtedly realized. At that time Harry Kellar was the most celebrated conjurer in the entire world. He did not require the services of additional magicians in his company, so Harry and I had served as minor assistants in some of the larger production numbers. I had quite enjoyed my role in the background, but Harry had chafed at his small handful of assignments. Chief among these was a novelty number that required him to don a leopard-pattern loincloth and heft large weights as Brakko the Strongman.

"Our duties were varied," I said, examining my fingernails with a careless air, "and I may say in all modesty that Mr. Kellar was most reluctant to see us depart."

"Was he, indeed?" Platt's smile broadened as he sent up a cloud of noxious black smoke. "I do hope that he will be able to carry on. Now, Mr. Hardeen, I seem to recall that you and your brother have some experience performing a magical act of your own devising. I regret to say that at present I have no need of a magical act."

"It is not simply a magical act," I said. "My brother has devised an entirely new form of entertainment, one that is certain to place his name in the very forefront of popular entertainment."

Platt unclipped the pince-nez and rubbed the bridge of his nose. "Not the escape act," he said wearily, closing his eyes. "I told you last time, there is simply no audience for such a thing."

Harry, who had showed uncharacteristic restraint during this exchange, now stepped forward and grasped the edge of Platt's desk. "I would be very pleased to offer a demonstration of my abilities," he said. "I guarantee that you will find it worth your attention."

Platt waved the back of his hand. "Please, Mr. Houdini. I do not allow every passing entertainer to audition here in my office. I should have no end of singers warbling the latest tunes and Shakespeareans declaiming from *Hamlet*. It wouldn't do to encourage such behavior."

Harry smiled as if Platt had made a delightful witticism. "Singers are a penny to the dozen," he said. "Actors can be found on every street corner. The Great Houdini, as my brother has said, is entirely unique. I fear that mere words cannot convey the power of what I am able to achieve upon the stage. Only a demonstration will suffice. Have you a pair of regulation handcuffs?"

"Handcuffs?" Platt leaned back in his swivel chair. "No, Mr. Houdini. I do not happen to have a pair of handcuffs lying about."

"You're certain? Perhaps a good set of Palmer manacles or a nice solid pair of Lilly bar irons? I would also settle for leg restraints or thumbscrews."

"Mr. Houdini, I do not keep such things about my person. What sort of establishment do you suppose I am running?"

Harry's face fell. "It will be difficult to demonstrate my facility with handcuffs if no handcuffs are forthcoming," he allowed.

"I shouldn't be surprised," said Platt, squaring a pile of documents on his desk. "Now, gentlemen, if you would be so good as to excuse me, I have some rather pressing—"

"Mr. Platt," I said, struggling to regain some purchase on his attention, "I beg that you give my brother some chance to demonstrate his value as an entertainer. I offer my assurance that he is the most exceptional performer in New York today."

"I must find a solution," Harry was saying, musing aloud over the strange absence of restraining devices in Platt's office. "I suppose that I could provide my own handcuffs in these situations, but people would naturally assume that they were gaffed in some way. What to do?"

Platt ignored him. "Hardeen, I've already told you that I don't place any stock in the entertainment value of a man who escapes from things. It's a silly notion. I know that you and your brother are fair magicians, but I don't have any need of magicians just now." He paused as a new thought struck him. "Is Mr. Houdini's wife seeking opportunities at present? I might have something coming open in the chorus at the Blair."

"She is fully booked at the moment," I said. "My brother and I—"

"Yes, yes," said Platt heavily. "I know all about you and your brother."

"I suppose it is a question of advertising my intentions in advance," Harry murmured to himself. "I could post a notice or handbill to the effect that the Great Houdini intends to accept any and all challenges to escape from regulation handcuffs. Then people would be forewarned to provide their own restraints. That might resolve the difficulty."

"Are there any other opportunities that might be suitable?" I asked Platt. "Anything at all?"

Platt reached across the desk for a folded sheet of paper. "I shouldn't think so," he said. "But don't despair, Hardeen. If your brother truly is the most exceptional performer in New York, the other agencies are undoubtedly clamoring for his services." He unfolded the paper and ran the pince-nez over the print.

"Perhaps there could be a trained locksmith on hand as I took the stage," Harry was saying. "He could confirm that the handcuffs had not been tampered with or altered in any way. It would lend an official touch to the proceedings. The Houdini Handcuff Challenge. That would look well in print." He glanced at me. "Don't you agree, Dash?"

"Harry, perhaps we might confine our attention to the matter at hand. Mr. Platt is consulting his books to see if—"

"I'm afraid there's nothing," said Platt, tossing the folded sheet onto the desk. "Unless, of course, your remarkable brother happens to have a cast-iron stomach."

"Pardon?"

"A cast-iron stomach. The Portain Circus has an opening in two weeks' time. I'm looking to send a man with a cast-iron stomach."

"I don't quite follow you," I said.

"A stone-eater," Harry said impatiently. "An omnivore." He made an exaggerated chewing motion. "Someone who will eat whatever the audience throws at him."

"Precisely," said Platt. "I have the honor to represent Mr. Bradley Wareham, who earns a fine living in this manner. At present, however, he is indisposed."

My hand went to my midsection. "A stomach complaint, by any chance?"

"Not at all. A gouty foot, as it happens." Platt snatched a handbill from amid the clutter on his desk. "Mr. Wareham is proving to be a difficult man to replace. Listen to this: 'For the amusement of all present the Man with the Cast-Iron Stomach will ingest all manner of small objects presented to him by the audience, including rocks and gravel, potsherds, flints, bits of glass, and other savories. Upon conclusion of the display, this Gustatory Marvel will allow onlookers to strike his stomach to hear the rattling of the strange objects within.'" Platt lowered his pince-nez and regarded us with a bemused expression. "I don't suppose this is an act you might be willing to undertake."

"Certainly not," I said. "The talents of the Brothers Houdini lie in an entirely different sphere of—"

"Would I be able to take my wife?" Harry asked.

"Harry!" I cried. "What are you thinking? You're not a—"

"The Portain Circus is a very reputable organization," my brother said evenly. "If I could establish myself in the company, I might be able to win a spot more in keeping with the usual run of my talents. Moreover, I would be able to rescue Bess from her servitude in the chorus line at Ravelsen's Review."

"Your reasoning is flawless," I said with considerable asperity, "except for the part which requires you to eat rocks and glass. How do you propose to overcome that little difficulty?"

Harry turned to Platt, who had been pulling contentedly at his clay pipe during this exchange.

"You say that I would have two weeks to prepare?" Harry asked.

Platt folded his hands. "Yes, Mr. Houdini. Two weeks. But I warn you, this act is no place for an amateur. Do you really think you're up to it?"

By way of an answer, Harry reached across Platt's desk and plucked the clay pipe from his fingers.

"Harry!" I cried, as he placed the smoldering bowl into his mouth. "Don't—"

But he had already bitten off the bowl of the pipe at its stem and was now happily chewing on the glowing contents.

"What did he say?" Platt asked, as Harry tried to speak through a mouthful of clay and burning embers.

"I can't be certain," I said, "but I believe it was 'Hoonga-boonga.'"

2

A MOST DELICIOUS POCKET WATCH

"Harry," I said, as we jumped onto an omnibus heading back across town, "what were you thinking? You're no stone-eater! You can't possibly be ready to tour in two weeks' time! You'll only ruin your health in the attempt!"

"I'll do nothing of the sort," he said, settling himself onto a wooden seat near the back. "I shall apply the same rigorous conditioning and training techniques that have made me the world's foremost escape artist."

"But—"

"Dash," he said calmly, "the Portain Circus would be a vast improvement over our current run of bookings. You know that perfectly well. As for my lack of experience, I shall simply ask for some pointers from Vranko."

"The Glass-Eater? How long has he been on the bill at Huber's now? Five years? Six?"

"Seven," said Harry.

"Seven years. Vranko isn't exactly a headliner, Harry. Not after seven years at the dime museum."

"Perhaps, but he can certainly instruct me in the rudiments. My startling natural charisma will do the rest."

"Of course," I said. "Your startling natural charisma. How careless of me to overlook that."

Harry gripped the arm rail as our driver whipped the horses

around a corner. "Dash, I just want to have Bess working alongside me again. I hate to think of my wife thrown among those wolves at Ravelsen's, helpless and vulnerable."

"Harry, do you recall that theater manager in Loon Lake? Bess nearly chewed his ear off for daring to suggest that she use a more 'enticing' shade of rouge. Your wife could scarcely be described as helpless or vulnerable."

"Even so, Dash. I can hardly be faulted for wishing to take her out of the chorus line."

"She enjoys it, Harry. This wouldn't have anything to do with her pay packet being heavier than yours, would it?"

He colored. "Certainly not! I am delighted that my wife's talents are so highly prized!" He drew back from the open window as a hansom cab clattered past in the opposite direction. "In any case, the disparity is only temporary and will soon be rectified." He tugged at the corners of his bow tie. "Yes, a temporary disparity. I believe we are approaching your stop, Dash. I shall collect Bess at Ravelsen's and join you at Mama's. We have much to discuss."

"Harry, be careful of how you break this news to Bess."

He looked at me with surprise. "You don't think she'll be pleased?"

I stood up as the omnibus slowed. "I'd approach the matter with caution, if I were you. Use your startling natural charisma." I descended the wooden stairs and made my way north on foot.

The rain had slackened by the time I reached my mother's apartment on East 69th Street. As I approached the familiar building I found my friend Biggs lounging in the doorway with a cigarette. It was not often that I saw him away from his compositor's desk at the *New York Herald*, and he retained the hunched and focused attitude that marked him as a working journalist. He wore his customary baggy tweed suit with an open waistcoat and a loosely knotted wool tie, but even so his appearance was markedly spruce. His thinning red hair, which usually resembled a thatch of chick-weed, had been neatly pruned and swept back. His nails were carefully groomed and polished, and his cheeks fairly glowed with ruddy vigor.

I gave a two-tone whistle as I approached. "Biggs!" I cried. "Who's the lucky girl?"

"Augusta Clairmont," he replied without hesitation. "I don't clean up for just anyone, Dash. We don't all share your foppish disposition."

"Augusta Clairmont?" I asked, climbing the front steps and pulling open the outer doors. "Jasper Clairmont's widow? Isn't she just a bit old for you, Biggs?"

"She invited me to dinner last night," he said, following me inside. "I spent the better part of yesterday afternoon receiving the attentions of my tonsorialist. Shave, haircut, steam—the works." He ran a hand through his hair. "It'll be days before I regain my usual sickly pallor."

"But I thought Mrs. Clairmont had gone into seclusion after—after—"

"Her husband's suicide? She did go into seclusion. She only sees her closest friends and relatives now, but there were special circumstances last night. That's what I've come to speak with you about. I believe you can help me, Dash."

"How so? I must say, you're being very cryptic, Biggs."

"Do you think so? I'm so pleased. I'm hoping that an air of mystery will make me more appealing to the fair sex. Why don't you invite me inside, and I'll tell you all about it."

Biggs refused to answer any more questions as I led him through the main doors and up the stairs. I couldn't imagine what interest Augusta Clairmont, the famous society hostess, could possibly have in my friend, nor could I conceive of why Biggs might require assistance from me.

I did, however, recall the circumstances of the death of Jasper Clairmont some three months earlier. The news had dominated the headlines for nearly a week and remained a subject of speculation and salacious gossip. Clairmont, a shipping magnate who wielded enormous power in the city's financial circles, had shot himself through the head while locked away in his private study. Almost at once, rumors began to surface of ruinous business failures, illicit liaisons, grave illnesses, and various other dark portents, each of which was put forward in its turn as a possible explanation for the tragedy.

"I still don't understand what connection there can be between you and the Clairmont family," I said as we neared the top of the stairs. "You weren't even assigned to Mr. Clairmont's death, as I recall."

"No, I wasn't," he answered, his breath growing short with the effort of climbing so many steps. "Why must your mother live on such a damnably high floor?"

"Why is it that you always insist on calling for me here, anyway? You know I live at Mrs. Arthur's boarding house now."

"I'm aware of that, Dash."

"Well, then?"

"Is Mrs. Arthur the finest cook in all of New York?"

"No, but—"

"No, she most certainly is not. Your mother holds that distinction, and the last time I called upon her she gave me the most extraordinary lemon cake I've ever tasted. I still dream of it."

"I believe it's a raisin bundt today, but you know perfectly well that my mother will never be content with a slice of cake at this hour. She'll insist on giving you dinner."

Biggs made a show of seeming surprised. "Dinner, you say? How could I have been so thoughtless as to appear on your doorstep at the dinner hour? What an unpardonable breach of courtesy! You must think me a terrible—"

"That'll do, Biggs," I said, pausing at the kitchen door. "Hardly your most convincing performance, in any case."

"No," he agreed, as I led him into the kitchen. "I really must remember to leave the theatrics to you."

We found my mother hovering at the stove, as always, and

the rich aromas of simmering meats and cooling breads filled the room. She paused just long enough to pinch Biggs's cheeks and comment on how thin he was looking before commanding him to take a chair at the kitchen table. After a moment or two of clattering through the silver drawer, she set an extra place and ladled out two steaming bowls of cabbage soup. This done, she turned back to the preparation of a Chicken Debrecen.

"Come now, Biggs," I said as he bent low over his bowl, "you're lapping up that soup as if you haven't eaten in a week. Surely Mrs. Clairmont puts on a respectable table?"

"Very respectable," Biggs agreed. "Although dinner was not the main feature of the evening."

"No?"

He looked up from his soup bowl. "Not at all. That's what I came to tell you. You see, Dash, I've seen a ghost." He lowered his head and went back to eating his soup.

I lifted my eyebrows. "Have you, indeed?"

"Several of them, in fact. Mrs. Clairmont might as well be running a hotel for departed souls. The place was fairly swimming with apparitions."

"A séance," I said quietly. "Augusta Clairmont invited you to a séance. You've been table-tipping with the upper classes."

He nodded. "The poor woman has resolved to make contact with her late husband. She can't accept the fact that he did himself to death. It seems she wants to hear it from his own lips, if you please."

I glanced at my mother. "It's difficult to lose a husband, Biggs," I said. "If Augusta Clairmont chooses to sit in a dark room and console herself by reading auguries in a saucer of tea leaves, who am I to criticize?"

"This was no ordinary séance, Dash. I know a bit about that type of jiggery-pokery. A group of people gather in the parlor after supper and decide that it would be a jolly lark to try to communicate with the spirit world. So they lay their hands on the table and wait for the spirits to arrive. After a while the table begins to sway and finally gets up sufficient motion to tap with one leg. Then a question is asked—"Is that you, Uncle Chester?"—and an answer is given by the tedious process of reciting the alphabet and waiting for the table leg to tap at a certain letter. It can take an eternity to get a simple yes or no. I had a lady friend once who went in for that type of thing. She dragged me along on more than one occasion. It seemed to me that we were collectively pushing the table without really realizing it. In our eagerness to have something happen, we were causing the table leg to come down at the right moment." He looked up as my mother filled his soup bowl again. "Thank you, Mrs. Weiss. Delicious, as always. Anyway, Dash, I hope you don't think that I'm completely benighted where this type of thing is concerned. I know a bill of goods when I see one."

"I take it there was no table-tipping at Mrs. Clairmont's."

"No. She'd never tip her own table, in any event. She's a very wealthy woman. She'd hire someone to do it for her. Listen, Dash, I know it sounds like a lot of hokum, but there were some remarkable things that happened last night. Truly remarkable."

"And there will be a rational explanation for each of them, Biggs."

"I would have thought so," he said. "I spent the whole day digging for answers. You know I can be a real brass-plated bloodhound when I have to be, but this has me stumped." He pulled out a leather-bound notebook. "You've heard of Lucius Craig?"

I shook my head.

"Apparently he has Mrs. Clairmont wrapped around his finger."

"He was the medium?"

"The what?"

"The medium, Biggs. The spirit guide—the one who makes contact with the supernatural realm. You'll need to learn the lingo if you intend to keep up."

"That's why I've come, Dash. You and the ape man have

done a bit of medicine show fakery, haven't you?"

"Biggs, you really must stop calling him that."

"Oh, I shall. Just as soon as he evolves into something vaguely human. I imagine your brother would have given the estimable Charles Darwin a few uneasy moments. Natural selection seems to have looked the other way when it came upon Harry Houdini."

"Biggs. Really." I glanced again at my mother. Thankfully, she was too absorbed in her cooking to pay any heed.

"Sorry, Dash," said Biggs. "I forget myself sometimes."

It was a familiar rant. Harry and Biggs had nurtured an intense dislike of one another since childhood, and neither showed any sign of growing out of it. Biggs had often found himself on the receiving end of Harry's bullying nature, and unlike me, he had never grown comfortable responding in kind. As we grew older, however, Biggs learned to use words every bit as forcefully as his fists, and this was an arena that left my brother at a decided disadvantage.

"So," Biggs continued, dabbing at his lips with a napkin, "have the two of you worked the spirit angle or not?"

"There was a brief period when we were travelling with an outfit called Dr. Hill's California Concert Company. We were doing tent shows through Kansas and Oklahoma, and everybody wanted to see a spook show because the Davenport Brothers had passed through and caused a sensation."

"The Davenport Brothers? Something to do with a 'spirit cabinet,' right?"

I nodded. "The cabinet was a great big bureau with swinging doors on the front. It was set on a raised platform at center stage. Inside there was a long wooden bench. The brothers, tied hand and foot, were placed inside the cabinet, facing each other. There was a number of tambourines and trumpets and such placed on the floor at their feet. At a signal from the brothers, their assistants lowered the stage lights and swung the doors closed. All at once the audience heard strange noises—jangling tambourines, strumming guitars, that sort of thing. Disembodied hands poked out through openings in the cabinet and musical instruments could be seen floating in mid-air."

Biggs snorted. "So they'd freed themselves from the ropes! Where's the mystery in that? Your brother does it all the time! It's a simple escape!"

"You'd think so, wouldn't you? But at regular intervals during the demonstration, the assistants threw open the doors. Inside, the brothers were seen to be securely fastened, breathing hard as though deep in a trance, with their heads bowed and their eyes closed in concentration. When the doors swung shut, the strange happenings started up again—instantly."

"A clever act," said Biggs. "Nothing more."

"The Davenports rarely—if ever—laid claim to supernatural powers, but their audiences were quick to form that impression, and the brothers did little to dispel the notion."

"Sounds like overripe boilings to me."

"The public seemed to like it, and it opened the way for a number of imitators. Harry and I were given the job of presenting something similar for the benefit of Dr. Hill's company. We were in Topeka at the time, and we spent a couple of days—"

We both turned at the sound of thudding footsteps on the back stairs. I recognized the sound. It was my brother, having collected Bess at Ravelsen's, returning home for the evening. By the reverberation of Harry's tread, I knew that Bess had not responded warmly to his latest career plan, and that his "uncomprehending world" tirade would not be long in coming. After a moment, the kitchen door flew open, and Harry stormed into the room, followed by Bess.

"Dash!" he cried. "She will not listen! She does not wish to join the Portain Circus! Is this not madness? You must explain it to her! I cannot tolerate another day in the dime museum! Am I not the man whom the *Milwaukee Sentinel* called the 'most captivating entertainer in living memory'? Yet I am squandering my youth working a ten-in-one! My talents are being wasted!"

He threw himself down in a chair. "I feel as if I am alone with my genius in an uncomprehending world."

"Harry," I said, indicating Biggs. "You remember—"

But he was too caught up in his jeremiad. "I am the world's all-eclipsing and justly celebrated master of escape! I have struggled for years to attain my present level of perfection in my craft! And now I have an opportunity to reach a broader audience, and my own wife would prefer to remain where she is! Madness! Dash, perhaps you can explain the importance of this new opportunity! She will not listen to me!"

"Harry," I said again, "we have a—"

"Must I remain at the dime museum until I am old and gray, entertaining the groundlings for mere table scraps? Ridiculous! I am accused of being a jealous husband! Absurd! I am proud of my wife's attainments! But at the same time I must endeavor to do what is best for my family, as every man must! Is it not vastly preferable that husband and wife should be together? This seems to me to be beyond dispute! I would even go so far as to say—"

As was often the case when my brother was well along on one of his harangues, it fell to Bess to quiet him. "Harry," she said, laying a hand on his arm. "Stop."

That was all it took. My brother blinked once or twice, as though emerging from a trance, then looked down at her with a curious expression. "What is it, my dear?"

"We have a visitor."

Harry turned and registered for the first time that there was another person in the room. "Biggs," he said, puzzled.

Biggs had stood to pull out a chair for Bess. "Hello, Houdini," he said. "Nice to see you again, Mrs. Houdini."

"Thank you, Mr. Biggs," said Bess, smiling in a way that even a brass-plated bloodhound couldn't possibly have resisted. "And how are you this evening, Dash?"

"I'm well, thank you."

My sister-in-law had come directly from Ravelsen's, wearing

a cloth overcoat over her stage costume. Her chorus girl outfit was a gauzy, tight-fitting concoction of short bloomers, purple stockings, and a glittery sash. It was designed for ease of movement and showed her bare arms and stockinged legs to advantage. Although not quite as revealing as the familiar sugarplum fairy getup she wore on stage with Harry, it had much the same impact. Take my word for it.

Harry took his usual place at the table while Bess chatted brightly about the goings-on at Ravelsen's. Mother served each of them a bowl of soup, while Biggs and I were given plates of Chicken Debrecen. Harry and Biggs regarded one another warily across the table.

"Biggs," Harry said at last, "if you've come to drag my brother off to one of your bawdy houses, I'm afraid you'll have to go alone. I need him for an important rehearsal this evening."

"Oh, undoubtedly!" cried Biggs. "It's apparent that all of New York is crying out for the debut of Harry Houdini's latest miracle! Have you reserved the Palace yet?"

Harry's face darkened. "It is only a matter of time, Biggs. Only a matter of time."

"Strong words from Harry Keller's hod carrier. Or was even that job too demanding?"

Harry slapped his hands on the table. "I'll have you know that Mr. Kellar—"

A stern voice cut his words short. "That will be enough, boys."

Biggs and my brother looked up to see my mother standing over them with her hands on her hips. "That will be enough, boys," she repeated. "Don't make me separate you."

"Yes, Mama."

"Sorry, Mrs. Weiss."

Harry folded his arms and stared fiercely at the opposite wall. Biggs beamed happily as my mother served him another portion of whipped potatoes. "You'll spoil me, Mrs. Weiss," he said.

"You looked as if you could use a little something on your stomach," she answered.

"Biggs has been asking about spook shows," I said, hoping to cajole my brother out of his foul humor. "I was just telling him about that night in Topeka."

"Oh, I remember that night," Bess said. "Very strange. I wouldn't care to go through that again."

"Nor I," Harry said with a shake of his head. "I don't know why I ever agreed to it."

Biggs, his curiosity roused, set down his fork and leaned forward. "Agreed to what? What's all this about, anyway?"

"It was supposed to be a simple spook show," I said. "With a few ghosts and goblins dancing against a black screen. In the end it became something more. I'm trying to remember how we billed it. What was it, Harry?"

He closed his eyes as if picturing the handbill. "'Professor Harry Houdini, the man who sees all, will give a Spiritual Séance in the Open Light,'" he intoned. "'Grand, Brilliant, Bewildering, and Startling Spiritualistic Display and other Weird Happenings presided over by the Celebrated Psycrometic Clairvoyant. Assisted by Mlle. Beatrice Houdini.'" He opened his eyes and gave a sidelong glance at Bess. "You see, my dear. Even then I always took care to share the stage and billing with you."

Bess, chewing a forkful of chicken, did not reply.

"What does 'psycrometic' mean?" asked Biggs.

"We were never quite sure," I admitted. "It was a term the Davenports seemed to favor. We copied everything from them, except for the part about performing in the open light."

"Well, that was the point," Harry said. "I had hoped to present the thing in a fair and open manner, not like these cork-show Merlins who can't even make a tambourine jangle unless the room is pitch black."

"You're getting ahead of me," Biggs said.

Harry, who seldom had the chance to tell Biggs something he didn't know, leapt at the opportunity. "It's very simple," he said. "In your ordinary séance room or spirit show, the so-called psychic will offer up a number of modest little parlor tricks. A ringing bell, perhaps. Or a scrawl of writing on a chalk slate. He dresses up these minor effects as 'manifestations,' and they are presented as indications of contact with the spirit world."

"That much I understand," said Biggs, bridling a bit at being on the receiving end of a lecture from Harry. "But what does that have to do with Topeka?"

"I planned to do something unique," Harry said. "When Dr. Hill asked me to present a spirit show, I hoped to show that the Great Houdini was capable of doing such things under the glare of the stage lights. It—thank you, Mama—" He looked up as Mother served him a plate of chicken. "It seemed to me that if I could do these things in the open light, it would open the audience's eyes to how easily such deceptions are practiced. I should have known better."

"You couldn't have known how they would respond, Harry," said Bess.

"What happened?" asked Biggs, flashing another broad smile as Mother placed a slice of raisin bundt cake before him.

"I was too effective," said Harry. "Too brilliant. It is a familiar problem."

"It wasn't so much brilliance as careful planning," I said. "Harry and I knew all along that we'd need to soak up some of the local color if we were going to pull this thing off. We spent a couple of afternoons mooching about in the town, listening in on gossip, reading old newspapers at the library. As it happened, there had been a rather gruesome killing some months earlier—a bar fight gone bad—and the locals were eager to talk about it."

"Don't forget the cemetery," said Harry. "That was my idea."

"Yes, we went to the cemetery and copied down the names from the tombstones that appeared to be the most recent."

"What'd you need those for?" Biggs asked.

"I'm surprised that a brass-plated bloodhound such as yourself has to ask," I said. "We were priming the pump. We had prepared a few props and gimmicks, but we wanted to be certain that our patter was up to scratch."

"We needn't have worried," said Harry. "My startling natural charisma carried the day."

"Even so, I was eager to make sure we were properly prepared. We knew the house would be full that night. Our Celebrated Psycrometic Clairvoyant handbills had been posted far and wide. It was a big theater—quite possibly the largest crowd we've ever played."

"Surely not!" cried Harry. "Have you forgotten our appearance at the Belasco?"

"No, Harry, I haven't forgotten the Belasco. However, since we were serving as assistants to Harry Kellar at the time, I'm not sure we can claim credit for filling the seats—although you were wonderfully engaging as Brakko the Strongman." I turned back to Biggs. "As I was saying, it was probably the largest crowd who had ever assembled for the specific purpose of seeing the Houdinis. We started the demonstration with a rough approximation of the Davenport act. We invited a committee of audience members to come up and tie Harry to a chair. They made a good job of it, with his hands double-knotted at the back. Then we brought in a cabinet of cloth screens—the same one we used in the Trunk Substitution Mystery—and drew the curtains in front of Harry's chair. I stepped away from the curtain and asked the members of the committee if they were certain that they had tied him securely. The words were barely out of my mouth when the weird happenings commenced."

"They were rather good," Harry recalled, smiling.

"Weird happenings?" Biggs asked.

"First the audience heard a loud klaxon horn from within Harry's cabinet. Then the horn itself was flung into the air. Next there was the strumming of a mandolin. After a moment, we could see the mandolin itself hovering above the enclosure."

"Harry had escaped," Biggs said matter-of-factly. "Quite simple."

"It might have seemed so at first," I allowed. "But each time there was a strange manifestation, I would fling open the curtains to show Harry still securely tied to the chair, his head lolling on his chest, as though in the thrall of unseen forces. But as soon as I drew the curtain again, we would hear another sound or see another strange apparition. After a time, the whole cabinet started to shake and pitch as though possessed by a restless spirit. Finally the screen fell forward in a heap, and there was Harry, free of the ropes, taking his bows."

"I couldn't resist," Harry admitted. "I couldn't allow them to think that those feeble sailor-hitch knots could hold me. I told the audience that I had been untied by spirit hands."

"I admit it sounds like a very clever act," Biggs said, "but I don't see much of a difference from the Davenport act."

"Ah!" Harry cried. "That would have been true if we had let it rest there, but I was not content to be a mere imitator!"

"That's where things got a bit out of hand," I said. "We decided to give them a spirit message service."

"Pardon?" asked Biggs.

"It's what they call it when the medium brings forth messages from the other side—for specific individuals in the audience."

"Messages?" asked Biggs. "From the dead, you mean?"

"Or so they claimed," said Bess, taking up the thread. "On the face of it, the entire thing seemed outrageous. If I had not seen it for myself, I wouldn't have believed how effective such a display could be. Imagine if you went along to the theater one night, and the gentleman on stage called out your name across the footlights and delivered a few words that he claimed to be a private message from a dead relative of yours. Your grandfather, for example."

"I would say that he was a charlatan," Biggs declared. "Such things are not possible."

"So you might think," Bess continued, "but what if the message contained some private, deeply personal piece of intelligence—something that no stranger could possibly have known? A pet name, for instance, or a memory of some birthday or anniversary?"

Biggs hesitated, stirring the crumbs of his bundt cake with his fork. "I still wouldn't believe it," he said.

"Nor would I," said Bess, "but a fair number of people in Topeka were persuaded otherwise."

Biggs set down the fork. "You told them that you were communicating with their families?"

"Not in so many words," I said. "We brought the lights low, and Harry walked forward and stood alone at the edge of the stage. He looked out over the audience and told them that he could see spirit forms hovering in their midst. His voice quavered as he said this, and his hands were seen to tremble."

"I was mesmerizing," said Harry.

"It was one of his more remarkable displays," I agreed. "He spoke in a quiet, reverent voice and kept his eyes closed and his body rigid, as though the exertion of this contact with the other side was threatening to overwhelm him. Then he started to call out names. 'Mr. Alexander Botham. I sense the presence of your wife. She is here with us tonight. She is happy on the other side. She wishes you well. Mrs. Mabel North, your daughter Helen is being well looked after by her spirit family. Your mother is with her, and your Aunt Catherine.'"

An expression of distaste passed over Biggs's face. "That's cruel, Houdini. Giving people false hope that way. You got those names off tombstones."

Harry nodded and his eyes grew unfocused. "It was unforgivable," he said quietly.

"Believe me, Biggs," I said, "we've both had occasion to think better of what we did that night. At the same time there was something quite moving about it. I found I couldn't take my eyes off the faces in the crowd. There was something extraordinary in the way they kept glancing at one another, half afraid, yet half hoping that Harry might call upon them. If we had stopped it there, I might actually have persuaded myself that we had given them a strange form of consolation. But we took it too far."

"How do you mean?" Biggs asked.

I glanced at Harry. He looked away. "After half an hour or so, Harry suddenly drew back, and his eyes went wide with alarm, as though he had sensed a new and dangerous presence in the theater. He walked to the lights and peered out over the heads of the crowd, focusing on something that only he could see. 'Who is this?' he said. 'It is a man, but who is he? He is badly injured, I can see. He walks in a halting manner. He does not speak, yet I can sense that his soul is restless and troubled. He draws closer. What do I see? Why—why—it is horrible! His throat is cut! The blood flows freely from the wound, and he—'"

"The dead man," said Biggs. "The one who'd been killed in the bar fight."

"Exactly," I said. "And it caused an uproar. By the time Harry called out the man's name, women were screaming from the balcony. Men were on their feet with their fists raised, ready to fight off the angry spirit. There were some who fainted dead away and others who ran from the theater." I shook my head at the memory. "I've never seen anything like it."

"It was inexcusable," said Harry. "It was only then that I realized how easily one might prey upon the fears of the public. I might have become a considerable success as a medicine show huckster, but I could not bring myself to walk that path."

"Oh, come now, Houdini," said Biggs. "I saw you jump off a bridge once, and I've always been convinced that you stayed underwater longer than necessary just to throw a good scare into the crowd. Isn't it much the same thing? Aren't your escapes just another form of spook show?"

I expected that the accusation would send Harry into an indignant bluster. To my surprise, he appeared to weigh the question carefully. "There is an important difference. When I do my escapes, the audience feels a degree of fear because they themselves are afraid of what I am facing. They are afraid of being confined. They are afraid of dark places. They are afraid of drowning. But they are afraid on my behalf, not for themselves. And when I am successful, it is as though they have seen their fears conquered. Not so with the spiritualists. There is nothing honest in what they do. They do not conquer death. Instead they feed upon the fear of death. Such false coin must be nailed to the counter at any cost."

Biggs looked at my brother as if for the first time. "You sound almost human, Houdini."

Harry had gone back to his Chicken Debrecen. "No need to trouble yourself over it."

Biggs grinned and leaned back in his chair. "Do you know anything about a man named Lucius Craig?"

Harry snorted. "A charlatan."

"You know him, then?"

"By reputation only. But what a reputation! It is said that he has the power to float to the ceiling! That he can elongate his body! That he is resistant to all forms of pain!" Harry leaned forward in a confidential manner. "It is even said that he can walk through walls!"

"Harry," I said, "you don't believe any of that, do you?"

"Of course not, but what a *chutzpanik*!"

"Pardon?" asked Biggs.

I thought for a moment. "Someone who possesses an unparalleled degree of gall and brazen nerve."

"A charlatan!" Harry repeated, brandishing his fork. "But is it not fascinating that a man should be able to convince so many people of such abilities? What a showman he must be!"

"I had dinner with him last night," Biggs said.

Harry's eyes brightened. "Did he float to the ceiling?"

"Certainly not. But he did some rather astonishing things, and for the life of me I can't figure out how he could have done any of them."

Harry waved his hand impatiently. "Of course not. You are a blockhead."

"I'm a blockhead?" cried Biggs incredulously. "This from a

man who can scarcely walk without dragging his knuckles on the ground? My dear Houdini, I have a pair of socks back in my room with more brains than you have." He gestured at the remains of Harry's dinner. "That chicken, though dead, could undoubtedly defeat you in a contest of wits! And you have the gall to call me—"

He broke off as my mother turned from the stove and raised a finger of warning.

"Mr. Biggs," said Bess, laying a hand on his arm. "Harry didn't mean it that way. It's a term used in medicine shows and dime museums to describe the uninitiated. A blockhead is simply another term for a ticket-holder."

Biggs glanced at me. I nodded.

Harry appeared to be ignoring us. "So many blockheads," he said. "An entire planet filled with them. It is no great feat for a clever magician to prey upon willing and susceptible minds. If people want to believe in ghosts, it is not difficult to provide a ghost for them. I might just as readily claim that I am able to read minds because I am able to divine which card has been chosen from a shuffled pack. But Lucius Craig, there is a different matter."

"You don't mean to say you put any credit in his nonsense, Houdini? Even you couldn't be quite so"—Biggs cast a wary eye at my mother—"even you couldn't be quite so... open-minded."

"Do I believe that he can float from an open window? No. Do I believe that he can stretch his body to twice its length? Of course not. Yet he has been received as an honored guest in the homes of the Vanderbilts and the Astors, while I struggle to earn my keep as a sideshow attraction. That in itself is remarkable, would you not agree? I should like to know how he does it."

Bess had been watching her husband with considerable interest during this exchange. "How do you know so much about Lucius Craig, Harry?"

"Houdini knows many things," he said.

The answer did not entirely satisfy her. "Harry," she said, "you promised you would have nothing to do with spiritualists ever again."

"And I shall not. I don't think his modus operandi would be particularly suitable for a married man, in any case. He seems to have a habit of attaching himself to wealthy widows."

"Just so," said Biggs. "He finds a rich society matron and attaches himself like a leech."

"Yet it is said that he accepts no payment for his services," Harry offered.

"That's true," Biggs admitted, "but he would hardly require a fee, would he? He allows himself to accept the lavish hospitality of his hostesses, and he is continually showered with extravagant gifts from grateful clients. It seems he's been making his living in this manner for years."

"Still," Harry returned, "who but a widow would have need of the services of a man who claims to contact the dead? And who but a wealthy one would have the resources to pursue the matter?"

Biggs raised his chin. "Houdini, you almost sound as if you have a certain sympathy for this man!"

"He fascinates me," Harry said. "That is all."

"Don't be fooled, Biggs," I said. "I've heard him argue the other side of this matter with equal vigor. If you're looking for someone to help you with your story on the mysterious Mr. Craig, Harry's your man. Not me."

Biggs's distaste at the prospect of collaborating with my brother could be plainly read on his features. "It's not a story," he said, "at least not yet. I was there last night as a favor to a friend."

"A friend?" Harry asked.

"Mrs. Clairmont's son, Kenneth. He and I were at school together."

"School?" Harry turned to me. "Then you must know him as well, Dash."

"I believe Biggs is referring to New Haven, Harry."

"Oh." Harry rolled his eyes. "College."

"Kenneth and I weren't terribly close," Biggs continued, "but he always seemed a decent sort of person. Quiet, very studious. In any event, Kenneth seems to think that I can be of some use. He's concerned over the influence that Lucius Craig is exerting on his mother and asked me to look into the man's background. Our files turned up very little, I'm afraid. After last night's demonstration, I decided I'd better ask someone with a bit more experience in the spirit realm."

"Very well," said Harry. 'Tell me everything. Begin with last night's séance. Omit nothing, no matter how seemingly insignificant." He leaned back in his chair and assumed an expression of utmost concentration, with his eyes closed and his fingers steepled at his chin. "To a great mind, nothing is little."

Biggs glanced at me and raised his eyebrows.

"You'll have to excuse him," I said. "He thinks he's Sherlock Holmes."

Harry waved a hand for silence. "Data! Data! Data! I can't make bricks without clay!"

Biggs sighed. "Actually, Houdini, I've come to take Dash for a drink at the Waldorf. I suppose you'd better join us."

Harry opened his eyes. "Surely this is no time for carousing, Biggs. If you'd care to have my assistance, I am willing to give it. If not, Dash and I have an important rehearsal."

"I'm meeting Kenneth Clairmont there."

"Ah." Harry nodded. "Our young client. Very good."

"He's not a client, Houdini. He's a friend of mine and he's asked for help. However, if you are too busy with your rehearsing, I'm sure that Kenneth will understand. I should hate to deprive the Broadway season of its newest sensation."

Harry's brow darkened but he said nothing.

Biggs glanced at his pocket watch and rose from the table. "We'd best be getting along," he said. "I told Clairmont I would meet him at the Peacock Alley." He turned to my mother and took her hand. "Mrs. Weiss, once again you have surpassed yourself. The meal was delectable. There is none finer to be had in all of New York."

Mother blushed. "You were getting too thin. It is not good, the empty stomach walls rubbing together."

"I'll bear that in mind. Come along, Dash. You, too, Houdini—if you're coming. It's nearly half past seven."

"What an exceptional watch," said Harry.

Biggs patted the watch pocket of his waistcoat. "Thank you," he said. "It belonged to my grandfather."

"Swiss?"

"Yes."

"Might I see it?"

Biggs unhooked the watch from his chain and passed it over. "It came to me through my father," he said. "The case is white gold, and the face is hand-painted ivory. You can see the inscription on the inside cover."

Harry examined the watch with elaborate care. "A remarkably fine timepiece," he said. "This might be just the thing for my new act."

"Your act? I hardly think so."

"No? I assure you, it promises to be the sensation of the new Broadway season. Allow me to demonstrate." With a flourish, Harry threw back his head, parted his lips wide, and dropped the watch into his mouth.

"Houdini—!" cried Biggs.

"A most delicious pocket watch," Harry said, amid loud crunching noises as he worked his jaws. "How very delectable. There is none finer to be had in all of New York."

"Houdini, what the devil—!"

Harry swallowed with exaggerated relish. "Ah!" he patted his stomach. "I believe that a drink at the Waldorf might be just the thing to wash it down."

Without another word, he turned and made his way down the back stairs.

≈ 3 ≈

A TRICK OF THE HINDU FAKIRS

WE WERE NEARLY AT THE WALDORF, RIDING IN AN OPEN CALASH, by the time I persuaded Harry to return the watch. Make no mistake, Harry could easily have eaten the watch had he wished it, as there is a fair amount of truth in an omnivore act. From my vantage, however, I was able to see that he had simply palmed the watch and substituted a small chicken bone, which accounted for the crunching sounds that had so alarmed Biggs.

"You're a primate, Houdini," Biggs said, wiping the watch on his coat sleeve before returning it to his pocket. "You really are."

"One day you will plead for the honor of an interview," Harry said serenely. Biggs slumped back against the hard leather seat and glowered for the remainder of the journey.

The Waldorf-Astoria had only recently opened, as I recall. Today, of course, the original building is long gone, knocked down to make room for the Empire State Building, but at that time it was one of the most splendid buildings in New York. I barely had time to register the gleaming marble expanses and ornate staircases as Biggs rushed us through the main reception area. We hurried past the grand clock at the center and made our way toward the Peacock Alley bar.

As we pushed through a set of etched glass doors we were greeted by the low murmur of male voices. The dim lights were made to seem even dimmer by the dark wood panelling and low tin ceiling. Heavy plumes of cigar smoke hung in the air, all but obscuring the faded Venetian tapestries on the rear walls.

Biggs hesitated in the doorway for a moment, allowing his eyes to adjust to the gloom. Upon spotting his friend seated alone at a table near the back, he waved aside the maitre d' and led us past the bar.

"Kenneth!" Biggs cried as we approached the table. "What's that you're reading? The *Herald*? I'm surprised they allow such a liberal sheet in here!"

"Not so liberal as all that, Biggs," the young man answered. "I've just been reading your screed on the events in Manila Bay. You're becoming something of a saber-rattler."

"Well," replied my friend, "it sells the newspaper."

"That's a rather feeble justification for war, Biggs."

"My editor takes a different view. He'll soon tire of the conflict, I expect."

"Let us hope so."

Kenneth Clairmont was a slight, pale man of roughly my own age, with clear, intelligent eyes behind a pair of round spectacles. He wore an understated brown suit of fine Scottish wool with a black mourning band on the arm. Along with the newspaper there was a book on the table in front of him—the latest novel by Richard Harding Davis—and I guessed that Clairmont was a man who preferred reading to the usual bar room chatter.

Biggs made the introductions as we took our seats. Clairmont greeted us with enthusiasm and signalled for a steward. "I'll have another Walker's and soda," he said, lifting his empty glass. "I imagine my learned friend here will take the same. Hardeen, what can I offer you?"

I shuddered at the thought of what a drink would cost in such a place. "Nothing for me, thanks," I said.

"Absurd!" cried Biggs. "The same for Dash, as well."

"Excellent," Clairmont said, smoothly maneuvering past my embarrassment. "I should be thought a poor host otherwise. How about you, Houdini?"

"I do not drink," Harry said.

"Not at all?"

"I have embarked on a rigorous course of muscular expansionism. Alcohol has an inhibiting effect."

"You don't say?" Clairmont lifted his empty glass and examined it critically, then turned back to the steward. "Better make mine a double measure, then. Will you take a glass of minerals, Mr. Houdini?"

"Mineral water is fine," my brother said.

The steward nodded and moved away while Clairmont rose to greet a pair of older gentlemen who were approaching our table. From their conversation, I gathered that the two had been colleagues of Clairmont's late father. The young man spent several moments in earnest conversation, then resumed his seat. "This place was a great favorite of my father's," he said, by way of explanation. "I'm forever running into his friends and associates. I don't know why I keep coming back, to be honest. I never came here before."

"It is a natural thing," said Harry quietly. "When our father passed, I found myself walking through the park each day along the same path where he took his exercise. Each day I would be stopped by people from the neighborhood who knew him. They would tell me stories of things he had said and done— small things, but they meant a great deal to me. It is a comfort at such times to know that one is not alone."

Clairmont nodded, and once again I caught Biggs staring at my brother with transparent surprise, as though Harry had suddenly shown himself to be fluent in ancient Sumerian.

"I suppose we must all find a way of coming to terms with our ghosts," said Clairmont, glancing up as the server returned with our drinks. "Biggs tells me that you have some experience in this line—ghosts and spiritualists and all that."

"A bit," I said. Clairmont listened attentively as I recounted much of what I had told Biggs about our spook show days. He asked several questions and seemed particularly intrigued by the manner in which we had been able to transform idle gossip into seemingly miraculous spirit revelations.

"So it was all fakery?" he asked when I had finished.

"Certainly," I said.

"Very artful fakery," Harry added.

"Have you ever known of a genuine medium?"

Harry leaned forward. "Lucius Craig, you mean?"

"Exactly. Could he be the genuine article?"

"No," I said. "There is no such thing."

Harry swirled the water in his glass. "I wonder."

"Mr. Clairmont," I said, "just because a man rattles a tambourine doesn't mean he is trafficking with the spirit realm. You are in a fanciful frame of mind because of your recent loss, and perhaps this has left you more receptive to Mr. Craig's blandishments than you might otherwise have been. I can assure you that you will not find answers in the séance room. You may safely send Mr. Craig on his way."

"I wish it were that simple," Clairmont said, raising his glass to his lips. "My mother is quite taken with him. She has been very distraught since my father—since my father—" He set down his glass and stared down at the tabletop for a moment. "Well, I suppose you know all about it. My father took his own life—suddenly and without warning of any kind. My mother simply cannot accept that he should have done this. Her health has always been fragile, and I have worried that the strain might prove too much to bear. I am studying medicine, as it happens, and have been able to care for her to some extent, but she is not a strong woman." The corners of his mouth turned down slightly as he took another sip of his drink. "I fear that fetching powders for my mother may be as close as I come to an actual medical practice."

Biggs looked up at this. "What do you mean, Kenneth?"

"Father's death has forced me to reconsider my choice of career. There is a place waiting for me in the family firm."

"The shipping business? You've always loathed it!"

The young man shrugged. "I hardly have a choice in the matter. My father is gone, and my uncle is of no use. If the business is to stay a family concern, I must step in."

Biggs shook his head. "But your medical studies! What about—?"

"My father always wished me to abandon them," Clairmont said briskly. "It seems he's won the point after all. In any case, it has no bearing on the matter at hand."

"Lucius Craig?" asked Harry.

"Money," answered Clairmont. "My father's money. As you may know, my father amassed a considerable fortune over the course of his lifetime. It is to be expected, then, that my mother should attract her share of suitors once her mourning period has ended. Make no mistake, my mother is a charming woman, and I would be quite delighted if she were to find companionship after a suitable interval, but it is my nature to be cautious on her behalf."

Harry drummed his fingers on the table. "You think she is liable to fall prey to fortune hunters?"

"She has too much common sense for the average Lothario, and up to this point she has limited her social engagements to a small circle of family intimates. It is possible, I suppose, that she might in time form an attachment to one of this group. My father's friend Dr. Wells, for instance, has been spending a great deal of time at the house, and our family lawyer, Mr. Edgar Grange, has been seen about the place rather more often than his official business might dictate. But these are both men of considerable means. If they evince a social interest in my mother, I like to think that their intentions are genuine. Lucius Craig is a different matter entirely."

"So I've heard," said Harry. "How did your mother meet him?"

"It was at a dinner party given by one of her friends, Mrs. Watkin. As it happens, the occasion marked the first time that my mother had ventured out of the house since my father's passing. She had heard a great deal about the remarkable Mr. Craig, and her curiosity got the better of her. Mr. Craig did a few of his minor miracles that evening, and my mother—"

"Were you present?" asked Harry.

"I was."

"Describe these minor miracles, please."

Clairmont laced his fingers behind his head as he collected his thoughts. "As I recall, it was only through the most persistent pleadings from Mrs. Watkin that Mr. Craig was persuaded to give any sort of demonstration. He made a great show of reluctance, then agreed to make what he called 'a modest effort to commune with the spirits.' He asked that each member of the party place some small object into a hat at the center of the table. He was very careful to specify that the objects be personal in nature. The items were gathered while Craig himself stepped out of the room. When he returned—"

"He was able to identify the owner of each object," Harry said, "and he was able to reveal some private fact about each person."

"Exactly! You've seen him perform the feat?"

"I've done it myself," Harry said. "It is not terribly difficult."

"Come now, Houdini," said Biggs. "How have you been able to bring off such a thing?"

Harry waved his hand as if batting at an insect. "Later," he said impatiently.

"Well, Mr. Houdini," Clairmont continued, "I can't vouch for your abilities, but by the reactions of my mother and the other guests, you would have thought that Mr. Craig had parted the Red Sea. My mother happened to be carrying a stickpin that had belonged to my father. When Mr. Craig grasped it, he seemed to know this at once. 'This belonged to the late husband of the charming Mrs. Clairmont,' he said. 'Her husband was obviously a man of great cunning and intelligence, who also had a deep appreciation of life's bounty.'"

"A deep appreciation of life's bounty," said Biggs with a snort.

"Who would disagree with such a thing? He was simply telling your mother something she wanted to hear."

"I would have agreed with you, but when it came to be my turn Mr. Craig did something that left me absolutely baffled. I had taken care to provide an object that I felt certain would stymie him. Instead of putting forward my collar stay or something of that nature, I borrowed a fountain pen belonging to Mrs. Watkin's butler, Lachley."

"Very clever," Harry said, appraising Clairmont with fresh interest.

"My little deception proved ineffective. Craig puzzled over the fountain pen for some time, then he looked at me and said, 'Young Kenneth seeks to confuse the matter. This is not the pen of a young student, but that of an older man, a man born to serve others with dignity and grace—though perhaps a bit overly fond of the fruits of the vine.' And poor Lachley, who had been standing close by with a tray of fruit cups, nearly collapsed from embarrassment. It was a triumph for Mr. Craig, but ever since that day he has been wary of me. This has not prevented him from attaching himself to my mother, however."

"How did this come about?"

"Well, Mr. Houdini, it was clear from the first that my mother had been captivated by the possibility of contacting my father's spirit through Mr. Craig. That very evening she drew him aside and acquainted him with the unhappy circumstances of my father's death. She knew that he claimed to have the power to speak with departed souls and wished to know whether it might be possible to reach my father in this manner. Mr. Craig professed to be ambivalent, saying that such communications are not always possible and adding that my father might not yet have completed his 'translation' to the other side. But my mother would not be dissuaded, and Mr. Craig eventually agreed to visit us at our home the next day."

Harry fingered the rim of his glass. "Did he conduct a séance?"

"Hardly, Mr. Houdini. That's what's so infuriating about this man. He husbands this so-called gift of his as though it were some precious metal that wears away with use. It is only with the greatest reluctance that he will make any sort of demonstration at all, such as the trick of matching the objects with their owners. He continually dangles the promise of a séance before my mother, but there has always been some reason to prevent it. He will say that there is a negative energy permeating the room or that the stars are in an unfortunate alignment. He does just enough to sharpen the edge of my mother's interest but no more. The result, of course, is that she must continue to entertain him in high style, in the hope that he will become able to use his powers on her behalf."

"I take it that he is now a regular visitor at your home?" I asked.

"It is more than that, Mr. Hardeen. He has taken up residence. My mother insisted on it. At first he would simply call in for an hour or two. In time he began to accept small gifts and he would occasionally pass the night in one of the guest rooms. Soon enough, however, we had reached our present circumstance, which finds him installed in a suite of rooms and given the run of the house. As if that wasn't sufficient imposition, we must also give lodging to his young daughter, Lila."

"His daughter travels with him?" I asked.

"He claims that she is a catalyst for his psychic energies, so of course nothing will do but that she is entertained in the same high style as he. She is an odd little girl. Quiet and watchful. She makes me uncomfortable."

"How long have the Craigs been living at your house?" Harry asked.

"Nearly two weeks. It seems an eternity."

"Two weeks?" Harry was obviously surprised.

"Yes, and it is only just recently that he has condescended to favor us with a séance. He has spent a great deal of time converting Father's study to suit his needs, with my mother consenting to his every whim."

"Your father's study? The room in which he died?"

"Precisely. My mother has allowed it to be transformed into a séance room. She has even ordered an absurd table built to Mr. Craig's exacting standards."

"Octagonal," said Harry. "With a round pedestal base."

Clairmont nodded. "Yes, exactly. You seem to know a great deal about these matters, Mr. Houdini."

"I hope to know more presently. I take it that Mr. Craig made his first attempt to contact your father's spirit last night?"

"Yes. He had postponed long enough, to my way of thinking. After much agonizing he intimated that he would be ready to make an attempt to 'cross the eternal divide,' as he phrased it. That's why I invited Biggs. I wanted an independent observer, and I thought that the presence of a newspaper reporter might have a moderating effect on Mr. Craig. In the end, Biggs was just as baffled as I was."

"Hardly surprising," said Harry. "Tell us what you saw. Or what you believe you saw, in any case. Start at the beginning. What time did the evening commence?"

"At seven. Mother arranged that we should all have a light meal beforehand. Mr. Craig did not join us. He claimed that he required an hour of absolute isolation in order to summon his reserves of psychic energy."

"But there were others present?"

"Yes. We needed to fill out the numbers for the séance. Eight people were required, according to Mr. Craig. One for each side of the octagonal table. There was Dr. Richardson Wells, whom I mentioned earlier. He was my father's closest friend. Also Mr. Edgar Grange, our lawyer, who seemed in a foul mood over Mr. Craig's increasing influence over my mother."

"Who else?"

"My uncle, Sterling Foster."

"Your mother's brother?"

"What possible difference can all of this make, Houdini?" asked Biggs impatiently.

Harry fixed Biggs with an expression of mild reproach, as though correcting a recalcitrant schoolboy. "Unless Mr. Craig is a genuine psychic, he will require a confederate of some sort. I must learn all I can about everyone who was present."

"But he has a confederate," I said. "Lila. His daughter."

"She wasn't in the séance room last night," Clairmont told me. "In fact, the cook tells me she was down in the kitchen the whole time, eating her dinner."

"The girl wouldn't be the confederate during the séance, in any case," Harry said. "He would turn to someone who seemed above suspicion. Tell me, where did the various guests sit during the séance?"

"Well," Clairmont said, gazing up at the ceiling as he pictured the scene in his mind, "Mr. Craig sat nearest the door, and my mother was seated to his right. Next to her was Dr. Wells, and I sat on his right. Next there was Mr. Grange, and then Uncle Sterling, and finally Biggs. That's right, isn't it, Biggs?"

"That is only seven," said Harry. "Surely Mr. Craig would not have allowed the séance to proceed with an empty place."

"No," Clairmont agreed, "he was most insistent that the so-called psychic circle be completed. At the last moment our butler Brunson was summoned to fill the remaining place. He did not seem terribly pleased by this added duty. He indicated to my mother that his services might be of more practical use in seeing to the coffee and port."

Harry smiled. "A wise man. What time was it when the séance began?"

"Nearly nine o'clock. Mr. Craig was already seated at the table when my mother led the guests upstairs. Each of us took a place at the table—"

"Pardon me," Harry said, leaning forward suddenly. "Did Mr. Craig himself indicate where each of you was to sit?"

"No," Clairmont answered. "My mother did, but I believe that the seating arrangement was made in accordance with Mr. Craig's wishes."

"Very good," said Harry, closing his eyes. "Proceed."

"As you will appreciate, after so many delays and evasions, I was on fire with curiosity to see what Mr. Craig was going to do. For all my skepticism, I could not help but wonder if he might succeed in some fashion. Was it possible, I wondered, that I might feel some faint glimmer of my father's presence here in the very room where he died? My mother, for her part, took her place by Mr. Craig's side as reverently as if taking Holy Communion. It pained me to see her so completely in his thrall. I felt embarrassed in front of my friends."

"You had no cause," said Biggs quietly.

Clairmont did not appear to have heard. "The lights had been dimmed as we entered the room, but there was a sufficient number of candles lit so that it was possible to make out what Mr. Craig was doing. There was an arrangement of cloth screens forming a sort of tent over his chair. The fabric was so sheer as to be translucent. The screens offered no concealment of any kind, but Mr. Craig claimed that they helped to focus his powers."

"The spirit screens are a common feature of the séance room," Harry said. "Did Mr. Craig also play music of some kind?"

"He did. He produced a most unusual music box and set it going as we entered the room. The melody was quite soothing. When we had taken our places, Mr. Craig spent a few moments with his head lowered in prayer, then told us that we would begin with a small experiment designed to bring our energies into balance. He called this the 'invocational.' He passed a block of paper around the table and instructed each of us to take a sheet. We were told to write down a single word—a name or place or thing—that held some private significance. These slips of paper were folded into small squares and dropped into a hat at the center of the table. Mr. Craig then reached in and drew out the folded slips one by one. I expected that he would open each paper and read it, but instead he simply pressed the folded squares to his forehead. After a moment or two, he was able to divine the word that was printed on each slip of paper."

A change came over my brother during Clairmont's narrative. At the outset he had been content merely to ask questions; now, at the mention of the folded squares of paper, he grew increasingly agitated. "But that's a simple billet—"

"Harry," I said, "let Mr. Clairmont tell his story in his own way. We don't want to color his account."

"First rule of journalism," Biggs agreed.

Harry leaned back, obviously annoyed.

Clairmont took a swallow of his drink before continuing. "Upon concluding this feat, Mr. Craig announced that he would undertake a tentative contact with the spirit realm. This contact, he went on to explain, was intended merely to gauge whether the spirits might look upon our gathering with favor. He brought forth a small chalk slate, such as one might find in an ordinary schoolroom. He explained that on occasion it was possible for a spirit presence to manifest a message upon a slate of this kind. If we were to receive such a message, he claimed, we would know that the spirits were with us, and we might continue with our experiment."

Once again, Harry's emotions got the better of him. "Slates!" he cried. "Dash, do you hear? Spirit slates! I've never heard such—"

"Quiet, Harry," I said. "Let him finish."

Momentarily disconcerted by Harry's outburst, Clairmont soon collected himself. "Now that our energies were in balance, Mr. Craig told us, it was necessary to establish a 'circle of psychic force.' We were instructed to place our hands upon the table so that the tips of our fingers would be touching those of our neighbors. We were also told to position our feet so that they would touch those of the person on either side. Mr. Craig explained that this was necessary to form a conduit of energy, though it was tacitly understood that we were establishing control over the hands and feet of everyone in the circle—and

Mr. Craig in particular—so as to preclude any suggestion of trickery. From that point forward, Mr. Craig would not have been able to move about without alerting the person on either side."

"Or so he would have you believe," said Harry. "In fact—"

"Harry." I held up a finger in warning.

"Forgive me," he said. "Please carry on, Mr. Clairmont."

"Prior to our joining hands Mr. Craig had extinguished the candles and placed the chalk slate beneath the table. We now sat in darkness for some moments, with our hands spread upon the table, listening to the strange melody coming from the music box. After a time Mr. Craig began to call to the spirits. I can't remember all of what he said, but he repeatedly urged the spirits to use his being as the instrument of their communication, so that the others might know of their presence. His entreaties seemed to go on for quite a long time."

"Did you hear any other sounds while this was going on?" Harry asked. "Apart from the music and the sound of Mr. Craig's voice?"

"At one point I thought I heard a distant whistle—or perhaps a clanging noise from the kitchen—but I can't be certain."

"How long did Mr. Craig continue to speak?"

"It can't have been more than fifteen minutes. Then he went quiet, and though I could not be certain in the darkness, I had the impression that his head had slumped forward, as though he had been exhausted by his labors. When he spoke again—to ask that a candle be lit—his voice sounded weak and strained. By the candle's light we could see that Mr. Craig appeared pale and shaken by his efforts. He told us that he had sensed a powerful spirit presence. He reached under the table and drew forth the slate. We could see that a single word had been scrawled upon its surface."

Harry and I leaned forward. "What was the word?" I asked.

"Petal."

Harry raised his eyebrows. "Petal?"

"Yes. It was a pet name that my father had for my mother. You can imagine the effect that this had upon her. She was fairly thunderstruck."

"Indeed she was," Biggs confirmed. "I thought she might faint dead away."

"Petal," I repeated. "And you say that Craig's hands and feet were under control at the time?"

"His hands and feet were touching those of the people on either side of him. That is absolutely certain."

"Very interesting." I glanced at my brother, who did not seem to be paying attention. "Harry, how do you suppose he managed that?"

"Pardon?"

"I was asking how Craig managed to produce a message on the spirit slate without using his hands or feet."

Harry did not appear to hear me. "Dash, do you recall Mr. Bithworth from Father's congregation?"

"The cobbler? Of course, but what——?"

"A nice man, Mr. Bithworth. I must remember to pay him a visit."

Biggs shot an exasperated look at my brother. "Houdini, if it wouldn't be too much trouble, Kenneth was trying to give us his impressions of last night's séance."

"Of course. My apologies. Please continue, Mr. Clairmont."

"Well, there's not much more to tell, actually. Mr. Craig declared that the spirits were no longer cooperative and brought the evening to a close. However, we extracted a promise that there would be a further experiment as soon as possible. Mr. Craig claimed that he would need a day or so to allow his energies to refresh themselves. At length it was agreed that we would conduct another séance tomorrow evening."

"How interesting," Harry said. "And no doubt he promised that there would be a physical manifestation of your late father—assuming the conditions were favorable."

Clairmont's eyes widened. "He did say something to that

effect, Houdini. How did you know?"

Harry grinned. "It is the way of these things."

"Do you mean to say you've seen this sort of thing before?" Clairmont's expression brightened. "Do you think you might be able to expose these tricks?"

Biggs shook his head. "Houdini is a clever magician, I'll grant you. So is Dash, if it comes to that. But what we saw last night was an entirely—"

"It is not so very difficult," Harry said.

"You think you could do as much, Houdini?" asked Biggs.

"I believe I could."

"What utter codswallop!"

A smile played at Harry's lips. "Perhaps a small demonstration would be in order." He placed his hands on the table and fixed Clairmont with a level gaze. "Mr. Clairmont, you and I have never met before this evening, is that correct?"

"Of course not, Mr. Houdini. I—"

"Then would it surprise you greatly to know that I have already managed to establish a close psychic rapport? Would you be alarmed to know that I am able to read your mind as easily as I might read a book?"

Clairmont glanced at me. "Hardeen, is he serious?"

"Harry is always serious," I said.

"I shall be pleased to offer an exhibition of my strange and wondrous talents," my brother continued. "First, however, I must gather my spirit forces. I shall do so in the washroom. While I am away, you may order me another glass of minerals." With that, Harry excused himself and slipped away.

"He gets worse every year," said Biggs, watching Harry retreat toward the rear of the bar. "I don't know how or why you tolerate him, Dash."

"He doesn't seem so bad," said Clairmont, withdrawing a silver cigar case from his pocket. "He must be fascinating to watch on stage. A bit rough, perhaps, but a commanding presence, nonetheless."

"Life with my brother is never dull," I said, accepting a flat-nosed diplomat cigar from Clairmont. "I can assure you, there is a reason for everything he does."

"Dash has been making excuses for Harry since we were boys," said Biggs, leaning forward as Clairmont offered a light. "Dash always had the brains in the family, yet he plays down his own talents so that his brother's monstrous ego may be allowed to thrive." He sat back and sent up a stream of smoke. "Honestly, Dash, you are getting too old to be trailing along in your big brother's shadow."

"You don't understand," I said, drawing a light for my own cigar. "However vain and boastful he may appear, he believes every word that he says. When Harry claims that he is going to be the most celebrated entertainer in the world, he believes it to be the literal truth." I leaned back as the end of my cigar began to glow. "And I suspect he may be right."

Biggs shook his head. "Because he can do some clever things with ropes and chains? That sort of thing is fine for the dime museum, but I can't see that it will carry him any further than that."

"I wouldn't be so certain," said Clairmont. "Novelty acts are enjoying a vogue at the moment. There is a troupe of performing dogs holding the stage down at Proctor's. Who's to say that Houdini might not have some modest success along these lines?"

"Modest," said Biggs. "That is a word seldom used to describe anything to do with Houdini. He has the most titanic—"

"I have returned to amaze and fascinate you," said Harry, appearing suddenly at Clairmont's elbow. "A brief spell of meditation has brought my psychic powers to the very peak of readiness." He took his seat and reached for his glass of mineral water. "Mr. Clairmont," he resumed, "you professed amazement that Lucius Craig was able to cause the word 'petal' to appear on a chalk slate, is that not so?"

"That's right, Houdini."

"Very good. Although I do not have a chalk slate with me this evening, I think we might essay a demonstration along similar lines. Would this be acceptable to you?"

Clairmont tapped the ash from his cigar. "It certainly would."

"Excellent. I want you to fix your mind on some detail about your late father. Try to fix on something generally not known to the public. It must be simple—one word, really—so that it may be easily transmitted by the delicate mechanism of thought transference. Later, when a closer rapport has been established, it may be possible to achieve success with longer messages. For now, simplicity is the key. Your mother's maiden name would do nicely, or perhaps the name of the town where your parents had their honeymoon. Have you something in mind?"

Clairmont nodded.

"Good. Now close your eyes and concentrate on your chosen message. Try to empty your mind of everything else, as any stray thought might compromise the experiment."

Although Clairmont seemed uncertain as to whether to take Harry's theatrics seriously, he closed his eyes and composed his features into an expression of earnest concentration. Harry reached across the table and grasped Clairmont's wrists. "Focus your thoughts," said Harry, dropping his voice to a dramatic register. "Whatever strange sounds you may hear—whatever I may say or do—you must keep your eyes closed and your mind clear of all thoughts but the message. I will now endeavor to place myself into a trance-state."

"A trance-state?" asked Biggs. "What sort of nonsense is that?"

"It is not nonsense at all," Harry said. "It is a trick of the Hindu fakirs. I do not expect that a mind such as yours will comprehend the subtleties of my art, but I must ask you to keep silent. Your disbelief creates a climate of hostility that may compromise our success." With this, my brother closed his eyes and commenced to hum.

This continued for some moments. After a time, Harry began to vary his pitch and make strange guttural noises at the back of his throat. Biggs looked at me with a bemused expression, as if to ask how much longer this might last. I nudged Harry's leg under the table. He ignored me.

By now, the gentlemen at the tables adjacent to ours had paused in their conversations to peer over at the strange young man in the black suit and red bow tie who appeared to be chanting and holding the hands of his companion. "Uh, Harry——?" I began.

Just then, Harry's head slumped forward, as though entering a Hindu trance-state. His hands, still grasping Clairmont's wrists, gave a sudden spasm, knocking a glass of mineral water into Biggs's lap.

"What the——!" Biggs cried, as a steward hurried forward with a cloth. "For heaven's sake!"

"It's all right," I said to the steward, taking the cloth and passing it to Biggs. "My brother is attempting to demonstrate that he is able to read minds."

"Very good, sir," said the steward.

Harry's head snapped up, though his eyes were still closed tight. "The spirits are uneasy this evening," he intoned, his voice quavering, "but a picture begins to form. I can almost reach out and grasp it. Who is there? Can you hear me? Who is it who comes before us?"

A small knot of onlookers had now formed beside our table. To his credit, Kenneth Clairmont managed to keep his eyes closed and his expression composed, even as my brother's tremulous voice rose in pitch.

"The picture remains cloudy," he continued, "as though the spirits are repelled by a skeptic in our midst."

Biggs, still dabbing at his trousers with the cloth, paused and shot a baleful look at my brother.

"Spirit friends! The Great Houdini beckons to you! Present us with some small token or sign of your presence! I feel that you are almost within reach now, that I might almost reach out and grasp—just a bit further—yes! I have it!" At this, Harry's head slumped forward once again.

After a moment or two, Harry released Clairmont's wrists and sat upright. "You have done well, Mr. Clairmont," Harry said, resuming his normal speaking voice. "Your energies are most powerful."

Clairmont's eyes blinked open, and he flushed as he saw the gathering of spectators beside our table. "Houdini? Exactly what is it you hoped to accomplish by all of this?"

By way of an answer, Harry removed his jacket. "When I asked you to focus on a message, many disparate thoughts passed through your mind, did they not? There was some difficulty in selecting an appropriate one."

"Well, yes, but—"

"Can you tell me what word or name you selected?"

Clairmont hesitated. "Well, I thought of my father's middle name. Ellsworth."

Harry smiled serenely and stood up, so that the men from the surrounding tables might have a better view. Thrusting his left arm in the air, he unfastened his shirt cuff.

"Ellsworth, you say? A most unusual name."

"Houdini," muttered Biggs, "don't make a spectacle. You're embarrassing Kenneth."

Harry, needless to say, was relishing the attention. He raised his voice so as to be heard more clearly by the impromptu audience. "Would it not be stunning if our spirit guides have been able to divine your message?" he declaimed, rolling back his sleeve. "Our experiment was a difficult one, and it must also be said that a public house does not provide the most favorable atmosphere for such an undertaking. Nevertheless, I believe that the Great Houdini has been able to produce yet another miracle."

"Miracle?" asked Biggs. "What—?"

Harry silenced him with a gesture. Reaching across the table, he scooped a handful of cigar ashes from the glass tray. He studied them intently for a moment, as if appraising their quality. Then, with a vigorous sweep of his hand, he rubbed the ashes across his inner forearm, creating a thick smear across the pale flesh.

"Houdini!" cried Biggs. "This really is too—"

"Behold!" cried Harry, turning his forearm for Biggs and Clairmont to see. There, standing out in relief against the gray ash, was a crude handwritten message: *Ellsworth.*

A wild ovation went up among the crowd that had gathered by our table. Harry acknowledged the applause and hoots of approval with a deep bow, then turned back to face Biggs and Clairmont, whose expressions attested to their astonishment.

"Well done, Houdini," said Clairmont as the crowd of onlookers dispersed. "I dare say that would have done credit to Lucius Craig himself!"

Even Biggs could not contain his enthusiasm. "How'd you manage it, Houdini?"

"It is a small matter," Harry said. "Such things are well within the power of the Great Houdini. I merely attuned my mind to Mr. Clairmont's psychic—"

"It's a carnival trick," I said.

Harry shot a withering look in my direction. "Dash, why do you insist upon—"

I ignored him. "We've been doing that one since we were in short pants. Of course, we used dirt instead of cigar ash. All you have to do is write the word on your arm with a thin piece of soap. The dirt sticks to the soap and the word shows up plain as day. That's what Harry was doing when he stepped away to 'gather his spirit forces.' He simply went to the washroom to find some soap."

"Clever," said Biggs, "but that hardly explains how he knew what Kenneth was thinking. How could he possibly have known that Kenneth would choose his father's middle name?"

"A simple matter," Harry said. "Nothing more than a convergence of energies."

"Probability," I amended. "Remember Harry's instructions?

He wanted you to think of a single word. He mentioned maiden names and honeymoon destinations—thereby ensuring that you wouldn't make either of those two choices. But Harry knew that the mention of those two possibilities would turn your mind down similar avenues. The two most likely considerations in that instance would be your father's middle name or his place of birth. These are the two answers that show up time and again."

"Extraordinary!" cried Clairmont. "Now that you mention it, I very nearly did select Father's place of birth. Now I wish I had. That would have confounded you, Houdini."

Harry sighed and rolled back his other shirtsleeve. As he rubbed a second handful of cigar ash onto his forearm, the word "Albany" rose up from the dark smear.

Clairmont roared with laughter. "Bravo, Houdini!"

Biggs appeared nonplussed. "But now you've run out of arms, Houdini. Suppose he hadn't chosen either of those two words?"

"Harry would have improvised," I said. "He'd have distracted you with a deck of playing cards, then scrawled the word onto the face of one of the cards and brought it into play when you weren't looking."

"It rarely happens, though," Harry said.

"But how in the world did you know Mr. Clairmont's middle name?" Biggs asked. "I couldn't have told you what it was—I didn't know myself until tonight. And I certainly wouldn't have known where he was born."

I looked at my brother. "How did you know, Harry?"

He shrugged. "Do you recall the two older gentlemen who exchanged greetings with Mr. Clairmont earlier? I happened to notice that they were leaving as I excused myself from the table. I simply caught up with them and struck up a conversation. I doubt if they even realized that I had extracted any information from them."

Clairmont let out another roar of laughter. "You are precisely the man I need, Houdini! The two of you must join us for Mr.

Craig's séance tomorrow evening. I'm certain your presence will greatly enliven the proceedings. If nothing else, I can promise you a fine dinner with plenty of wine—" he checked himself. "And minerals for you, of course, Mr. Houdini. Will you come?"

Harry and I glanced at one another. "We'd be delighted," I said.

"We have no other pressing business on hand at the moment," Harry added.

"Excellent! I shall look forward to receiving you at—"

"What about the balance?" Harry asked.

Clairmont stubbed out his cigar. "The balance?"

"If Dash and I both attend, there will be two extra sitters at Mr. Craig's séance. Mediums are quite particular about such things. He is sure to object if the numbers are out of balance."

Clairmont considered the problem. "Well, I'm quite certain that Brunson, our butler, will be only too pleased to surrender his place. That frees one chair. As to the other...Biggs...I am afraid I must withdraw—"

"On one condition," said Biggs. "You must agree to meet me here afterwards and give a full accounting."

Clairmont grinned with relief. "Done."

Biggs turned to Harry with an expression of glee. "Well, Harry," he said, "I'll bet that even the Hindu fakirs wouldn't be able to tell you what I'm thinking now."

"A simple matter," Harry said evenly. "You are filled with a new sense of admiration for the powers of the Great Houdini."

"Not quite."

"I think I can take a stab at it," I said, setting down my cigar. "You're wondering what the celebrated Mrs. Augusta Clairmont, doyenne of New York society, is going to make of the Brothers Houdini."

"Exactly," said Biggs, sending up a smoke ring. "Harry Houdini faces his greatest challenge to date—the oyster knife and the finger bowl. I'm only sorry I won't be there to see it."

4

THE MYSTERIOUS DR. WEISS

"Harry," I said, as we made our way on foot to the Clairmont residence the following evening, "I do wish you'd come along with me to see Mr. Sanders."

"Don't be absurd!" cried Harry. "Our evening clothes are hand-tailored!"

"If by that you mean that Mama was able to run them up on her sewing machine, then I suppose they are. But I doubt if any of Mrs. Clairmont's other guests will be wearing tailcoats fitted with a special pouch for the concealment of rabbits and doves." I fingered the shawl collar of my dinner jacket. "At least Mr. Sanders was able to give my trousers a bit of a touch-up."

Harry pursed his lips. "Mrs. Clairmont will have to take me as she finds me, Dash. We can't all be strutting peacocks."

"Speaking of strutting peacocks, why are you walking so strangely? Have you hurt your leg?"

"No," he said. "My leg is fine. I am simply eager to arrive on time for our dinner engagement."

"We'd have plenty of time if you hadn't disappeared for half the day. Where were you, anyway?"

"I had business to address."

"What sort of business?"

"Private business," he said. His hand went to the right-hand pocket of his coat.

"Harry, what have you got there? Don't tell me you've brought Selma." Selma was an aging, somewhat flatulent, lop-eared rabbit who often appeared from Harry's top hat.

"Selma is resting comfortably at home, Dash. You needn't worry yourself about that."

"Then what have you got there?"

"Just a precaution." Harry increased his pace as we approached the north end of Gramercy Park. "Come on, Dash. Try to keep up."

I had no difficulty keeping pace with my brother, as he knew perfectly well. Throughout my life I have been a walker, and it was my habit in those days to walk several miles each day. I could not begin to count the number of times I have crisscrossed Gramercy Park, enjoying the restful elegance of its brownstones and shade trees. Until that night, however, I had never crossed any of the thresholds.

The late Jasper Ellsworth Clairmont, who did rather well for himself in the shipping business, had lived on the west side of the park in a graceful home with fine stone columns and an elaborate cast-iron porch. A pair of bilkin torches threw a guttering light over the path as we approached. As we passed an expensive brougham standing in front of the house, I paused to neaten my collar in the reflection of the carriage's gleaming brass palm plate.

"Dash! This is no time to preen your feathers!" cried Harry, pulling my elbow.

"Harry, it's bad enough that our clothing smells of rabbits. At least my tie should be straight."

"If you spent half as much time practicing your sleights as you do arranging your hair, you'd be a headliner by now." He dragged me up a set of broad stone steps and pulled at the door chime.

A pair of heavy, oval-paned doors swung inward, and we stepped into a large entryway, the chief feature of which was a heavy wooden staircase winding up to a minstrels' gallery.

A ruddy-faced butler took our cloaks, and I don't think I'm imagining it when I say that his nose wrinkled a bit as he accepted Harry's top hat.

"Your name is Brunson, is it not?" Harry asked as the butler led us toward a reception room.

"It is, sir."

"Would you ask Mr. Kenneth Clairmont to join us for a moment before we go through to meet the others? I should like a private word with him."

"Of course, sir." Brunson withdrew, leaving us alone in the entry hall.

"What's this about, Harry?" I asked. "I don't want to keep Mrs. Clairmont waiting."

"Just a minor precaution, Dash. I wish to ensure the success of our examination of Mr. Craig."

"Houdini!" called Kenneth Clairmont, strolling through from the reception room. "Good of you to come! Nice to see you again, too, Hardeen!"

Harry put a finger to his lips. "Quiet! Do not use my name too freely!"

"Pardon?"

Harry stepped closer to Clairmont and grasped his elbow. "Tell me, have you mentioned our names to Lucius Craig? Have you told him that you have invited a pair of professional magicians to observe his actions this evening?"

"Why, no. You specifically told me not to do so. I've only said that a pair of school friends would be joining us."

"Excellent! Then it is not too late!"

"Too late? Too late for what?"

By way of an answer, Harry reached into his coat pocket and produced a monocle and a false moustache. "I must conceal my true identity from Mr. Craig at all costs," Harry explained, fixing the monocle over his right eye. "If he should learn that the Great Houdini is among the sitters this evening, he will be on guard. Indeed, he might even refuse to proceed!"

"Uh, Harry," I said, "I'm not sure this is entirely necessary."

"We cannot be too careful," he insisted, fixing a luxuriant black moustache onto his upper lip. "It is our best chance of exposing Mr. Craig's trickery. You must not use my name during the evening. You may refer to me as Dr. Weiss."

Clairmont watched with raised eyebrows as my brother straightened his moustache. "You're quite certain about this, Houdini?"

"Harry, is that Uncle Herman's monocle?"

"Don't worry, Dash, I've brought a disguise for you, too! Here is a false nose!"

"Harry, I don't want to wear a false nose."

"But it has a wart!"

"Be that as it may, I'm not going to wear it. The whole idea is absolute foolishness."

Harry gazed at the false nose wistfully, then put it back into his pocket. "Very well," he said. "It is not essential to my plan for you to be incognito as well. Your fame is not quite so transcendent as mine. I merely thought—"

"Gentlemen?" Brunson, the butler, had reappeared at the doors to the reception room. "If you'll pardon me, Mrs. Clairmont wondered what had become of you." The butler's eyes came to rest upon my brother's upper lip, which had been clean-shaven not five minutes earlier. If the sudden sprouting of a handlebar moustache struck him as odd, he gave no outward sign.

"Of course, Brunson," said Kenneth, glancing at Harry with an uncertain expression. "We're just coming now." Squaring his shoulders, he led us from the room.

We were shown through to a large and brightly appointed reception room, where a woman whom I took to be Mrs. Clairmont stood waiting to greet us. Behind her was an imposing oil portrait of a grim-faced man who could only have been her late husband.

"Mother," Kenneth said, "here are the two friends I

mentioned. This is Dash Hardeen, and this, uh, this is Dr. Weiss."

"It is so good of you to agree to fill out our little circle," said Mrs. Clairmont, greeting us with genuine warmth. "When Kenneth said that Mr. Biggs would not be joining us this evening, I was afraid that we would not have a sufficient number of sitters. I am delighted you were able to step in, and no doubt Brunson is relieved to have been freed of the obligation to fill the extra chair. I do hope that our demonstration this evening will be of interest."

Mrs. Clairmont was tall and slender, with long hair of brilliant white. With her pleasing high cheekbones and sparkling gray eyes, it was plain to see that she had been a beauty in her youth. Like her son, she had an easy, gracious manner that went a long way toward putting us at our ease. Though Harry and I could not have been the sort of young men she was accustomed to receiving in her home, there was nothing in her manner to hint that we were unwelcome.

"Allow me to introduce my brother, Mr. Sterling Foster," Mrs. Clairmont was saying, indicating a stooped figure near the fire. Sterling Foster made no move to acknowledge our presence. He stood at the far end of the room with a glass of whiskey in hand, glowering at us as though we might have been debt collectors. Like his sister, he had bright eyes and strong features, though the broken veins tracing his bulbous nose spoke of a more dissolute lifestyle.

"I don't see why I have to participate in this foolery," he grumbled. "Lucius Craig can go and hang himself for all I care."

"Where is the mysterious Mr. Craig?" I asked, scanning the room.

"He is upstairs in my late husband's study," Mrs. Clairmont answered, ignoring her brother's grousing. "He requires a period of silent meditation before a demonstration. We shall wait here for the others." She signalled to the butler, who moved forward with a tray of wine glasses.

Kenneth and I each accepted a glass while Harry busied

himself examining a shelf of books. "Is wine not to your liking, Dr. Weiss?" Mrs. Clairmont asked, noting that Harry had not taken a glass. "We have other spirits, if you would prefer."

"Thank you, no," my brother answered. "As a medical man, I prefer to keep my mind clear." He tapped the side of his head, indicating the fine and presumably delicate organ operating within.

"What a shame," said Mrs. Clairmont. "It's a most unusual vintage."

The ringing of the door chime interrupted Harry's reply, and a moment later Brunson appeared to announce a pair of fresh visitors.

Dr. Richardson Wells was a dark-haired giant of a man, with a swag belly but powerful arms and shoulders. His skin had a coppery tinge that spoke of much time spent out of doors, and he appeared uncomfortable and somewhat confined in his formal attire. Mr. Edgar Grange, by contrast, had a pallid, drawn face that appeared never to have seen the light of day and the languid manner of a man unused to physical exertion of any kind. Kenneth had mentioned that Grange had taken over the family's business concerns in the months since Jasper Clairmont's passing, and it took no great feat of imagination to picture him hunched over a ledger volume, tallying up a column of figures.

"Ah! Grange! There you are!" called Sterling Foster in a voice thickened by whiskey. "Need to speak to you. Most urgent." With this, Foster shuttled the lawyer into a corner for a whispered conference. Judging by the sharp gestures and grim expressions, the subject under discussion was not pleasant.

"Weiss, eh?" Dr. Wells was saying to my brother. "What sort of practice are you in, sir?"

"Practice?" Harry asked, adjusting his monocle.

"I'm a general practitioner, myself," said Dr. Wells. "Had a country practice for many years."

"Yes!" Harry's head bobbed eagerly. "I am also a general practitioner."

"Ah!" cried Dr. Wells. "A kindred spirit! Where did you do your practicals?"

A spark of fear began to show in Harry's eyes. "Europe," he said. "Budapest, to be precise."

"Budapest? How very interesting! I can't say I know much about Hungary. It must be fascinating!"

"Dr. Weiss was just telling me of the most fascinating article he saw in *The Lancet*," said Kenneth Clairmont, endeavoring to save my brother from himself. "It had to do with the vasomotor changes in tabes dorsalis and its influence on the sympathetic nervous system."

"Indeed! Interested in nervous disorders, are you?" asked Dr. Wells.

"Isn't everyone?" said my brother.

"Well, Kenneth here certainly is." He clapped Kenneth on the back. "So, you're keeping up with your studies, boy? They've managed to teach you a thing or two in New Haven?"

"A thing or two, yes," Kenneth answered.

"You know there'll always be a place for you with me, if you should want some seasoning when you finish. I could use a pair of fresh legs on my rounds."

A cloud passed over the young man's face. "Well, I'm not certain that will be possible in the present circumstances."

"Nonsense!" cried Wells. "You're a born sawbones. Never saw anyone with such a ready grasp of anatomy. It's been that way since you were a pup."

"See here, Wells," said Edgar Grange, extricating himself from his conference with Sterling Foster, "you know perfectly well that young Kenneth will be joining the family firm soon enough. With Jasper gone, it's all the more urgent that we have a member of the Clairmont family at the helm."

The remark prompted a surly exclamation from Sterling Foster, who moved off toward the sideboard and reached for a whiskey decanter.

"Gentlemen," said Mrs. Clairmont in a bright but firm tone,

"we agreed that there would be no talk of business this evening. My plans are too important."

"Sorry, Augusta," said Dr. Wells, finishing off his glass of wine. "When are we going to have another go in the spook room, anyway?"

"We shall be joining Mr. Craig after the meal. Gentlemen, if you will follow me." With that, our hostess led us through to the dining room.

"I hope you've built up an appetite," Kenneth said as we made our way down a long corridor. "My mother has a rather exaggerated view of what constitutes a light supper."

"So does mine," I replied, "but as it happens, I'm so hungry I could eat a—good lord!"

It is fortunate that I did not actually proclaim my willingness to eat a horse, as my hostess would undoubtedly have produced one. In later years, when I had achieved a modicum of fame, I became accustomed to dining in high style at some of the finest establishments in Europe—at considerable cost to my waistline. At that time, however, I had never seen a table laid out in the fashion that awaited us in Mrs. Clairmont's dining room, nor would I have many more chances to enjoy the lavish gilded-age groaning board style of hospitality. The table was dressed with the finest linen beneath the soft glow of an alabaster gasolier. Each place was set with a square of cloth folded into an intricate crown imperial, and a bewildering array of seventeen pieces of silver. Mrs. Clairmont directed each of us to his place, then Dr. Wells held her chair as she settled herself to the right of the head of the table. The place of honor, I noted, was held vacant.

Even now, I can still recall the delicious smells that rose from the vast assembly of dishes on offer. Kenneth Clairmont, perhaps noting my perplexed expression, took care to name each of the dishes, adding a word or two of comment so as to remove any further confusion. "Ah! What have we in the soup tureen? Mock turtle! How pleasant! And for the fish course? Salmon

Restigouche, I see. A particular favorite of Mr. Grange's, as I recall. And what about the entrees? There's a brace of partridges, I see, and a wild duck. Is that Grenadine de Veau? You really must try that, Mr.—er, Dr. Weiss. The cook has a wonderful talent for veal."

On and on it went, with Kenneth offering helpful assistance at each stage of the meal, and Harry and myself struggling to do justice to the astonishing bounty before us. Brunson and his staff managed the silver serving platters and rolling carts with unobtrusive skill, although there had been some minor distress as we sat down over a missing chair. Brunson dispatched an assistant to fetch a replacement, and the rest of the meal passed without any noticeable disruption. More than once I looked down to find that my setting had changed or my glass had been filled without my having noticed.

Mrs. Clairmont kept the conversation light and the wine flowing, though her brother partook of neither. A decanter of whiskey had been set at his place, and he spent the duration of the meal steadily draining it, growing more and more truculent with each swallow. Mr. Grange, by contrast, drank nothing but ate ravenously, occasionally glancing at the table and furnishings with a certain proprietary interest, as though contemplating a purchase. Dr. Wells, for his part, spent much of the meal attempting to extract information on the state of European medicine from my brother, whose faltering replies were skillfully embroidered by Kenneth. As Biggs had foreseen, there was an uneasy moment when Harry attempted to address a lobster galantine with a pair of snail tongs, but once again Kenneth Clairmont managed to salvage the situation. "I see," he declared with a note of admiration, "is that how they do it in Budapest, Doctor?"

I must say that there were no further gaffes from my brother during the meal, largely because he had been stunned into immobility by the sight of a sautéed rabbit, which had been made to stand upright with its paws crossed in a disturbingly lifelike way, with a sprig of cauliflower tucked in where its tail had been. The greenish tinge behind my brother's monocle and false moustache told me that his thoughts were with his beloved lop-eared Selma.

Presently, when the remains of a magnificent prune flory had been cleared away, the gathering repaired to the sitting room for port and cigars.

"You must forgive me, Mr. Hardeen," said Mrs. Clairmont, taking my arm as we walked back down the central corridor, "I haven't had a chance to say more than two words to you all evening."

"I'm afraid I would not have been much of a conversationalist," I replied. "Not while my attention was absorbed by that wondrous saddle of mutton."

"I do like to see my guests well fed. Now, tell me, Kenneth mentioned that you are a friend from school. Are you a newspaper man, like that young Mr. Biggs who was here the other night?"

"Well, I have studied journalism," I said, which was, in fact, the truth. "At present, however, I am involved in the theater."

"The theater! How exciting! In what connection?"

"Management," I said.

"You must see all the new plays. Tell me, is the latest Sardou as wicked as I've heard?"

"Actually, I haven't—"

"And what about this clever young Harry Houdini?" asked my brother, stroking his moustache. "I hear he is poised to become the toast of New York!"

"Never heard of him," I said drily.

"No? But I understand he has just completed an engagement at the Belasco."

"Doesn't ring a bell."

"Can it be? I understand that no less a journal than the *Milwaukee Sentinel* was inspired to remark that—"

"Tell me, Mrs. Clairmont," I said, turning away from my

brother, "when might we expect to begin our sitting with Mr. Craig?"

"Very shortly, I expect. It is Mr. Craig's habit to fast prior to his demonstrations, but Brunson informs me that he has ordered a Coquette de Volaille to be ready in one hour's time."

"He's what?" cried Edgar Grange. "Augusta, this man has made himself too much at home. He is too free with your hospitality." He reached out to take a cigar from the humidor Brunson had offered.

"Not at all, Edgar," Mrs. Clairmont answered. "Lucius Craig is above material wants and desires."

Mr. Grange continued to voice his objections as Brunson made his way around the room with the humidor. Harry, listening intently, gave me a withering look as I reached out and selected a belvedere. "Dash," he whispered, "tobacco is a—"

I cut him short. "A serious obstacle to the proper development of the mental acuities. I know, Harry. But it's a damned fine cigar."

"Is it?" He considered the humidor for a moment, then took a fat imperial from the center.

"Harry?" I said. "What are you—?"

"When in Rome," he murmured, leaning forward to accept a light from Brunson.

"But Harry," I said, as he began choking violently on the first draw of smoke, "you've never so much as—"

"Look, Mr. Hardeen! Is that not an interesting set of books on the mantelpiece?" Leading me away from the others, Harry resumed in a low voice, "Don't look so shocked, Dash. I just wanted to see if these cigars were as good as you claimed." With that, Harry turned the cigar over, examined the burning end carefully, and then popped the entire thing into his mouth. He chewed twice, then swallowed.

"Harry!" I cried.

"Nothing to it," he said happily. "How very delectable!"

"But that was a very expensive cigar! If you were going to

practice your act, you could have done just as well with a penny cheroot!"

"I suppose, but I doubt if Mrs. Clairmont keeps such things about the house. After all—"

"You aren't quite like the other doctors I've met," came a drink-sodden voice. We turned to see that Sterling Foster, whiskey glass in hand, had crossed the room to join us, having apparently witnessed Harry's strange display.

"Er, no," Harry began.

"We, uh—"

He waved aside our attempts to explain ourselves, sloshing a fair measure of whiskey onto the carpet. "I couldn't help overhearing. You needn't worry about me, I'll keep your secret. What are you, some sort of circus performer?"

Harry puffed himself up a bit. "I am no mere circus performer," he announced. "I am the eclipsing sensation of—"

"Yes," I put in. "He's a circus performer."

"Wonderful! You may be able to expose this man Craig!" He gulped at his whiskey. "I had thought that was what that chap from the *Herald* might have been planning the other night, but he seemed just as flummoxed as the rest of them." He waved his glass to indicate the others in the room. "Hooked like trout, they were. Me, I think he's just a circus tout, like you. You might be just the thing to knock him down a peg. Set a thief to catch a thief, I say."

Harry began to protest the remark, but I restrained him.

"You wouldn't object to seeing Mr. Craig exposed, then?"

"Object? Far from it. That man is the very worst kind of charlatan. He's playing on my sister's bereavement, giving her hope where none exists. Her husband is dead. We all have to accept it. So long as this man dangles the hope of communicating with Jasper, Augusta won't be able to think of anything else. It's cruel, I say."

I stepped closer, lowering my voice. "You were present at the séance the other night, I understand."

"Yes."

"Why didn't you accuse Mr. Craig of being a fraud then and there?"

"Oh, the man is very clever. I'll admit to that straight off. I don't know how he does the things that he does, but I know perfectly well that he's not communicating with any spirit presence."

"I quite agree," said Harry in a conspiratorial tone. "It may interest you to know that we are not alone in thinking so. I understand that the Great Houdini himself has taken an interest in Mr. Craig."

"The Great Houdini?" Foster asked. "Who might that be?"

Harry's cheeks reddened. "Why, he is the justly celebrated star of—"

"You won't have heard of him," I said, motioning for Harry to lower his voice.

Foster did not appear to be listening. "Once a man is dead, there's an end of it," he declared, with yet another mighty swallow of whiskey. "I know that as well as I know my own name." His eyelids fluttered for a moment as he struggled to keep hold of his thoughts. "If that Lucius Craig has any ideas about getting his hands on my sister's money, he'd better think again. I know a thing or two about him. He'd better tread carefully."

"I hear tell," said Harry, still lagging a step behind, "that the Great Houdini is highly—"

"You know a thing or two about him?" I asked, silencing Harry with an urgent gesture. "What sorts of things might those be?"

Foster glanced from side to side in an exaggerated show of confidentiality. "About that daughter of his. Not all she seems, is she? The high and mighty Mr. Craig thinks he's getting one over on us, but I'm not fooled. I know things. Believe me, I know things."

"His daughter? What about his daughter?"

Foster's shoulders twitched and he glared at us with sudden

ferocity, as though we had insulted his honor. "Say! Who are you to be asking me questions? Baggy-pants circus touts, that's what you are! I ought to have you turned out of here!"

"But we were only—"

"Better yet, I'll see to it myself, you baggy-pants circus touts!" He set his jaw and took a menacing step forward, cocking a fist as he advanced.

"Mr. Foster, there's no need—"

But it was too late. With a grunt, Foster squared his shoulders and threw a vigorous left hook. It is difficult to say which of us he was attempting to strike, but Harry and I both stepped aside easily, leaving Foster to pitch forward under the momentum of his swing. Harry's arms darted out but failed to stop our assailant's forward progress. Foster took three lurching steps and collided with a Hepplewhite side table, upending a bowl of fruit and walnuts as he slumped heavily to the floor.

"Don't think you're getting one over on me," he declared, resting his head against the overturned bowl. "I know things." His eyes closed, and his breathing subsided into a contented snore.

Harry gazed down at the sleeping form. "What do you suppose he meant by that?"

"Don't ask me, Dr. Weiss," I said. "I'm just a baggy-pants circus tout."

5

THE LIGHT MILITIA

THE SUDDEN INDISPOSITION OF STERLING FOSTER CAUSED LITTLE stir. Brunson and a pair of the serving staff converged on the fallen figure with brisk efficiency, bearing him away as though tidying an upended cuspidor. Dr. Wells and Mr. Grange made a point of looking elsewhere as the operation was carried out, while Kenneth Clairmont murmured a quiet word of apology on his uncle's behalf. Mrs. Clairmont, her hand at her throat, remarked only that her brother had been "most unaccountably run down of late." I had the impression that such displays were not uncommon in the Clairmont household.

Within moments of Foster's unceremonious departure, a slight, red-haired girl could be seen hovering tentatively at the entrance to the room. She could not have been much more than thirteen or fourteen years old, with pale features framed by ringlets. Her bright, green eyes swept the room with a level, direct gaze. Mrs. Clairmont rose and moved across to greet her.

"Lila," she said, "I don't believe you've met everyone." She led the girl to the center of the room. "Lila is Mr. Craig's daughter," she told us.

The girl said nothing but nodded to Harry and me.

"Is your father ready for us upstairs?" Mrs. Clairmont asked.

Lila gave a nod in reply and leaned to whisper something in Mrs. Clairmont's ear. The older woman smiled. "I am told that Mr. Craig is pleased with the equipoise of energies," she announced. "Perhaps this will be the evening that we succeed in reaching my dear husband. Kindly follow me to the séance chamber." She turned to the butler, who had just returned from overseeing the removal of Sterling Foster. "Brunson?"

"Madam?"

"In light of my brother's sudden infirmity, I shall require you to occupy the empty chair in tonight's circle."

A slight tremor washed over the butler's features. "How pleasant, madam."

Harry drew me aside as Mrs. Clairmont led us through to the grand staircase. "At last I am going to meet the famous Lucius Craig," he whispered, as we climbed past a gallery of oil portraits lining the stairs. "Apparently his psychic powers have not alerted him to the presence of a formidable adversary!"

"Harry, we're just here to observe. Don't do anything crazy."

"Of course not. However, it is only sporting to alert Mr. Craig to the fact that he is being watched by an expert in the arcane arts!"

"Harry, I don't know what you're planning, but—"

"Mr. Hardeen? Dr. Weiss? There you are!" Mrs. Clairmont waited for us in the doorway of a room at the top of the stairs. "Come along, gentlemen. I'm eager to introduce you to our honored guest." She beamed happily as we passed through the doorway.

We found ourselves in a large and comfortably furnished gentleman's study. Cluttered bookshelves lined three walls, jammed with worn volumes, loose papers, and odd curios such as an African fertility carving, a battered whale harpoon, and an array of brass weather instruments and wind gauges such as might be found on the bridge of a merchant vessel. A fourth wall opened out onto a tall bay window, before which stood a polished maple desk. The surface of the desk was absolutely bare and had been recently polished to a high gloss. I suppressed a shudder as I recalled that this was the spot where

Jasper Clairmont had taken his own life.

An octagonal table stood on a thick pedestal at the center of the room, exactly as Kenneth Clairmont had described, with a ceramic tray, a pad of paper and a chalk slate arranged on its surface. Eight chairs were circled about the table, with the one nearest to us partially enclosed by an arrangement of sheer cloth screens. A bright carpet of an odd plum-colored Indian design was spread out beneath the table, and I guessed that the floor coverings had been changed immediately following the family's tragedy.

A slender figure stood at the windows with his hands clasped behind his back, gazing down into the street below with an air of intense fascination.

"Lucius?" called Mrs. Clairmont. "I've brought our visitors."

Lucius Craig turned from the window and greeted us with a faltering smile. He was tall and round-shouldered, with reddish hair running to gray, and a pair of wide-set, sunken eyes that gave the impression of peering down from a great height. He crossed the room with a curiously weightless, almost spidery, movement, waving one hand as though conducting a symphony.

"Good of you to come," he said in a soft, feathery voice. "So good of you to indulge me. There is a decided chill in the air this evening. It bodes well."

I noted that Lucius Craig spoke with a trace of a British accent, though unlike any I had heard before. I speculated that he had spent time in Ireland or perhaps Scotland. His head bobbed agreeably as he was introduced to me and Harry, but his fingers seemed to shrivel under the force of our handshakes, as though physical proximity was somehow painful to him.

"I do hope that the spirits might favor us with a manifestation this evening, Mrs. Clairmont," Craig was saying. "I am so hopeful after the promising results we obtained the other night. Now, if I might ask you to take your places at the table. Dr. Weiss, you shall be there, and Mr. Hardeen, may I ask you to sit beside him?"

We took our places around the octagonal table as Craig stepped over to a large music box and set it in motion. A tinny rendition of a Mozart étude filled the room.

"Ah!" cried Craig, waving his fingers to the music. "Very soothing! Just the thing!"

"This is the celebrated Lucius Craig?" I whispered to Harry. "I expected a more commanding presence—something almost demonic. He seems like a dithery old schoolmaster."

"It's often the way with mediums," Harry answered. "They appear harmless so as not to invite suspicion. I guarantee that there is more to him than meets the eye."

I watched as Craig lingered by the music box, swaying to the music with a dreamy expression on his face. "There would have to be," I said.

When the rest of us were seated Craig spent a further moment or two fussing over the screens behind his chair, explaining that the arrangement of fabric was needed to form a crucible for his energies. This done, he settled himself between Mrs. Clairmont and Mr. Grange, smiling with happy contentment.

"Now, then," he began, laying his hands on the surface of the table, "it is my fervent hope this evening that we shall journey into unknown realms. However, since Mr. Hardeen and Dr. Weiss were not with us for our previous effort, we must again take care that we bring our minds into alignment before we can begin. As with the tuning of a musical instrument, our vital forces must be brought into accord. For the moment, we shall leave the lights as they are, though if we are to ascend to the next level as the séance progresses, we shall have to extinguish them entirely. Do you understand?"

Mrs. Clairmont nodded her agreement, though my brother—even behind his moustache and monocle—appeared decidedly agitated.

"I would like each of you to take a slip of paper from this pad," Craig continued. "Allow yourself a moment or two to clear your mind of all stray impressions, then jot down a word or phrase on the slip of paper. It should be a thought that comes naturally to mind—do not confuse matters by straining over an old memory or a lengthy maxim. The message should be brief and direct. As I said, this is merely an exercise—a means of clearing the palate before we move on to the main feature of the evening."

My brother grew more and more restive during Craig's remarks. "Brief and direct," he muttered, bending low over his slip of paper.

Craig waited for a moment while the others scrawled out their messages. "That is excellent," he said when each of us had finished. "Now, you would oblige me if you would each add your initials at the bottom of your message. Good. Now, we finish by folding the slips in half, then in half again. Excellent. Let us place the papers in this tray." He watched as a shallow ceramic tray was passed around the table. "Very good," he said when the tray made its way back to him. "We are ready to proceed."

"I shouldn't wonder," Harry grumbled. I shot him a warning glance.

Resting his hands on either side of the tray, Craig closed his eyes and remained motionless for a moment. Then, without opening his eyes, he dipped his fingers into the tray and withdrew one of the slips of paper. Pressing it to his forehead, he concentrated for a further moment before a smile spread across his features. "A fitting invocation," he said. "The message comes from our hostess, and it reads, 'Success.' I do hope so, Mrs. Clairmont."

Craig unfolded the message and set it aside before dipping his fingers into the tray once more. "Here is a message from our friend Mr. Grange," he said, pressing the next folded slip to his forehead. "It reads, 'Violet.' And here is an offering from Mr. Brunson, unless I'm mistaken. His message is 'Remember the Maine.' Dear me! How very patriotic! Let us see, I believe this next slip of paper holds a rather longer message. 'Unnumbered spirits round thee fly.' A line from Pope, is it not, Kenneth? How does the poem continue? Ah, yes. 'Unnumbered spirits round thee fly, the light militia of the lower sky.' Now, then, what have we here...?"

The demonstration continued in this manner for some moments, with Craig plucking each folded slip from the tray, pressing it to his forehead and, after a moment's concentration, reading out the words printed within. As he successfully divined each particular message, Craig unfolded the paper billet, scanned the contents to confirm his reading, and then tossed it aside before moving on to the next. I could not help but marvel at the easy, conversational manner in which he carried out the feat. There was no suggestion of performance about his actions and nothing in his bearing to convey pride or satisfaction in the demonstration. Instead, his attitude was that of a humble supplicant who considered himself fortunate to be taking part in a remarkable happening. The distinction, I realized, was an important one, for it shifted the emphasis of the gathering away from any examination of his deeds. Instead, we were invited to join in his apparent wonder at a power greater than ourselves.

"I believe this is the message from our friend Dr. Wells," Craig was saying. "The sentiment is brief and, I dare say, painful. It simply says, 'Toothache.' My sincere sympathies, Dr. Wells."

From across the table, the doc tor nodded ruefully and rubbed at his jaw.

"Yes," Craig continued, "that can be most"—a pained expression passed over his face suddenly—"unpleasant. Very unpleasant, indeed."

"What's wrong, Mr. Craig?" asked Mrs. Clairmont. "You seem distressed."

The medium gripped the edge of the table. "A sudden shift of animus," he said. "Most extraordinary. I hope our experiment is not compromised."

"Dear me," said Mrs. Clairmont.

"Think nothing of it, dear lady," Craig continued. "Let

us continue." He pressed another folded slip to his forehead. "Another message begins to reveal itself, though not an entirely serious one, I see. It reads, 'Whiskey and soda.' "

This brought an appreciative bark of laughter from Dr. Wells.

"Very amusing, Mr. Hardeen," said Craig, unfolding the slip of paper. "I'm certain that Brunson will be pleased to accommodate you when our gathering has concluded. But what is this?" His features darkened once again. "How strange! How terribly strange!"

Mrs. Clairmont leaned toward him. "What is it, Lucius?"

"A strange challenge, though I cannot begin to fathom the meaning."

"What does it say?"

Craig unfolded the slip of paper and held it up for all to see. " 'Lucius Craig, your judgement is at hand!' "

Mrs. Clairmont gave an exhalation of alarm and sank back in her chair. Edgar Grange, meanwhile, fixed my brother with an expression of intense interest. "You're the only one we haven't heard from yet, Dr. Weiss," he said. "What is the meaning of this strange declaration?"

Harry adjusted his monocle. "I am afraid—" he began.

"See here," Craig interrupted, pointing at the slip of paper. "The initials are not those of Dr. Weiss. The message is signed 'H. H.'" He glanced around the table. "But who might that be?"

Harry rose from his chair and gripped the edge of the table. "Can you not guess?" he demanded, allowing his voice to sink to a dramatic register. "Can you not fathom who this mysterious H. H. might be?"

"I'm afraid I'm at a loss," said the medium.

"Then allow me to assist you," cried Harry, snatching the monocle and moustache from his face. "For, you see, I am none other than the Great Houdini himself!"

A confused silence greeted this revelation.

"The Great Houdini!" Harry repeated. "The renowned magician!"

Our fellow guests looked back at him with blank expressions. "The man whom the *Milwaukee Sentinel* praised as—"

"My brother apologizes profusely for any confusion that his behavior has caused," I said, stepping into the breach. "What he wishes to say—and undoubtedly would have said had his eagerness to be of service not gotten the best of him—is that as a professional magician he is privy to a great number of secrets of stagecraft and sleight of hand. Some of these secrets have suggested a means by which Mr. Craig's demonstration might have been accomplished by strictly conventional means."

Dr. Wells cleared his throat. "Do you mean to say you're accusing Craig here of being a fraud?" The prospect seemed to delight him. "You mean it was just a magic trick?"

"Yes!" cried Harry. "That is exactly—"

"Not precisely," I said, with a quick glance at Mrs. Clairmont, who appeared positively stricken. "Harry merely wishes to suggest, in the spirit of sportsmanship, that he might be able to duplicate the effect. Of course, he does not mean to imply deception on the part of our esteemed friend."

Dr. Wells grinned at my evasion, then looked at Lucius Craig. "Well, what do you say, Craig? Are you up to a little sporting challenge?"

The medium had been studying my brother intently. For a moment his features flashed with annoyance, but he soon mastered himself. "This young man intrigues me," he said with some of his old geniality. "I should like to see this so-called duplication, though I'm not entirely certain what Mr.— Houdini, was it?—I'm not entirely certain what Mr. Houdini seeks to prove. With sufficient application, any one of us might be able to copy a painting by Rembrandt. By your logic, that would render Mr. Rembrandt himself a forger."

"It's not quite the same thing," said Edgar Grange, rising to the challenge in a lawyerly fashion. "So far as I'm aware, Mr. Rembrandt claimed no spirit guidance for his works."

"Even so," Craig began, "I fail to see—"

"Gentlemen," said Mrs. Clairmont, "I will not permit any squabbling in this room. If Mr. Craig is willing to permit Mr. Houdini to proceed, then let us get on with it. If not, I am anxious to resume the séance."

Craig looked again at my brother. The medium's expression was that of a man preparing to step out onto a tightrope. "Very well," he said after a moment. "Let's see what this young man has to show us. I must repeat, however, that a magician's tricks have nothing to do with spiritualism."

"No?" Harry pulled at the points of his tie, a gesture he made before every performance. "Well, perhaps we should examine the matter more closely. Mr. Craig, if you would be so good as to exchange places with me, I think it will assist in our"—he glanced at Mrs. Clairmont—"with our experiment." Harry sat down and reached for the tray in which Craig had deposited the folded messages. "Mr. Craig has given us a fascinating display of what he calls spirit message reading. In the world in which I travel, it goes by a different name. We call it a billet effect."

"A billet effect?" asked Kenneth Clairmont. "What do you mean, Houdini?"

"Allow me to demonstrate." Harry reached into the ceramic tray and picked up one of the slips of paper. Quickly refolding it, he pressed it to his forehead. "Let us suppose that I am attempting to divine the message written on this piece of paper. After concentrating for a moment, I am prepared to tell you that the message is 'Success' and that it was written by Mrs. Clairmont."

"Which is exactly what Mr. Craig did, Houdini," said Dr. Wells. "I'm not sure where that gets us."

"No? Well, suppose I then unfolded the paper, as if to check that my reading had been correct. And suppose that instead of the message 'Success,' the paper actually held the word 'Violet' and the initials of Mr. Grange."

"Then you'd have been wrong, Houdini," said Wells. "Your

demonstration would be counted a failure."

"I think not," Harry said. "I should only have failed if one of you were to see the contents of the paper. If I were to set it aside, you would have no way of knowing what it said. Imagine, then, that I picked up another slip of paper"—again Harry reached into the tray—"and after a further show of concentration, I told you that the message was 'Violet,' with the initials of Mr. Grange attached."

Kenneth spoke up. "But that slip of paper wasn't Mr. Grange's at all," he said. "The previous one was his."

"Exactly," said Harry. "This slip of paper says, 'Remember the Maine,' and it is initialed by our good friend Mr. Brunson. But you would have no reason to doubt me if I told you that it said 'Violet,' especially with Mr. Grange himself confirming that this was the word he wrote. Meanwhile, this deception leaves me free to take up the next slip of paper and tell you that it contains the message 'Remember the Maine.'"

"I see?" cried Kenneth excitedly. "That's very good? You would only be pretending to reveal the message on each slip of paper. In reality, you would be telling us the contents of the previous message, the one you had opened moments earlier. You would always be one message ahead of what you were actually telling us."

"Precisely so," said Harry.

Edgar Grange cleared his throat. "It's very clever, Mr. Houdini, but it seems to me there's a fatal flaw in your reasoning. In order for your trick to work, you would have to know the contents of one of the messages before you could begin. To use your own example, you would need to know in advance that Augusta had written the word 'Success' on her paper. Otherwise you would have no excuse for opening that first slip of paper so as to put your system into effect."

"He's got you there, Houdini," agreed Dr. Wells. "In order to get one step ahead of the messages, you'd have to know what one of us had written in advance. I don't see how you'd be able to do that—not in these circumstances, at any rate. Not unless you can read minds after all."

Harry reached for the pad of paper and pushed it across the table. "Dr. Wells, I wonder if I might ask you to write down a number between one and one hundred. Any number at all."

Wells picked up the pad and reached for a pencil. "What's this supposed to prove, Houdini?"

"Only that it is not as difficult to read your thoughts as you might suppose. All I ask is that you write down the first number that comes into your mind. Do you understand? Ah, very good." Harry rose from his chair and walked toward the windows, turning his back to us. "Please be sure that the others are able to see the number that you have written, so that there is no misunderstanding afterwards. Next, take the slip of paper and place it into your pocket, so that there is no possibility of my sneaking a look at it. Have you done so? Good."

Harry turned and walked back to the table, carrying a candle holder from the desk. "Here is a pretty problem. I must find some means of apprehending what you have written on that slip of paper. How might I do this? There is one possibility. In ancient Mesopotamia it was believed that a man's eye retained a faint image—like the flicker of this candle flame—of everything he had ever looked upon and that if we only knew how to look, we might see these images as plainly as you might look upon your own reflection in a mirror. It is possible that if—"

"That's poppycock!" cried Dr. Wells. "The eye merely transmits images, it doesn't record them!"

"Does it not?" Harry moved around the table to where Dr. Wells was sitting. "Well, we shall know soon enough." He picked up the ceramic tray that held the discarded slips of paper. Dipping the candle he was holding, he touched the flame to the paper. As the scraps ignited, sending up an orange glow, Harry passed the tray back and forth in front of the doctor's face. "Watch closely, if you would, Dr. Wells," Harry said, "and please keep your eyes fixed upon the flames. I am trying to see if there is any trace of—ah ha! Excellent! How very interesting! How very interesting, indeed!"

"What is it, Mr. Houdini?" asked Mrs. Clairmont. "What was it that you saw?"

"Everything, my dear lady. Everything." He reached across for the pad of paper and jotted a quick note, then turned the pad face down on the table. "Do you still have that slip of paper, Dr. Wells? Might I trouble you to place it upon the table? Good. Would you read the number that you have printed upon it?"

"Forty-two," said the doctor.

"Very good. Mrs. Clairmont, may I ask you to turn over the pad of paper at the center of the table? Thank you. Now, would you read what I have written there?"

"Forty-two!" cried Mrs. Clairmont. "But that's wonderful, Mr. Houdini!"

"Excellent!" agreed Dr. Wells, as the others around the table made various noises of agreement. "But I still maintain that business about reading the image in my eye was a pure fabrication. How did you manage it?"

Harry sat down and folded his arms. "I might as well tell you," he said with a sigh, "because if I do not, my brother Dash undoubtedly will. You are correct, Dr. Wells. My claim of seeing the number through your eyes was nothing more than a magician's patter, meant to distract you from my true method. In fact, I knew what number you had chosen at the very instant you wrote it down."

"But how?"

"Simplicity itself. I followed the movements of your pencil."

Kenneth Clairmont picked up one of the pencils lying on the table. "You've lost me there, Houdini."

"Let me show you," said my brother, taking up the pad. "When I instructed Dr. Wells to write down a number, he was careful to hold the pad at an angle, facing himself, so that I would not be able to glimpse what he was writing. This was a worthwhile precaution, as it prevented me from seeing either the paper or the point of the pencil. However, it did not prevent me from seeing the other end of the pencil."

"I don't see how the other end of the pencil could tell you anything," said Edgar Grange.

"It told me a great deal. Observe: if I hold the pad facing myself and write the number 1, the other end of the pencil makes a sharp upward stroke. If I make a 2, the end of the pencil makes a half-circle, followed by a sharp horizontal stroke. A 3 is a pair of half-circles. And so on. The same technique may be applied to letters of the alphabet. It is very difficult to keep track of a longer piece of writing, but with practice, a number or a short message may be followed easily enough simply by reading the movements of the pencil."

"Incredible," said Dr. Wells. "Very good, Houdini."

Kenneth Clairmont rose from his chair and began pacing a slow circle around the table. "So you would have been able to do the trick of reading the slips of paper after all," he said. "You would simply have fastened your attention on one of us and read the movements of his pencil. Then you would have known what that person's message was, and you would have been able to use that knowledge as you pretended to divine each subsequent message, using the method you showed us earlier." He glanced at Lucius Craig, who had said nothing during Harry's demonstration. "That is most illuminating, Mr. Houdini. I must see if I can't learn to do that pencil-reading stunt myself."

"Actually, Mr. Clairmont, it may not be necessary to acquire that skill at all," Harry said. "I daresay that if you were to undertake the billet-reading trick, you might find simpler ways of catching a glimpse of one of the messages at the table. In a gathering such as this, it is almost always possible to sneak a look at someone's paper as they write. I took particular care to warn Dr. Wells to shield his message from my eyes. Mr. Craig issued no such warning. It would be no great surprise, therefore, to find that he had been able to glance at your mother's message without her knowledge of—"

Lucius Craig was on his feet in an instant. "See here, Houdini!" he cried. "I have remained silent throughout this curious spectacle, but this is too much! You have gone too far!" His hands went to his cheeks, as though trying to hold back a flood of emotion that threatened to overwhelm him. "You are a fascinating young man," he resumed in a more measured tone. "I have been as intrigued and entertained as the others by your interesting, if crude, approximation of the effects one sometimes experiences when moving among the spirits. But it is quite apparent that you do not fully understand these forces. It is one thing to a show us means by which the doings of the séance room may be mimicked by those such as yourself who possess no genuine psychic gifts. It is quite another thing, however, to state that your methods—the feints and dodges of a sideshow trickster—are the means by which true manifestations are achieved. I am not a performer like yourself, sir. I am simply a medium, a person who acts as a conduit between our world and the next. I can assure you, the spirits are not required to steal glances at a slip of paper or read the movements of a pencil."

"No?" Harry grinned broadly, warming to the challenge. "I defy you to demonstrate that you are able to produce the same effect in conditions set and monitored by my brother and myself!"

"You don't understand, Houdini," the medium answered. "The spirits cannot be made to dance for coins and leap through hoops of fire!"

Harry made to reply, but a glance at our hostess told him that he had drifted into dangerous waters.

"Gentlemen," Mrs. Clairmont said in a firm voice, "I will not have raised voices in this room."

Craig folded his hands. "You are quite right, Augusta," he said. "I have allowed my passions to get the best of me."

Mrs. Clairmont turned to my brother. "Mr. Houdini, I must say that your behavior this evening has been most peculiar.

You have presented yourself in my home under the cloak of an outlandish disguise, and yet you feel entitled to insult the integrity of one of my guests. What Mr. Craig seeks to accomplish is a thing of great importance to me. I will not have you make light of so sacred a matter."

I shot my brother another warning glance, hoping that he understood the precarious position into which he had thrust himself. He glanced back at me and tapped his nose with his forefinger, a signal we had devised for use in the escape act. It indicated that he was in trouble and needed help extricating himself.

I stood and rested my hands on the back of my chair. "I must apologize," I said. "I assure you that my brother did not mean to give offense. He has allowed his enthusiasm to get the best of him. This happens often, I am obliged to say, and if you knew him as I do you would know that he does not mean to attack Mr. Craig's beliefs. This is all very new and unfamiliar to us. We cannot help but respond in the light of our own training and experiences. We are magicians. We are accustomed to solving puzzles. It is our business to devise methods of performing effects that seem to be impossible. When we are presented with a set of circumstances that appear to defy logic, we are naturally inclined to address the matter as we would a vanished rabbit or a floating sphere. I hope that you will accept our apologies, Mr. Craig."

The medium drew in a deep breath, evidently weighing his words carefully. He rested the fingers of one hand on the séance table while the other stole to his coat pocket and withdrew a glass snuff shaker. He tapped a small quantity onto the back of his hand and dispatched it with a brisk intake of air. He repeated the process with the other nostril, leaving us all waiting while he gathered his thoughts.

"Your brother appears to be a wonderfully skillful magician," he began. "I am not. As I stated earlier, there is no need to suppose because a clever man like Mr. Houdini may be able to duplicate some of what transpires in the séance room that the original effects themselves are somehow rendered invalid. Just because a signature may be forged, it does not mean that there is no such thing as an authentic signature."

"Precisely so, Mr. Craig," said Mrs. Clairmont. "My very thought."

"I cannot entirely agree," said Edgar Grange, raising the timbre of his voice as if addressing a courtroom. "You will admit that it does rather strike at one's inclination to credit Mr. Craig's effects when one sees how easily they may be manufactured by a man such as Houdini. As much as he might wish to deny it, Mr. Craig is inviting us to believe in the veracity of his so-called contacts with the spirit world simply because there is no other explanation for the feats and effects which he is able to accomplish. It is all well and good to speak as if the thing must be taken on faith, but the fact remains that you are attempting to foster our belief with these seemingly inexplicable feats."

Lucius Craig's eyes flashed for a moment, and it was clear that he was having some difficulty mastering his temper. "You may see it that way, sir. If so, you have my pity. This is not a case to be tried in a court of law. This is my life's pursuit. My gift. It must be approached not with the aggressive tilt of the barrister but with the open mind and pleading soul of a supplicant at the gates of a new revelation. One makes most of the progress on one's knees."

Dr. Wells spoke up at this. "You mean to say that one must already believe in spiritualism in order to find confirmation? Sounds like circular logic to me. The dog chasing its own tail."

"An open mind," Craig said evenly. "An open mind and a questing soul. Is that so very much to require when one stands at the brink of a new epoch of human thought? Is it so very different from what your clergyman asks of you each Sunday morning?"

"See here," said Wells, "you're equating this spiritualism of yours with religion?"

"Of course," said Craig with a serene smile. "One that embraces all of the world's peoples. And such matters are decided within the human heart, not by cold proofs but by warming faith. I have no doubt that Mr. Houdini might also contrive some clever means of changing water into wine. Would that tear at your beliefs, Dr. Wells? 'Your judgement is at hand.' Wasn't that what Mr. Houdini said?"

The doctor opened his mouth to reply but thought better of it.

"Lucius," said Mrs. Clairmont, "last night you promised that we would attempt to reach my husband. Perhaps that might serve to set aside any remaining doubts once and for all. Is there any chance that we may yet make the attempt?"

Craig frowned as he considered the matter. "Mr. Houdini's display has unsettled the balance of spirit energy in the room. I fear that it would be dangerous to proceed. In any event, there would be little point in making the attempt with such an avowed disbeliever in our midst. It creates a negative aura that prohibits spirit activity."

"There it is again," Dr. Wells murmured. "One must already believe in order to find belief. One sees what one wants to see."

Kenneth Clairmont looked at me in despair. He had invited us to assess Lucius Craig's mediumship, but Harry had tipped our hand too early in the proceedings. If Craig could not be encouraged to continue, Harry and I would be of no further use.

"Mr. Craig," I said, leaning forward, "my brother is not so closed-minded as you assume. It is only that he has not yet found a medium worthy of his attention. Harry and I are professional magicians. The chalk slate and the floating tambourine hold no great mystery for us, as you will appreciate. But surely a man such as yourself has something to teach us? I assure you that we will free our minds of any preconceptions we may have brought with us tonight." I picked up the chalk slate from the table and wiped it with my sleeve. "We will present you with a blank slate."

Craig was not mollified. "I will not have Mr. Houdini prodding and probing at my every movement. I am not a circus dog."

I glanced at my brother. "Harry?"

"What my brother says is true," Harry said, with surprising sincerity. "There is much in this world that I do not yet understand. My mind is supple. I am prepared to weigh the evidence."

The medium shook his head. "Your actions tonight suggest otherwise, Mr. Houdini."

"I beg to differ. I have done nothing that a man of science would not do. There are several distinguished scientific bodies dedicated to examining this type of phenomena. In London there is the Society for Psychical Research. There is an American counterpart as well, operating in Boston, I believe. Many distinguished men have been drawn into their ranks. The physicist Oliver Lodge. The naturalist Alfred Russel Wallace. The philosopher William James. These are men of judgement and reason, but they are also men of discernment. They would require proof. If there is a single grain of truth in this matter, I will happily embrace it. Perhaps that proof may reside with you, Mr. Craig."

I glanced at him in the dim light, surprised to find that he seemed to mean what he was saying. It is strange now to recall these sentiments coming from the lips of Harry Houdini, who in later life would become the scourge of spirit mediums at home and abroad. In time his reputation as an anti-spiritualist crusader would grow to be nearly as great as that of his exploits upon the stage. In his youth, however, his mind was far more plastic. Though he could never have been called a believer, more than once I heard him express a wistful hope that there might yet be magic in the world.

Craig's hands fluttered to his lapels. "Very well," he said after a moment's consideration, "but first I must ask a favor of young Mr. Houdini."

Harry looked up. "A favor?"

"Indeed," said Craig, smiling contentedly. "I must ask that you tie me up."

"What?" Harry appeared truly shocked. "Tie you up?"

"Don't look so surprised, Mr. Houdini. I don't know what, if any, spirit phenomena we may expect when we resume our experiment, but whatever may happen, I do not want you to accuse me of having manipulated the conditions afterwards. I can think of no other proof against your skepticism than to allow you to bind me to this chair."

"Lucius, this seems very irregular," said Mrs. Clairmont. "If you are tied to the chair, how will we maintain the spirit circle? You must be able to touch the hands of the sitters on either side of you."

"That is so," said the medium, weighing the problem. "Suppose Mr. Houdini were to lash my wrists to the arms of the chair? I should still be able to grasp the hands of my fellow sitters, but I would not be able to move in any other manner. Would that satisfy you, Mr. Houdini?"

Harry considered the matter. "It would," he admitted. "It would, indeed."

Craig's mouth pursed with satisfaction. "Brunson? Have we any rope about the place?"

The butler nodded. "I believe there is some line for the washing, sir."

"Please be so good as to fetch it." The medium turned to my brother as Brunson departed on his errand. "Now, then, Mr. Houdini, I must once again emphasize that I do not know what will happen when we make our foray into the spirit realms, but I want there to be no doubt about my ability to perpetrate any type of fraud. You must tie me securely. Do you happen to know anything about ropes and knots? If not, perhaps one of the other gentlemen might—"

"I believe I am equal to the task," Harry said carefully. "I know a bit about ropes and knots."

"Excellent! Well, then, I await the outcome with great interest!" Craig linked his hands behind his back and drifted over toward the sideboard, helping himself to a small brandy from one of the decanters.

After a moment Brunson returned with a length of thin but sturdy braided hemp. Harry fell on the rope and examined it with careful attention, pulling to test its strength and examining the length for signs of wear. When he had satisfied himself, he asked that Mr. Craig be seated in the chair. The medium drained the last of his brandy and then settled himself with an air of amiable resignation. He placed his arms upon the rests, and there began the most thorough job of binding and trussing I have ever beheld. Harry did not so much tie the man's arms as seal them within a cocoon of hemp. The rope was cut into several lengths, and each of these was wrapped and knotted with a tidy precision that would have brought credit to a surgeon closing a wound.

"My goodness, Mr. Houdini!" cried Craig when the operation was complete. "I do hope you will be able to untie all of these knots once we've finished!"

"We shall have to cut you out," Harry said firmly. "When Harry Houdini ties a man up, he stays tied."

"So I gather," said Craig with a rueful smile. "In the circumstances, then, I must ask that each of you assist me in restoring the proper conditions for the continuation of our experiment. Mr. Grange, lock the door, if you would. We must not be disturbed at the crucial moment. Dr. Wells, put the lights down. Illumination is painful to the spirit presence. Kenneth, please take the chalk slate and replace it at the center of the table. Thank you, gentlemen. Brunson, please set the music box going once again. Yes, that is most pleasant. Good. Take your places, please. Let us begin anew. Perhaps we may enter into a realm that will astonish even Mr. Houdini."

Once more we joined hands around the octagonal table, with Mrs. Clairmont and Mr. Grange stretching their hands out a bit farther to clasp those of the confined Mr. Craig. The medium said a brief prayer and then closed his eyes for some further moments of silent contemplation. He had left a candle burning at the center of the table so that we might be able to find our places without difficulty. Now, having completed his meditations, he directed Brunson to extinguish the flame, plunging the room into total darkness.

In the sudden gloom I was aware only of the strains of Mozart rising from the music box and of the sound of Craig's voice. The medium spoke in his normal fashion, with only a slight measuring of his words to indicate the gravity of the circumstance. He discoursed at some length on the "mystic wonders" to be found in the spirit realm and the "glorious contentment" that awaited all who were ready to embrace this message.

After a time Craig began to address himself to the spirits themselves, calling out as if beckoning a reluctant friend to join in a dance. "Will you give us a sign?" he asked. "Will you manifest in some way? There are friends here who would be most grateful."

There was a sound near the bookcases. I strained my eyes against the gloom but could see nothing. Mr. Craig kept up his invocation, making it difficult to focus on any stray noises. "Are you there?" the medium continued. "Is that you? You are most welcome in this circle. We greet you with open hearts."

There was a soft clanking noise and then a strange glow was visible, a streak of greenish light against the sheer cloth of the medium's spirit cabinet. I heard a gasp from Mrs. Clairmont as several of the others shifted for a better view.

"Have a care, my friends!" Craig warned in an urgent tone. "Do not break the circle!"

"But what is it?" came Kenneth Clairmont's voice.

The medium gave him no response. "Come forward, if you can," said Craig, calling out to the glowing shape. "Do not be timid. We rejoice in your presence."

What I saw next thoroughly unnerved me. As the greenish illumination moved closer, growing brighter as it advanced, we heard another metallic sound, like a chain dragging across stone. Suddenly, and quite startlingly, we could make out the dim outline of a human form hovering in the air. Its back was turned toward us and the arms appeared to be folded. As we watched, it seemed to pulse and flicker like a dancing candle flame.

"My God!" came a gasp from Mrs. Clairmont. "Jasper? Is it—can it be you? Do you hear me?"

And then, uncannily, the figure whirled round, and we were confronted with the most ungodly sight I have ever beheld. The memory of it chills me even now. It was a face, human in form but demonic in aspect, with a sharp chin and nose, angled brows, and a pair of bright embers where the eyes should have been. One hand gestured wildly in the air, slashing at the empty space with a long-bladed knife, while the face contorted with malevolent glee.

Mrs. Clairmont gave a cry that seemed to shake the house to its foundation.

"Augusta!" cried Dr. Wells. "Are you all right?"

"Lights!" shouted Kenneth Clairmont. "Brunson, get the lights back up!"

All of this I registered only later, for at the sound of Mrs. Clairmont's scream I leapt from my chair and raced toward the strange apparition. As I neared it, however, I collided with a heavy, grunting figure, and both of us tumbled to the ground, our limbs tangled in a useless mass. At that moment, the lights were restored.

"Harry," I cried, pushing my brother away. "Get off! I was trying to see what that thing was!"

"As was I," he answered ruefully, rubbing at his head. "Whatever it was, it's gone now."

Harry pointed to the spot near the bookcases where the strange vision had appeared. Nothing seemed out of place. Meanwhile, Dr. Wells and Kenneth were hovering beside Mrs.

Clairmont, who had fallen into a swoon.

"Kenneth," Dr. Wells was saying, "fetch my bag from the front hall! Some smelling salts should do the trick."

"I—I'm all right, really I am," said Mrs. Clairmont in a feeble voice, as her eyes fluttered open. "What must you gentlemen think of me? I feel such a fool."

"Don't speak, Augusta," said Dr. Wells. "You'll be yourself shortly."

"You needn't fuss over me, Richardson. I assure you I'll be fine." She raised herself to an upright position. "Mr. Craig? Could that have been my husband?"

The medium was still bound securely to the chair, his face pale and anxious. "I could not say, I'm afraid. This was unlike anything I have ever experienced. The energies in this room are really quite unfathomable." He shuddered visibly, as though sensing a malign presence. "Perhaps someone might help me out of these ropes. Mr. Grange, would you—? Mr. Grange. Are you unwell, sir?"

Mr. Grange sat stiffly in his chair, his eyes wide with alarm. "Jasper," he said in a stricken voice.

At that moment, Kenneth Clairmont returned with Dr. Wells's medical bag. "Mother," he called, "are you feeling any better? I've brought—What's wrong with Edgar?"

Dr. Wells moved toward the lawyer. "Shock, I expect."

Grange gave a soft groan and appeared to be trying to shake off his indisposition. "Jasper," he repeated.

"Come on, now, Edgar," said Dr. Wells. "Here's a nice brandy for you. You'll get your strength back presently."

Then the lawyer slumped forward. It was evident—from the knife protruding from between his shoulder blades—that his strength would not be returning any time soon. A ragged gasp escaped from the dying man's lips. His left arm snaked forward across the surface of the table.

"Jasper," he groaned, as his eyes turned glassy. A spasm shook his body as his fingers strained to touch the spirit slate lying at the center of the table. It was only then, as Grange's eyes closed for the final time, that I noticed the message written in a faint, scrawling hand. I snatched up the slate, scarcely able to believe my eyes.

"Dash?" My brother looked up from Mr. Grange's side. "What does it say?"

I flipped the slate toward him and listened as he read aloud:

"Judgement is at hand."

~6~

A FLESH AND BLOOD KILLING

"Evening, Hardeen," said Lieutenant Murray, tapping the brim of his hat. "You're looking fit."

"You don't seem all that surprised to find me here, Lieutenant."

"Why should I be? Your brother sent me a wire. At home, I might add. I was off duty."

"Harry sent a wire?"

"Sure. It arrived as I was sitting down to a lamb stew. 'Man stabbed by ghost,' he says. 'Come at once. Great Houdini investigating.'"

"And yet you came," I said.

"Yeah," he said. "I came. I mean, I could have stayed home, I suppose, knowing that the investigation was proceeding with the Great Houdini at the helm, but I thought an official presence might be of some use." He sighed and took off his hat.

I had been acquainted with Lieutenant Patrick Murray for more than a year at that time, and if I had not known better, I would have attributed his disheveled appearance to the haste with which he answered the summons. Tall and beefy, Lieutenant Murray always managed to give the impression of having shaved and dressed in total darkness. His rumpled brown suit had acquired a few more gravy stains since our previous meeting, and he appeared to be wearing his collar inside out.

His eyes, by contrast, were sharp and piercing, in spite of the drooping lids and watery edges, giving him the aspect of a fierce, if bedraggled terrier.

Less than one hour had passed since the discovery of Edgar Grange's murder, and in the intervening time the circumstances surrounding his death had only grown more mysterious. Kenneth Clairmont confirmed that the door to the room had been securely bolted when he went to fetch Dr. Wells's medical bag, and a brief examination turned up no indication that the lock had been forced. The only other access to the room was through the windows, and these were also firmly secured from within.

Immediately following the unhappy discovery, several things had happened in rapid succession. First, Mrs. Clairmont had collapsed in a demure and elegant heap on the floor, requiring the application of lilac water to her pulse points. Next, the police were summoned to begin the process of examining, measuring, and recording every aspect of the scene. While awaiting their arrival, Dr. Wells and I had fetched a carving knife from the kitchen and used it to cut Lucius Craig free from his bonds. After Lieutenant Murray's appearance, as the others were shown downstairs, Harry and I were asked to remain behind to answer questions.

No sooner had the others left the room than my brother threw himself down on his hands and knees and began an energetic examination of the plum-colored carpet beneath the séance table. The police noted his strange behavior with a respectful interest but did nothing to disturb him, as though he might be a wealthy, if unbalanced, relation of the hostess.

Lieutenant Murray surveyed the scene for a few moments with his hands shoved in his pockets, then listened to a preliminary report from the leatherhead who had been the first on the scene. After a moment, he sidled up to me and jerked his thumb at the floor, where my brother had progressed to rubbing his fingers along the base of the séance table.

"What's he doing?" the lieutenant asked.

I watched as Harry plucked a splinter from beneath the table, sniffed it twice, and then carefully wrapped it in his handkerchief. "I believe he is examining the scene with the energy of a bloodhound," I said.

The lieutenant raised an eyebrow. "How's that?"

I shrugged my shoulders. "It's something he picked up in a Sherlock Holmes story."

"Ah." Lieutenant Murray led me to the bay window. "All right, Hardeen," he said. "Let's hear it. From the beginning. How did this happen and why are you and your brother in the middle of it?"

I spent the next twenty minutes or so relating the events of the evening for him and detailing the manner in which Harry and I had come to be included in the gathering. Lieutenant Murray interrupted several times to pose a question or seek clarification, and as I spoke he filled several pages of his notepad with dense printing. When I'd finished, the lieutenant closed up his notepad and looked back at the scene with a shake of his head.

"A ghost, you say?"

"Well, a glowing figure of some sort. An apparition, say."

"And this thing had a knife in its hand?"

"So it appeared." I shook my head, hardly able to believe what I was saying. "It was very difficult to see. It couldn't have been visible for more than a few seconds, and it kept flickering in and out. When I first saw it, I thought it was simply a streak of light. Then it resolved itself into that horrible figure."

"With a knife."

"Yes. With a knife."

"And when the lights came back up, the lawyer had been stabbed."

I turned to look at the séance table, where Edgar Grange's body was still being examined by the police physician. "That's right, Lieutenant. Incredible as it may sound."

The lieutenant flipped a page in his notebook. "It was completely dark before the ghost showed up?"

"I couldn't have seen my own hand in front of my face."

"And your hand wouldn't have been there, anyway," he said. "Not with all of you clutching one another in a circle around the table. That means that if one of you broke away to kill the lawyer—"

"At least two others sitting at the table would have known it," I said. "The person sitting on the killer's right and left would have had to release his hands. And his feet, for that matter."

Lieutenant Murray looked again at Harry, who was now fingering the scrollwork on one of the chair legs. "With all due respect, Hardeen, your account has to be taken with a grain of salt. You did just tell me that you and the rest of them saw a ghost in here."

"I didn't say I saw a ghost," I replied. "I said there was some sort of glowing apparition."

"Glowing apparition. Right. Well, whatever it was, there must have been some pretty considerable confusion when it appeared. I don't imagine everyone was paying the closest attention to what was going on around them. Somebody could have slipped free."

"It's possible," I agreed, "but the others are all insisting they kept hold of each other through the whole thing. Lucius Craig insisted on it. He seemed to feel that the minute the psychic circle was broken, the apparition would vanish. It seems our collective energy is what allowed it to manifest itself."

The lieutenant appeared bemused. "Your collective energy, you say?"

"I'm just telling you what was said."

Lieutenant Murray studied the table. "You and your brother don't seem to have been too concerned with collective energy," he said. "The two of you both broke away to go after this— what did you call it?"

"Glowing apparition."

"You have a real way with words, Hardeen. Anyway, the circle was broken at that stage. That must be when the killer struck."

I shook my head. "He couldn't have known that Harry and I were both going to jump up from the table."

"No, but it would have been a pretty safe bet that some sort of commotion would break out once the ghost put in an appearance."

I considered it. "The killer would have had to know in advance that there was going to be a manifestation. He'd have had to know about the ghost beforehand."

The lieutenant nodded. "Exactly."

I lowered my voice. "Lucius Craig," I said. "But he was wrapped like a mummy, Lieutenant. We had a devil of a time cutting him free afterwards. He couldn't possibly have stabbed Mr. Grange."

Lieutenant Murray did not reply. Instead, he stepped over to the body of Edgar Grange, which was still slumped forward across the séance table. Dr. Peterson, a short, round-faced man with a halo of startlingly white hair, was crouched nearby.

"Finding anything, Doc?" asked Lieutenant Murray.

The doctor straightened up and brushed off his knees. "The fatal injury was caused by a single knife thrust between the third and—"

The lieutenant waved his hand impatiently. "I can see that. Have you found anything I don't know?"

"It's a very peculiar case," the doctor said. "The killer was fortunate to have inflicted such a wound in total darkness. The thrust was not deep, but it nicked the carotid." He looked at me. "Young man, are you certain that you didn't hear the injured man cry out?"

"He may have, but there was considerable confusion in the room. The sound might have been mistaken for surprise over the appearance of the ghostly figure."

Dr. Peterson looked down at the body. "The wound must have been extremely painful. I'm quite certain he would have made a sound of some kind. Perhaps Dr. Wells might have been able to intervene."

"Or Dr. Wells may have been the one to inflict the wound in the first place," Lieutenant Murray said.

"Unlikely," answered Peterson. "A trained physician would have done a better job of it."

"Unless he couldn't see in the dark," Lieutenant Murray said.

"Yes," said Peterson. "I suppose that might account for it. Still, I would have expected—"

"Ah ha!" shouted my brother from the floor.

"What have you got there, Houdini?" asked Lieutenant Murray.

Harry pointed to a table leg. "A very distinct scratch mark where Mrs. Clairmont and Dr. Wells were sitting."

Lieutenant Murray bent down and studied the mark. "Looks like an old scuff mark to me, Houdini." He stepped across the room to the desk and returned with a letter opener. Bending down, he made a similar scratch above the one Harry had indicated. "See? The mark I made is brighter. The wood hasn't had a chance to age yet."

Harry studied the twin marks for a moment. "You may be right," he acknowledged. "Even so, my theory is still sound."

Lieutenant Murray straightened up. "Your theory?"

"Indeed." Harry crawled out from beneath the table, his face alight with excitement. "Might I ask you to step into the hallway for a moment, Lieutenant?"

"The hallway? Why?"

Harry put a finger to his lips. "All will be revealed," he said in a low voice. "Please follow me. I guarantee that you will find this most illuminating."

The expression on Lieutenant Murray's face told me that there would be grave consequences if that guarantee was not met. Nevertheless, the lieutenant had a quick word with Dr. Peterson and then followed Harry into the hallway outside the séance room.

"What's this about, Houdini?" he asked.

"Only this," said Harry with proud smile. "I have solved the case!"

"Pardon?"

"I have solved the case! I am ready to unmask the villain! He will rue the day that he crossed paths with the Great Houdini!"

Lieutenant Murray turned to me. "Hardeen, do you know anything about this?"

I shook my head. "Harry, how can you be so sure? The body isn't even cold yet. Don't you think you're being a bit—"

"The solution was evident from the first," Harry continued, ignoring my attempt at moderation. "Though it would not have revealed itself to the more conventional approach of the New York City police. No, this was a problem that required talents and abilities unique to the world's foremost self-liberator. When one is presented with a puzzle which appears to have no solution, one must turn to a master of puzzlement!"

"Harry," I said, noting Lieutenant Murray's rising color, "maybe you should get to the—"

"Eight people are locked within a room," he continued, stroking his chin. "One of them is murdered under cover of darkness. Yet it appears improbable that any of the remaining seven people could have accomplished the crime. How is it possible?"

"That's what my men and I are endeavoring to find out, Houdini," Lieutenant Murray said. "If you have anything to tell me, you'd best get to it. Otherwise, you're wasting my time."

"All in good time, dear sir! In order for you to appreciate the exquisite simplicity of my solution, I must acquaint you with the elegant chain of reasoning that produced it."

I watched as the lieutenant's jaw muscles tightened. "Harry," I said, "perhaps it might be best if we skipped over the elegant chain of reasoning."

"I would not dream of it," he said with a happy smile. "I could not ask the lieutenant to arrest the guilty party on my word alone. He must have the evidence!" He tugged on the points of his bow tie. "Now, then, as I approached the problem, I naturally asked myself if a killer could have entered from outside of the chamber while the eight of us sat in darkness. Perhaps the murderer slipped in through the windows or possibly through the locked doors." He gestured at the door to the study behind us. "After all, the door was secured by a simple Orkam shaft-clasp lock, with a mere three pins inside. One need not be the world's foremost self-liberator to pick this lock. An eight-year-old boy with a willow twig could undoubtedly have forced his way into the room."

"Flaherty," said the lieutenant, motioning to a sergeant standing nearby. "Go and round up any eight-year-old boys you happen to see carrying willow twigs."

"Right away, sir."

"I immediately discarded this possibility," Harry continued, oblivious to the lieutenant's sarcasm. "If the door had been opened, we should have seen the illumination from the hallway. The killer could not have entered through the door. Could he have entered through the windows? This seemed the most promising theory at first, but on closer examination, a grave problem emerged."

"The windows were locked from the inside," Lieutenant Murray said. "Houdini, as much as I enjoy listening to you state the obvious, I have a murder investigation to run."

"The window locks are no great obstacle, Lieutenant. A piece of filament or wire could easily be looped around the locking lever. If this wire were to run outside the window along a seam or hinge, the windows could easily be unlocked from the outside."

Harry had the lieutenant's attention now. "You're saying that the killer opened the windows by pulling a string?"

"I'm saying he could have." Harry stepped back as a pair of morgue attendants arrived carrying a stretcher. "Of course, he could also have had an accomplice inside who unlocked the windows and then locked them again afterwards. However, I do not believe this to have been the case."

"We'd have heard the windows opening," I said, "and we'd have seen light from the street when the killer passed through the curtains."

"Not to mention the fact that there's no ledge of any sort outside the windows," said Lieutenant Murray. "It's a good thirty-foot drop to the street."

"Exactly," said Harry. "That is why I have ruled out the possibility that the killer came from outside the room."

"Then we're back where we started," I said. "It was one of us. One of the seven people sitting at the table. Assuming we can rule out the Brothers Houdini, that leaves Dr. Wells, Kenneth Clairmont, Brunson, Mrs. Clairmont, and Lucius Craig himself. You're saying that one of them is the killer?"

Harry thrust his index finger into the air. "Not necessarily."

"That's enough cat and mouse, Houdini," Lieutenant Murray said. "If the killer didn't come from outside and it wasn't one of the people sitting around the table, then what other choice is there? Hardeen's glowing apparition, perhaps? I prefer a flesh and blood killer myself."

Harry turned away from us. "Sergeant Flaherty, may I ask you to gather up some of the newspapers from the rack beside Mr. Clairmont's desk?"

"Newspapers?" the sergeant asked, glancing at Lieutenant Murray.

The lieutenant held up his hand. "Hold on, Houdini. I won't have you giving orders to my men."

"You have asked me to name the killer. I intend to do better than that. I am going to produce him for you. All I require is a bundle of newspapers."

Lieutenant Murray hesitated, then nodded to the sergeant, who went off to do as Harry asked.

"I must ask that you do exactly as I say, but please keep your voices down until I give the signal. What you are about to see may strike you as peculiar, but the reasons for my actions will be apparent soon enough." Harry led us back into the séance room as he said this, his voice dropping to a low whisper as he approached the octagonal table. "Earlier I pointed out this scratch to you, Lieutenant," he continued, crouching next to the thick pedestal base. "It is worth noting that this table is quite new and was constructed to the exacting standards of Mr. Lucius Craig. It is an unusual piece of furniture, is it not? The octagonal shape is quite unconventional. So, too, is the exceedingly heavy base. Instead of four separate legs holding the table up, we have one extremely thick column of wood at the center. If Mr. Craig were here, he would undoubtedly tell us that the construction of the table forms a focus for the energies of the sitters. I believe there is an additional function, not generally known to outsiders. Ah, Sergeant Flaherty! Please spread the newspapers onto this tray. Excellent. Now, if you would be so good as to bring that pitcher of water from the sideboard. Thank you so much. Have you a match, Sergeant?"

"Wait a minute, Houdini," said Lieutenant Murray. "A match? What do you think you're doing?"

"All will become clear in just one moment, Lieutenant. Come along, Sergeant Flaherty. I believe we are ready to proceed. Please set fire to the newspapers, if you would be so kind."

The sergeant looked to Lieutenant Murray, who fixed my brother with a dubious expression. "You're sure this is necessary, Houdini?"

"You shall not be disappointed, Lieutenant."

Murray shrugged and nodded at the sergeant to proceed. In a moment, the newspapers were burning merrily. "Good," said Harry. "Now if we could direct some of the smoke toward the table, I believe the results will speak for themselves."

The sergeant used a discarded section of newspaper to fan smoke in the direction of the table.

"Now there is one more thing I must ask of you, Sergeant,"

said Harry. "If you would join me in raising a cry of 'Fire,' I should be eternally grateful."

The sergeant looked up from fanning the smoke. "You want me to yell 'Fire'?"

"Yes, only let us direct our voices toward the base of the table."

"Harry," I began, "this isn't going to—"

"Not now, Dash. We have a murderer to apprehend."

"But—Harry—"

"On the count of three, Sergeant. Now then: one, two, three—"

"Fire!" shouted the sergeant and Harry together.

"Thank you, Sergeant. I will trouble you once again."

"Fire!" they shouted again.

Harry rubbed his hands together with satisfaction. "Thank you so much. And now, Lieutenant, I believe it will be possible to introduce you to the murderer of Mr. Edgar Grange." Harry folded his arms and gazed expectantly at the séance table.

"Harry," I began again, "there is no—"

"Not now, Dash! I am waiting for the murderer to reveal himself." Harry beamed happily at the table. "Any moment now!"

Lieutenant Murray turned to me. "Hardeen? Can you explain what your brother is trying to achieve?"

"I believe I can," I said, "though I hope I'm wrong." I looked at Harry, who was still gazing expectantly at the séance table, as though waiting for it to burst into song. "Harry, I'm afraid you may have miscalculated."

He shot a quick glance in my direction, his happy confidence beginning to fray a bit at the edges. "Just a moment longer," he said. "I'm sure of it."

"What does he think is going to happen?" Lieutenant Murray asked.

"My brother has concluded that the murderer of Edgar Grange is hidden in a secret compartment within the base of the table," I explained. "Harry believes that the concealed killer will smell the smoke, hear the cries of fire, and conclude that the house is burning. At that point—"

The lieutenant finished the thought for me. "At that point he will emerge from his place of concealment and fly into the waiting arms of Sergeant Flaherty." He stroked his chin. "I believe I read that story as well. Was it Dr. Thorndyke?"

"Holmes," I said. " 'The Norwood Builder.'"

"Funny, I'd have sworn it was Thorndyke." He turned to the sergeant. "Flaherty, I think we can safely extinguish the flames now."

"Wait, Lieutenant," cried Harry. "There is still a chance that—"

"Put out the flames, Flaherty."

Harry gave a theatrical sigh as the sergeant poured water over the embers of the newspapers. "Perhaps he didn't smell the smoke," he said, still clinging to a shred of hope.

The lieutenant walked over to the séance table and took hold of the edge. With a sudden effort, he heaved the heavy table onto its side. "Hello?" he called, bending over the upended pedestal. "Anyone in there?" He rapped on the solid wood with his knuckles. "Come on out. Harry Houdini is waiting to apprehend you."

Harry appeared crestfallen. "Perhaps I was mistaken in my assessment of the situation," he admitted.

"Perhaps so," said Lieutenant Murray. He turned back to Dr. Peterson. "You have anything else for me, Doc?"

Peterson snapped his black bag shut. "Not until I finish up downtown. Are you done here?"

"Not yet. I'll let you know."

"Lieutenant," said Harry, "may I suggest that we—"

"No," said Murray shortly. "You and your brother are going back downstairs to join the others. I'll be through questioning in a couple of hours. I suggest you just make yourselves comfortable in the meantime."

"But we can be of assistance! We have unique talents and abilities that—"

The lieutenant signalled to a uniformed officer. "Marsden, take these gentlemen back downstairs, would you?"

Harry made to offer another plea, but I restrained him as the officer escorted us to the exit.

"Oh, Hardeen?" the lieutenant called after us.

I paused in the doorway. "Yes?"

"If you see this thing again, this—what did you call it?"

"A glowing apparition."

"Right. If you see it again, tell him I need to ask him some questions."

The sound of the lieutenant's laughter followed us all the way down the main stairs.

7

THE SANGUINARY SPIRIT

"THE GALL OF THAT MAN!" CRIED HARRY, HELPING HIMSELF TO A portion of scrambled eggs at breakfast the next morning. "After all we've done for him in the past! He'd still be trying to solve the murder of Branford Wintour if not for us! He'd still be trying to crack the Case of the Deadly Damsel!"

"The case of the deadly damsel?" I asked, stirring my black tea.

"Francesca Moore," said Harry, his cheeks reddening slightly. "I have recorded the business in my note-books under that title."

"Have you? I must say, Harry, that's quite vivid."

"Well, I have a certain theatrical flair, as you may know."

"Hadn't noticed."

Harry was referring to an unfortunate chain of events some months earlier, when an assistant to the great magician Harry Kellar had been murdered under seemingly inexplicable circumstances during a performance of the Floating Lady effect. Harry and I realized that Lieutenant Murray's investigation had taken a wrong turn, and through a combination of persistence and happenstance we had been able to uncover the identity of the killer.

"The lieutenant is just jealous," Harry said, chewing thoughtfully on a piece of sausage. "He is afraid that the Great Houdini will show him up once again."

"Patrick Murray has one of the finest records in the history of the New York City Police Department," I said. "Of the many hundreds of cases in which he has been involved, only two have required the assistance of the Brothers Houdini. And there is nothing to say that he wouldn't have solved those two on his own eventually."

Harry snorted. "I don't know why you place such confidence in that man, Dash."

It was nearly two o'clock in the morning when Lieutenant Murray dismissed our small band of suspects from the Clairmont house and we were instructed to return at noon for a further round of questioning. It was clear from his tone that the lieutenant would have preferred to conduct those interrogations at the precinct house, but Mrs. Clairmont's standing in society would not permit him to be so high-handed with her guests. Harry and I had attempted to confer with him over the findings, but he had wished no further aid from the two of us.

I had returned to my room at Mrs. Arthur's boarding house and fallen exhausted into my bed, but sleep would not come. I could not put the events of the evening out of my mind. Each time I closed my eyes, a vision of that strange, glowing spectre rose up behind my lids, brandishing its gleaming blade. What was it? How had it come to appear in the room? Could it possibly have been responsible for the death of Edgar Grange? I turned these problems over in my mind until the first brightening of dawn appeared at my window.

"The problem does not seem so very difficult to me," Bess was saying, as she poured out another cup of tea for Harry.

"No?" I asked.

She set the pot on a clay trivet. "Well, I don't mean to say I've worked out every detail, but I think that Harry must have been on the right track last night."

My brother beamed at her. "Thank you, my dear."

"How do you mean?" I asked. "You think the murderer really was hidden in the base of the table?"

"No, of course not. But it stands to reason, however, that the murderer was hidden somewhere in the room when the séance began. If what you've told me is true, no one could have entered the room after the lights were lowered. You'd have seen the light from outside."

"That's true," Harry agreed. "I said as much to Lieutenant Murray."

"If the murderer didn't come from outside the room," Bess continued, "he must have been inside the room the whole time. Naturally, that suggests that the killer was one of the other seven people sitting at the table."

"That is clearly the impression that Lieutenant Murray has formed," I said.

Bess nodded in agreement. "It would seem the logical conclusion, but it doesn't explain how one of you could have broken away from the circle without alerting the others. Wasn't Mr. Grange sitting next to Lucius Craig?"

"He was," Harry confirmed. "He was sitting to the left of Mr. Craig."

"And who was sitting on Mr. Grange's left?"

I looked up from buttering a piece of brown toast. "I was."

Bess favored me with a winning smile. "It begins to look quite bad for you, Dash. Did you kill Edgar Grange?"

"Not that I recall."

"No," she agreed. "You don't seem the murderous type. And we must rule out Mr. Craig, because Harry had tied him to his own chair."

"The man couldn't have moved an inch in any direction," Harry said proudly.

"So where does that leave us?" Bess took a sip of tea. "Dash didn't kill Mr. Grange. Lucius Craig didn't kill Mr. Grange. None of the others could have killed Mr. Grange without breaking the circle. Therefore, the killer must have been hidden elsewhere in the room."

"I'm not quite so sure," I said. "There was a great deal of

confusion when that figure appeared in the room—whatever it was. Lieutenant Murray asked last night if it might have been possible for one of the guests to take advantage of the chaos to break away from the circle. After all, Harry and I did so. We went after the ghost the instant we spotted it."

"Yes, but you didn't know that was going to happen in advance. No one could have, except possibly—"

"Lucius Craig," Harry said.

"Exactly," she agreed.

"And he was tied to the chair." Harry gripped the arms of his own chair for emphasis. "He couldn't move."

Bess smiled at him over the rim of her tea cup. "Which is why I think there must have been someone else hidden in the room."

"My exact thought!" Harry cried. "And it seemed to me that the séance table was the most logical place of concealment. Kenneth told us the other night that Craig had ordered it made to his own standards. It seemed perfectly logical to me that there should be a secret compartment hidden in the base."

"I don't know about that, Harry," I said. "It would have to have been an awfully small person to fit in there."

"Lila Craig," Harry said. "She's nothing more than a slip of a girl. And didn't Sterling Foster give us the impression that there was more to her than meets the eye?"

"He did," I agreed, "and then he slipped to the floor in a drunken stupor. I'm not sure how much weight I would lend to anything that Sterling Foster says."

"Even so, Lila Craig is the daughter of the medium, which certainly gives us reason to be suspicious of her. And we do not know for certain where she was at the time that the ghost made its appearance."

"Harry's right," said Bess. "It only makes sense that Lucius Craig works with an accomplice, and his daughter would have to be the most logical choice. She appears to be above suspicion because she wasn't in the room at the time. But what if they devised some means of hiding her in the room before the séance began? Perhaps she wasn't hidden in the base of the table, as Harry supposed, but there must have been other places in the room where she might have hidden. What about under the desk?"

Harry appeared to be taking enormous gratification from the fact that Bess was supporting his theories. He gave me a happy grin, much as he did after his inevitable victories in our boyhood wrestling matches. "Yes, Dash, what about that? Maybe she was hidden under the desk! Or perhaps behind a hidden panel concealed in one of the bookcases! Wouldn't that be something? Perhaps there is a secret corridor leading to the murderer's lair!"

Bess reached over and patted his hand. "I'm not sure I would go quite that far, Harry."

I pondered the matter. "You're saying that Lila Craig could have been hidden somewhere in the room while the rest of us took our places at the séance table. At the critical moment, after the lights went down, she emerged from her place of concealment wearing some sort of glowing sheet. Is that it?"

"Yes!" Harry cried. "Exactly!"

"What is it, Dash?" Bess asked, noting my apparent skepticism. "Have you some other explanation?"

"No," I said. "I most certainly do not. If this had been an ordinary séance, I would have no trouble accepting the idea that Lila Craig had been responsible for whatever floating trumpets and chalk slate messages we might have seen. But this was no ordinary séance. A man was murdered. Do you really mean to suggest that a girl of thirteen stabbed Edgar Grange to death?"

Harry frowned and looked over at Bess.

"Dash," she said, "you have always been too chivalrous for your own good. Do you really mean to say that no mere girl could have done such a thing?"

I held up my hands in resignation, having learned long ago not to argue with my sister-in-law on the subject of what a woman might or might not do. Bess firmly believed that there were few things that a man could do that a woman could not do just as well. Apparently her views were broad enough to encompass murder.

"I would not think of contradicting you," I said. "I would just like to know more about the matter before I accuse Lila Craig of Mr. Grange's murder. I would like to know more about Lucius Craig, first of all. We know very little about his background. If I knew more, perhaps I could suggest a motive. The same goes for the others—Dr. Wells, Kenneth, Sterling Foster, Brunson—"

"But Sterling Foster wasn't even in the room at the time!" Harry cried.

"Neither was Lila Craig, so far as we know," I said. "As for Brunson, he had no way of knowing that he would be asked to fill the empty chair at the table, but I'd still like to know more about him. We have a few hours before we have to appear at the Clairmont house. I'm going to call in on Biggs at the *Herald* and see if he's found anything else in the files."

"That's a good idea," said Bess. "Harry, you should go down to Huber's and tell Albert that you won't be able to cover your slot today. As for me, I'd better be getting over to Ravelsen's." She looked at Harry, steeling herself for the torrent of objections that usually accompanied any mention of her work in the chorus line.

Instead, Harry simply stared into his tea cup. "Yes, dear," he said.

"Harry? Are you all right?"

He gave no sign of having heard.

Bess looked at me and raised her eyebrows. "Harry," she said. "I have signed a long-term, binding contract with Ravelsen's. What do you think?"

"Yes, dear."

"We shall be touring throughout Europe and the Far East. I shall not return for five years. Does that sound acceptable to you?"

He stirred his tea.

"The touring manager has asked me to share accommodations with him, as a matter of economy. I'm certain it will be all right. What do you think?"

Harry was studying the back of his hand as though it might hold the answer to the riddle of the Sphinx. Bess reached across and tapped him on the shoulder. "Harry. What are you thinking?"

He looked up and blinked rapidly, as if emerging from a pool of water. "Dash," he said, "did you get a good look at it last night? That—that phantom?"

"No," I said. "I didn't."

"Nor did I. It was very dark, of course, and everything happened so quickly. But I can't escape the feeling that—I can't quite shake the impression that—"

"What?" Bess asked.

He covered her hands with his. "You will think I am talking nonsense, but there was something about that apparition that defies explanation. I am not a fanciful man, Bess. I am not given to wild flights of imagination. But there was something about that figure that rattled me." He looked from her to me and back again. "I know how a spook show works. Dash and I still have our costumes from the old Graveyard Ghouls act. Black cloth with the white bones and skulls painted on the front. All we had to do was dance about in front of a black screen, and the audience was prepared to swear that a pair of skeletons had returned from the grave. Is it so much to suppose that Lucius Craig and his daughter have worked out something along those lines? It seems the only logical explanation, and yet—" He shook his head.

"I know what you're trying to say, Harry," I said. "I know a fair bit about stagecraft, but I can't think how anyone could have produced a ghost like that one. For one thing, it seemed to be floating. For another, you could almost—you could—"

"See through it," Harry said.

"That's right," I said. "You could see through it."

Bess fixed us both with an incredulous expression. "You're imagining things," she said. "You've been taken in by a master deceiver."

I looked at Harry, who did not appear convinced.

"I'm supposed to be the master deceiver," he said.

"Dash!" cried Biggs, glancing up from his compositor's desk at the *Herald*. "I turn my back on you for just one moment, and you land in the middle of a murder drama! I really shouldn't leave you unsupervised!" He climbed down from his stool as I tossed my trilby onto the battered stand in the corner. "How is Mrs. Clairmont bearing up?" he asked. "This must have been a terrible shock."

"Dr. Wells had given her a sleeping draught when we left last night. He was doing everything possible to protect her from the more troubling details."

"Then he will have to be certain that she doesn't see a copy of this morning's *World*," Biggs said. "I'm afraid the story made quite an impression, though I can't understand how they got it into print before we did." He passed a folded newspaper to me.

"'A Sanguinary Spirit,'" I read, scanning the headline. "'Gramercy Park Séance Results in Murder.'" I glanced up. "That's quite a headline," I said.

"I recognize the style. Sounds like the work of Ben Michaels. He's always been a bit florid. Skip to the third paragraph."

"'The police investigation, under the diligent supervision of Lieutenant Patrick Murray, has not yet identified any suspects in the brutal slaying. A source close to the investigation was heard to remark that Lucius Craig, the noted spirit medium, was assisting the official force in their inquiries. "Mr. Lucius Craig is an expert in all things pertaining to the unusual and the arcane," said an observer of the case. "He will surely be able to help the investigators navigate these most unusual circumstances."' I tossed the paper aside in disgust. "And who might this observer be, do you suppose?"

"Lucius Craig himself, obviously," Biggs replied. "The man is seeking to burnish his reputation with the sensational details of this tragedy. He must have phoned Michaels in the middle of the night."

"And if the police should prove unable to solve the case—?"

"Then there are those who will be willing to believe that the spirit of Jasper Clairmont was responsible."

"And Lucius Craig will be remembered as the man who conjured up the so-called sanguinary spirit. This will only make him more notorious and therefore more sought after by the gullible likes of Mrs. Clairmont. Either way, Craig garners a great deal of the notoriety upon which he thrives. Biggs, I came here this morning because I was hoping that you might—"

Biggs cut me off with a wave of his pen. "I know, Dash, you want to go through the morgue and see what you can dig up on each of the guests at the séance. I've already done the preliminary work. Come along." He led me through a warren of offices to a dim basement chamber arrayed with row upon row of dusty wooden filing cabinets.

"Here," Biggs said, pointing to a manuscript table at the center of the room. "I've already pulled out the relevant packets."

"Did you find anything of interest?" I asked.

"I've only just glanced through them," he admitted. "You may find something that wasn't apparent to me, but it all looks fairly innocent. The dead man appears to have had an uneventful career as a partner in the firm of Larwood and Grange, having begun his professional climb as a junior clerk at Tammany Hall. His wife passed away nearly six years ago, and in the intervening years he seems to have lived quietly. One occasionally finds him mentioned among the first-nighters at various opera functions, but otherwise he's kept to himself."

"What about Dr. Wells?"

Biggs nudged a fat packet over to me. "An interesting character—I thought so when I met him the other night.

Richardson Wells comes from a well-heeled family in Boston, but upon completing his medical degree he packed himself off to the West. First Colorado and then California, where he spent most of his career."

"Any idea why he left Boston?"

"There seems to have been some sort of family scandal over a broken engagement. I haven't been able to obtain the details. In any event, he has only recently returned to society."

"How recently?"

"Four or five years ago. He and Jasper Clairmont became friendly at the Union League Club." He looked over the edge of the file at me, as if reading my thoughts. "No, Augusta Clairmont wasn't the one who broke his heart all those years ago, if that's what you're thinking."

"He seems rather fond of her now."

"Perhaps, but Wells is no money-grubber. He may have turned his back on the family fortune, but he made one of his own in California. Seems he made some wise investments in two or three of the better mining concerns."

"So he has no need of the Clairmont millions?"

"One can always use a few more millions, I suppose, but Wells does not give the impression of having a great concern for money."

"Still," I said, "the other night Kenneth led us to believe that both Dr. Wells and Mr. Grange were showing a social interest in Mrs. Clairmont. Isn't it possible that—"

"A love triangle, Dash? Is that what you're suggesting? That Wells and Grange were rivals for the hand of the Widow Clairmont and that one of them decided to eliminate the other?"

"Is it really so outlandish, Biggs?"

He rubbed at the corner of one eye as he considered the matter. "No," he said slowly, "I suppose not, but I'm having trouble believing such a thing of Dr. Wells. He doesn't seem capable of murder."

"I would tend to agree, but I'm trying to examine all of the possibilities. What about the brother-in-law?"

"Sterling Foster? He wasn't even in the room at the time of the murder." He looked at me closely. "Was he?"

I shrugged. "If we set aside the 'sanguinary spirit' theory, as I am compelled to do, then Grange was murdered either by someone at the table or by an unseen intruder. Suppose Foster had been able to find a way into the room. What sort of motive might he have had?"

"None, I should think. I'd have thought it far more likely that Foster would be murdered himself."

"How's that?"

Biggs opened another file. "Mr. Foster has not made a great success of himself, as you may have gathered last night. He began with good prospects, took an engineering degree at Heidelberg, came home and settled into a civil post. But he soon fell into bad habits. He spends and drinks freely and for years has relied entirely on the largess of his brother-in-law. At one stage Mr. Clairmont tried to find a suitable place for him in the shipping firm, but Foster showed no great aptitude for it. He turned latterly to the stock exchange and lost a considerable fortune—not all of it his own—in a reckless speculation last year. Now he seems to fill his days lounging about his sister's place."

Biggs pushed the file across the table to me, and I glanced through it. "He doesn't live at the Clairmont house, surely."

"He keeps a bachelor flat directly across Gramercy Park, so as to be within staggering distance of his sister's dinner table. Now that Mrs. Clairmont has come into her late husband's fortune, Foster has been doing his best to get a share. He's trying to get himself appointed in some sort of advisory capacity to oversee the handling of the estate."

"That explains why he was in such heated conversation with Edgar Grange last night. The two of them appeared to be arguing over something when Harry and I arrived."

"No doubt Foster was trying to pry another fat check out of the estate. I saw much the same display. I understand most of the money is still tied up, and a good deal of it will pass straight to Kenneth—on the condition that he enters the family firm."

"The family firm," I repeated, fingering the ragged edge of a yellowed clipping. "Biggs, when we met Kenneth the other night, you seemed greatly surprised that he appeared willing to give up his medical aspirations."

"I've known Kenneth for some time, Dash, and he has always been determined to become a surgeon. He has a talent in that direction and his instructors saw great promise in him. But he's the only son and heir apparent to the Clairmont shipping empire, and his father simply wouldn't hear of him entering another profession, no matter how honorable."

"Harry and I have chosen a rather different path from the one our father envisioned for us. Surely Kenneth might have defied his father."

"If Mr. Clairmont had lived, I have little doubt that Kenneth would have stuck to his guns. You heard him the other night, though. He doesn't feel he can turn his back now that his father is dead. He considers it his duty to look after his mother."

I recalled that my father had extracted a deathbed promise from Harry and me to look after our mother. Even in our hardest times, we always managed to send home a small portion of whatever meager earnings we had.

"Biggs, is there some manner in which the death of Edgar Grange releases Kenneth from his obligation to enter the family firm?"

My friend's head snapped up. "That's a rather devious thought, Dash. Are you suggesting that Kenneth murdered Edgar Grange so that he might pursue a career in medicine? It seems a rather inauspicious start to a life of healing, wouldn't you say?"

"I'm only trying to figure all the angles," I said. "Everyone else seems to have a possible motive—or at least some form of grudge against the dead man. If we are to rule out Kenneth as a suspect, we must at least be candid in assessing what he stands to gain."

Biggs shook his head. "I don't see how Grange's death changes things for Kenneth. His father's finances are now thrown into further disarray, and he will now have an even more difficult time fighting off the grasping claws of his father's competitors—not to mention those of his uncle, Sterling Foster. Apart from that, I do not see a great change in his prospects."

"What about those of Mrs. Clairmont herself?"

"What a mind you have, Dash!" Biggs said, shaking his head. "You imagine that Mrs. Clairmont plunged a knife into the lawyer's back? It's a pleasing image, I'll admit, but I just can't feature it. Mrs. Clairmont as a kind of Lizzie Borden in pearls? You see how frail her constitution is, Dash. Moreover, there can't be any motive."

"Why not? We know nothing of how Grange had been managing her husband's affairs. Perhaps he had been dipping his hands into the pot. Maybe she found him out."

"She would surely have other forms of recourse than murdering him in a room filled with seven other people."

I sighed. "You're right, of course. But I can't help but feel that there is more beneath the surface. She seems so blind in her devotion to Mr. Craig's mediumship, I cannot help but feel that she is not quite in her right mind."

"What about Lucius Craig himself? Surely his motives are as strong as anyone's."

"I should have thought that was apparent. Kenneth said as much the other night. Craig has been exerting a great influence over Mrs. Clairmont, which in turn would naturally place him in a position to influence the disposition of the Clairmont fortune. Edgar Grange had some harsh words for Mr. Craig last night. He objected to the manner in which Craig was assuming control over the household. If Grange himself had designs on the Clairmont fortune, that would bring the two men into direct opposition."

"Which would give Craig a motive, albeit a shaky one, for murdering Edgar Grange." Biggs reached across the manuscript table for his notepad. "You say he was tied to a chair at the time of the murder?"

"Yes," I said. "Even Harry would have had trouble freeing himself, and when the lights came back up, Craig's bonds did not appear to have been disturbed in any way. It would be useful to know if Craig has any background as a magician."

"I wish I could help you there," said Biggs, "but I've noticed something very curious about our Mr. Craig."

"What is that?"

"He doesn't seem to have existed prior to the year 1888."

"Pardon?"

"There is simply no record of the man," Biggs explained. "It's as though he sprang into being just over ten years ago, clutching a snuff shaker in one hand and a chalk slate in the other."

"He must have changed his name," I said. "He is a performer of sorts. Perhaps he found it expedient to adopt a separate identity for his spiritualist endeavors."

Biggs indicated the wall of battered wooden filing cabinets where the packets of theatricals were kept. "That was the first thing that occurred to me," he said, pulling open a file drawer, "but our system of records makes allowances for such things. For instance, when I consult the packet marked *Theodore Hardeen*, I find a notation informing me that the subject's name at birth was, in fact, Ferencz Deszo Weiss." Biggs cocked an eyebrow. "Ferencz?"

"Named for a relative back in the old country, I'm told."

"It suits you," Biggs said drily. "In any case, I've consulted our records on immigration and all other likely sources—including prison records—and I can find nothing on Mr. Lucius Craig prior to a town meeting in 1888. Barely a decade. He is not exactly a young man, Dash. What was he doing—and under what name—prior to that date?"

"How odd. It's as though his past has been wiped clean."

"Well put, Ferencz."

"You can forget you ever saw that," I said, "and I'll be good enough to forget that we used to call you Stinky."

"Fair enough. But I'm still baffled as to what Mr. Craig might have been doing for the first forty years or so of his life."

"Perhaps he was living in another country. That accent of his suggests that he's spent considerable time in some part of Britain. Ireland, do you suppose?"

"Scotland," Biggs said firmly. "I'd know those diphthongs anywhere. He has Scottish blood in him, as do I. The south, most likely. Auld Reekie, if I'm not mistaken."

"Auld Reekie?"

"Edinburgh. I've wired to a colleague at *The Scotsman* to see if their files are any more illuminating than ours. So long as Mr. Craig's past remains an enigma, it seems to me that there is more than one mystery hanging over the events of last night. It seems to me that it might throw some light on our endeavors if we were to discover why a man should completely obliterate all traces of his own past."

"Sterling Foster indicated that he knew something of Mr. Craig's history," I recalled. "He seemed pleased that Harry and I shared his suspicions of Craig's psychic powers. Of course, this was only moments before he took a swing at us and had to be carried from the house."

"Foster grumbled something of that sort in my ear, as well," Biggs said. "It had to do with the daughter."

"Yes, but he didn't give any specifics."

"Nor does the file. I can find no record of a marriage, far less a notation of the daughter's birth. Of course, this doesn't stop Mr. Craig from using his status as a widower to play upon the sympathies of his audiences."

"How so?"

"He makes frequent references to his 'dear departed wife' and 'the sainted mother of my dear Lila.'"

"I didn't hear him do so last night."

"No? I did. More than once. He keeps her portrait and a lock of her hair in a silver locket. Every so often he brings it out and gazes longingly in a manner calculated to melt the hearts of any wealthy widows who happen to be in the vicinity."

"You're a very cynical man, Biggs."

He pressed his mouth into a thin line. "Me? It's simply a pose to deflect attention from my staggering good looks."

"You've exceeded all expectations." I fished out my pocket watch and popped open the cover. "I'd better be heading to Gramercy Park," I said. "The lieutenant wanted us back for another round of questions."

"Ah, yes!" Biggs cried, his eyes alight. "The suspects are assembled once more under the watchful gaze of Dash Hardeen. How long can the murderer hope to remain at large now that our intrepid amateur sleuth is on the case? The cause of justice has found a sure and steady champion in this diligent and intriguing young man, whose rakish appearance conceals the shrewd intelligence of a—"

"That's enough, Biggs."

"I think not!" he said, leading me through the maze of offices back toward the press room. "After all, we still have not decided which of the suspects is most deserving of our youthful paladin's attention! Will it be the sinister Lucius Craig, whose claim of paranormal ability may conceal a darker and more earth-bound purpose? Or perhaps the bluff and genial Dr. Richardson Wells, whose youth in the rugged mining communities of California may hold the key to a surprising secret? And let us not forget the profligate brother-in-law, Sterling Foster, whose early ambitions have long since been sacrificed on the altar of Bacchus. Which of these three men had the motive and opportunity of plunging a knife into the back of the family lawyer? Or could it have been one of the less likely suspects—Kenneth Clairmont, Lila Craig, Brunson the butler, or perhaps even Mrs. Clairmont herself? How shall the brave young Dash Hardeen be able to—"

"All right, Biggs," I said, cutting him short. "I believe you've made your point. Besides, I wouldn't be surprised if Lieutenant Murray had already solved the case by now."

"Possibly," said Biggs, climbing back onto the stool behind his compositor's desk, "but just in case he hasn't, I'd like you to give me your word—"

"I know, Biggs," I said, reaching for my hat. "As soon as something breaks, you'll be the first to know."

~ 8 ~

WE PRECIPITATE A HOBGOBLIN

I SPOTTED HARRY ACROSS THE GREEN AS I ROUNDED EAST 21ST Street into Gramercy Park. His shaggy astrakhan coat would have made him conspicuous even among the crowds of Broadway, as did the fact that his gait resembled that of an elderly man.

"What's the matter with your feet?" I asked, easily overtaking him as he reached the front of the Clair-mont home.

"Nothing's wrong with my feet. Nothing at all."

"Then why are you walking like that?"

"Like what?"

"Like old Mrs. Brucher from the fruit stand."

Harry avoided looking me in the eye. "I have been doing some muscular expansionism involving weights strapped to my ankles," he said with an air of affected nonchalance. "Perhaps I have strained a tendon. Were you able to learn anything at the newspaper office?"

I spent a few moments reviewing my conversation with Biggs for him. Harry perked up when I mentioned the mysterious void in Mr. Craig's history.

"His background grows murkier all the time," Harry said. "I wonder if—Dash, isn't that Lila Craig playing in the park?" He pointed to the far corner of the green, where a slender, red-haired girl could be seen climbing in the sturdy branches of a maple tree.

"I believe so," I said.

"I should like to have a word with her," Harry said, crossing the street.

"She didn't strike me as a very talkative sort," I said, falling in beside him. "She didn't say a word to anyone except Mrs. Clairmont last night."

"She will speak to Houdini," Harry said. "The Great Houdini has a marvellous way with children."

Lila Craig scrambled down from the tree as we approached, cradling a yellow tabby cat in her arms. Again I was struck by her bright and knowing eyes, which seemed at odds with her broad, girlish face. She trailed a length of yellow yarn between her fingers, holding it out while the cat batted it.

"Hello, little girl," said Harry as we came up beside her. "I am the Great Houdini. This is my brother, Dash Hardeen. You may have seen us last night, partaking of Mrs. Clairmont's fine hospitality."

The girl said nothing.

Harry tried again. "It is a fine day, is it not? The sky is blue and the air is clear. What a marvellous day to be frolicking in the park. I am reminded of an exciting story. Would you like to hear it?"

Lila turned away and dangled the yellow yarn in front of the cat. Harry pressed on.

"Long ago, in ancient Mesopotamia, there was a celebrated young conjurer by the name of Ari Ardeeni. He had many wonderful powers. It was said that young Ari had the ability to transport himself from one place to the next in the twinkling of an eye! One moment he might be roistering in a stream, and at the next instant he could be seen dancing atop the highest mountain! Stranger still, it was believed that this handsome conjuror possessed the ability to change places with any being of his choosing—at the merest snap of his fingers! But of all these wondrous talents, there was one that young Ari prized most of all." Harry leaned forward in a conspiratorial manner.

"It was said that the handsome young wizard could conjure spirits and ghosts out of thin air!"

Lila Craig scooped up the tabby cat and began scratching its ears.

Harry soldiered on. "Now, there is no need to be alarmed," he said. "These ghosts and spirits were friends of young Ari, and would never have done anything to frighten anyone. They were jolly, happy spirits who loved to dance and play on their spirit clouds. Sometimes they brought candy for the children of the village. I this not delightful?"

The girl gave no answer. Instead, she set the cat on the grass and tried to push down its tail.

"Of all the many people in the kingdom, the young wizard had one very special little friend. A young girl in whom he confided all his secrets. Her name was Mila. The magical Ari would carry her up to the enchanted meadow on his flying carpet and share his mystic secrets. He thought it was glorious to have a friend such as this. And little Mila shared her secrets in return. She loved to tell Ari all about her toys and her cloth bear and her kitty cat. It must be wonderful to have a friend such as this, don't you think?"

Lila twisted the yellow yarn around her index finger and gazed off across the park.

"Of all the young wizard's many secrets, there was one which Mila wished to know most of all. This was the secret of making ghosts and spirits appear. How was such a thing possible? She puzzled over the mystery for many a long day, but she could not imagine how anyone could do it—not even Ari, with all his fantastical powers. One fine day, she plucked up her courage and decided to ask young Ari how he—"

"I need to go back."

It was the first thing either of us had ever heard her say, and I suppose the fact that she had spoken at all surprised us a bit.

"Go?" Harry asked. "But I haven't even told you about the dragon!"

Lila stood up, cradling the cat in her arms. "I need to go back," she repeated.

"But it's a very good dragon!" Harry insisted.

The girl set the cat down and watched as it darted away.

I took out my linen handkerchief and knotted the corner. I draped it over the crook of my right hand and made a sprinkling motion with the fingers of my left. Slowly, the knotted corner began to twitch and wriggle. "Lila," I said, "there have been some very strange things going on lately. I'm sure you've noticed."

She nodded.

"Do you know what happened last night?"

She gnawed at her lower lip. "Yes."

"Do you know how it happened?"

She shook her head.

"Neither do we," I said, as the knotted corner bobbed up and down. "My brother and I think it started out as a magic trick, like this one. It wasn't like any trick we'd ever seen before, though. We hoped maybe you could explain it to us. You seem like a clever girl. I bet your father has taught you some tricks here and there, right?"

She nodded.

"Like this?" The handkerchief was now floating above my right hand in the manner of a dancing puppet.

"Not like that."

"What sort of tricks, then?"

"I'm not supposed to tell."

"That's right. You're not supposed to tell. Magicians never tell their secrets. Your father is a very fine magician, isn't he?"

"He's not—" She gnawed her lip again. "He doesn't like it when people say he's a magician."

"No?" I untied the knot and poked the handkerchief down into my right fist. "I think he's a very fine magician. One of the best." I uncurled the fingers of my fist to show that the handkerchief had vanished. "I wish I knew how he did his tricks. Hold still for a moment—" I reached across with my left hand

and plucked the handkerchief from behind her ear. "Thank you. You would make a fine magician's assistant. Do you ever help out as your father's assistant?"

She watched as I spread the cloth over my palm and folded the corners inward. "Sometimes," she said.

"Do you? I thought as much. You strike me as a natural magician's assistant." I gripped the four corners and shook the handkerchief. Something rattled inside. "Did you help him last night?"

"Last night?"

I let the corners drop to show three walnuts cupped in my palm. "Sure. Last night. He did some tricks for us. I thought maybe you might have helped him."

Her eyes darted to the Clairmont house. "No," she said, fixing her attention elsewhere. "I was in the kitchen. The whole time."

I followed her eyes across the green. Lucius Craig could be seen standing in the bay window of Jasper Clairmont's study, gazing down with a stern expression, his hands clasped behind his back.

"I need to go back," the girl repeated. "Good-bye."

"Wait a minute," I called after her. She turned, and I tossed her the three walnuts one after the other. She caught them easily, then turned and hurried off toward the house, disappearing down the side lane that led to the kitchen entrance.

"What do you make of that, Harry?" I asked.

"The girl's afraid of her father," he answered. "She won't tell us anything."

"There's more to it than that," I said. "Something doesn't quite fit."

We fell silent as we crossed the green and mounted the broad stone steps to the Clairmont house. Harry pulled at the door chime and once again the oval-paned doors swung inward. Brunson, looking no worse for the previous night's drama, ushered us into the reception area. We divested ourselves of our hats and coats and were shown through to the drawing room. Richardson Wells and Kenneth Clairmont were helping themselves to tea from a silver service.

"Hardeen!" called Kenneth. "There you are! Lieutenant Murray was just asking if you'd arrived yet. He's upstairs with Lucius Craig at the moment. Dr. Wells and I were just wondering what further questions he might have for us today."

"I couldn't say," I answered. "We told him everything we could last night."

"Yes, but the two of you were up there rather a long time after the—the unpleasantness. He seemed to take a great deal longer with you than any of the rest of us."

"He was availing himself of our expertise in matters of the occult," said Harry. "We had a very interesting discussion."

"Actually, I believe the lieutenant was just being thorough," I said. "Harry and I have a slight acquaintance with him, so he may have questioned us a bit more closely than the rest of you."

"I see," Kenneth said, though he did not seem entirely satisfied.

"Where is your mother?" Harry asked. "I'm sure Lieutenant Murray will have additional questions to put to her, as well."

"His questions will have to wait," said Dr. Wells curtly. "Augusta is nearly beside herself with agitation. Her nerves have not been right since Jasper's death. I gave her a sleeping draught last night, but I'm afraid the shock of what happened may be more than she can stand. I have confined her to her sitting room." He stepped toward the fireplace as Brunson poured two cups of tea for Harry and myself.

"I don't see why the police should need to question my mother, in any case," Kenneth said. "She had nothing to do with Edgar's death. I refuse to believe that any of us could have done such a thing, and yet the other explanation is too fantastic."

"The other explanation?" asked Harry, reaching for the china cup Brunson offered him.

"The spirits, of course," said Lucius Craig, appearing suddenly in the doorway. "I don't know why you refuse to acknowledge what we all plainly saw. I've just been explaining it to the lieutenant. Last night the door between our world and the next was flung wide open. The manifestation which we all beheld came through as plainly as could be wished. There can be no point in seeking any other explanation."

"For God's sake, Craig!" said Dr. Wells, turning back from the fireplace. "A man has been murdered! It's time to drop this spirit claptrap once and for all!"

"On the contrary, Dr. Wells," the medium answered. "It is the only explanation that meets the facts."

A flush of angry red spread across the doctor's cheeks. "The facts, as you would have us believe them, are too ridiculous to consider. I'm quite serious, Craig. I have endured your foolishness these past weeks because it appeared to bring comfort to Augusta. As of last night, your usefulness is at an end. I don't know how you contrived to make that strange figure appear, but we can no longer tolerate this pretense of traffic with the supernatural. This is a matter for the police now. Surely they will demand to know what strings you were pulling while the lights were lowered."

Craig brought out his snuff shaker and tapped it on the back of his hand. "You are not the first man of science to doubt the evidence of his own eyes," said the medium, pausing to inhale the powder. "I have grown accustomed to dealing with skeptics of all descriptions. Soon enough you will have to embrace the truth, one way or another. What you saw last night was quite genuine."

Harry set down his tea cup. "Pardon me, Mr. Craig. If I understand you correctly, you are certain that what we saw last night was the ghost of Jasper Clairmont."

"I am."

"And you believe that the ghost of Jasper Clairmont murdered Edgar Grange?"

Craig pulled a handkerchief from his sleeve and dabbed at his nose. "You saw the message on the spirit slate. 'Judgement is at hand.' What other explanation could there be? How else could that message have appeared?" A smile played at Craig's lips. "After all, Mr. Houdini, I have no doubt that by this time you have made a rather thorough examination of the slate, have you not?"

Dr. Wells interrupted before Harry could reply. "Do you expect me to believe that the ghost of Jasper Clairmont descended upon us last night for the purpose of murdering poor Edgar? Even if one could credit such a preposterous notion, why would Jasper have wished harm to Edgar? They were the closest of friends."

Lucius Craig gave a languid sigh and lowered himself onto the settee. "It is not for me to say. Possibly Mr. Clairmont's spirit was resentful of Mr. Grange's attentions to our hostess."

Dr. Wells appeared genuinely shocked. "His attentions? What are you suggesting?"

"I am merely stating that Mr. Grange had been spending a good deal of time in Mrs. Clairmont's company."

"There's nothing unusual in that, Mr. Craig," said Kenneth. "My mother has been lonely since father passed. Both Mr. Grange and Dr. Wells have been very considerate in their attentions to her. For that matter, there is no one who has spent more time in her company these past weeks than you. Why should this 'spirit' have not taken his vengeance on you?"

"Because he recognizes that I am the conduit by which he will be able to communicate with his beloved wife," answered Craig. "He would not dream of severing that link. You will come to understand this as you learn more of the science of spiritualism."

"Science!" Dr. Wells cried. "There is no more science in this than in the ravings of a madman!"

Craig regarded him coldly. "There was a time, my friend, when the same was said of Copernicus and Galileo."

Kenneth's eyes went to the portrait of his father above the fireplace. "You speak of science, sir, and yet you are willing to ascribe the attributes of a crazed murderer to the spirit of my father." He paused, apparently struggling with his temper.

"You did not even know my father, Mr. Craig. I deeply resent the accusation."

At this Lucius Craig gathered himself on the settee and sat forward with a solicitous expression. "You must forgive me, Kenneth," he said. "When I spoke of your father's spirit, I was speaking in terms of an abstract problem, something to be considered within the ever-expanding horizons of what I know of the spirit realm. I did not stop to consider how my speculations might affect you on an emotional level. Let me explain myself more fully. It is my understanding that when a spirit makes its transition to the other side, there is a long period of adjustment—almost of rebirth, if you will. We cannot expect the entity to behave as it did during its time on the earthly plane. It is only half formed, and learning new ways of adapting to its circumstances. In this condition, its emotions and behaviors may be erratic and seemingly foreign to those who knew the spirit in life."

Dr. Wells reached forward to grip the back of the settee upon which Craig was sitting. "You're saying that the spirit of Jasper Clairmont, one of New York's most distinguished citizens, has killed his close friend and associate because he wasn't in his right mind?"

"I would not have phrased it so crudely, Doctor, but that is the gist of the matter."

The doctor leaned in close and spoke in a level tone. "Craig, I will see you turned out of this house and run out of town on the next train. You are the very worst kind of confidence man."

"Sir, you merely fail to—"

Craig's reply was cut short as the doors flew open and Sterling Foster burst into the room. "I don't see why that policeman needed to question me," he said angrily, making his way toward the tea service. "I wasn't even in the room at the time. I wasn't even in the house, as a matter of fact. The implication is outrageous." He poured himself a cup of tea and carried it to one of the armchairs. His face was pale and drawn, with a dirty smudge clinging to his jawline. It was clear from the gingerly manner with which he carried himself that he was feeling the effects of the previous night's excesses.

"Sterling," said Dr. Wells, "a man has been murdered. It is only right that the police should ask questions."

"But I wasn't there, I tell you! How am I supposed to know anything about it?"

Harry's ears had pricked up during this exchange. "You say you weren't in the house?" he asked.

"Of course not," Foster said. "I have my own rooms across the street."

"Can anyone confirm that you were there at the time?"

Foster wheeled around, sloshing a measure of tea onto the arm of his chair. "See here, young man! I've just answered a full slate of questions for the police! If you think I'm going to explain myself to you, you've got another thing coming!"

"Calm down, Sterling," said Dr. Wells. "We're all rattled by what's happened. We're trying to understand how such a thing could have occurred."

"I was in my rooms," said Foster pointedly. "Across the green. Even if I hadn't been, how could I have had anything to do with this thing? You were all locked away in the study. I couldn't have gotten in there even if I'd wished it!"

I looked at Kenneth. "Is that true? You grew up in this house, Kenneth. Is the room really as secure as it appears? Is it possible to get in by any other means?"

Kenneth shook his head. "That room was off-limits to me as a boy," he said, "so naturally I was powerfully curious to know what went on when my father locked himself away. I tried to find a way of spying on him. I even harbored a childish hope that I might discover a secret passage, but of course there was nothing of the kind. There is no way in or out of that room apart from the doors."

"Well, that puts the lot of you in a rather awkward position," said Foster with apparent satisfaction. "Either one of you killed

Edgar, or it was the work of Jasper's ghost."

"So it would seem," said Kenneth gloomily. "I can't say that I find much comfort in either of those two options."

A moody silence settled over the room as Sergeant Flaherty appeared to conduct each of us in turn into the presence of Lieutenant Murray. I passed the time looking through the leather–bound volumes near the fireplace, while Dr. Wells stirred at the coals with a metal poker. When it was Harry's turn to be led away for questioning, I took advantage of his absence to accept a cigarette from Kenneth. My brother's passion for physical conditioning left him with an abiding mistrust of tobacco, but in those days I still believed that a cigarette gave me an air of sophistication. I was happy to strike a pose near the mantelpiece, surveying the room though a cloud of fragrant smoke.

I had gotten through three of Kenneth's cigarettes before Sergeant Flaherty reappeared to take me upstairs to Jasper Clairmont's study. I found Lieutenant Murray seated at the séance table, with a sheaf of notes and reports spread out before him.

"Afternoon, Hardeen," he said. "Any more theories for me today? You and your brother aren't going to set fire to the room again, are you?"

"You must admit that it was an interesting solution to the problem," I returned. "It just didn't happen to be the correct one."

"Yes," the lieutenant allowed. "Unfortunately, I haven't anything better on hand at the moment. Why don't you tell me again what happened here last night?"

He sat absolutely still as I ran through the events of the previous evening in as much detail as I could recall. He did not make a single notation or even glance at the papers on the table before him, and I had the impression that he was waiting to see if my account varied from those of the others.

"I'll tell you what bothers me," he said when I had finished. "If I wanted to stab Edgar Grange in the back, I don't think I'd do it in a roomful of people."

"No," I agreed. "I can't imagine that you would."

"Obviously the killer wanted everyone to believe that Jasper Clairmont's ghost was responsible. For that he needed witnesses. Who benefits from giving the impression that there's a murderous ghost on the loose?"

"Lucius Craig," I answered. "He's already taken care to get his name in the newspapers."

"He killed a man to get his name in the newspapers? I don't buy it."

"Well, there may have been other motivations as well."

The lieutenant stood up and stretched his arms over his head. "I know. He may have had designs on the Clairmont millions. Still, if he was tied up as securely as your brother says—"

"Then he would have needed an accomplice from outside of the room."

"It seems so, though I can't figure how that could have been managed. Still, somebody had to be running around in a sheet or pulling strings or something. That was no ghost you saw."

"It wasn't someone dressed in a sheet, either, Lieutenant. It was too—too ethereal."

"Ethereal, huh?" He rubbed at his jaw. "You're a real fount of information, Hardeen. You really are. You're sure you didn't hear anyone moving around before this ethereal vision appeared?"

I stood up and walked to the music box cabinet. "Mr. Craig had the music playing from the beginning, and he was talking most of the time. It was difficult to hear anything else." I leaned over the music box and pushed the speaker trumpet aside on its swivel, then I lifted the mahogany lid to peer at the workings. Inside was a metal cylinder covered with grooves and notches, a pair of glass tubes, a metal disc with a series of holes punched in a spiral pattern, and a wooden pick arm that stretched across the spin shaft. I've always been fascinated by mechanical gadgets and longed to take the device apart to see how it worked.

"Your brother seems to think that Lucius Craig is the one

man who couldn't have done it," the lieutenant was saying. "I'm not sure I agree."

"He couldn't have done it alone, Lieutenant," I said, setting the music box going. "That much is certain."

"I'm not so sure," he answered as the first notes of Mozart filled the room. "Sergeant Flaherty?"

The sergeant, who had been standing by the open door, snapped to attention. "Sir?"

"Ask Mr. Houdini if I might have a few more moments of his time, would you?"

"Right away, sir."

'Tell me again what these screens are for, Hardeen," the lieutenant said, indicating the fabric tent surrounding Lucius Craig's chair.

"He claims that they help to focus the spirit energy in the room."

"Is Craig the only one who thinks so, or are there are other mediums who use this type of covering?"

"As I understand it, it's fairly typical for a spirit medium to use a screen of this type. What's unusual is that these particular screens actually provide less cover than one would expect. When Harry and I did our stint as mediums, we used a screen of opaque black cloth. When Harry went behind those curtains, he could do whatever he wanted without being observed by the audience."

The lieutenant stretched out his arm. "I can see my hand right through this material," he said.

"Yes, and there was never any sort of covering in front of the enclosure. He was only screened from the back and sides."

"Makes no sense."

"I've heard it explained in various ways. According to Harry, it's supposed to be like starting a fire in the woods. The spark has to be shielded from stray gusts of wind. The screens are meant to keep restless spirits from interfering."

"Restless spirits." The lieutenant narrowed his eyes. "Imagine that."

"It's just scene-setting. A platform magician will sometimes use his cape in the same way—hiding something from the eyes of the audience that doesn't really need to be hidden, just to make the effect look more mysterious than it actually is."

"Just to make it look good, eh?" He fingered the sheer fabric. "Maybe. Ah, Houdini! There you are!"

"How can I help you, Lieutenant?" my brother asked. "Is there some new discovery that requires my attention?"

"Not exactly, Houdini," the lieutenant said. "I wanted to ask you a favor."

"A favor? What sort of favor?"

The lieutenant fixed me with a strange expression. "Well, Houdini," he said, "I think you might actually enjoy it."

Five minutes later I was lashed to a wooden chair as securely as if dipped in a vat of plaster.

"You're quite right, Lieutenant," said Harry, stepping back to admire his handiwork. "I did find that rather agreeable."

"This is how you tied up Lucius Craig last night? With the double knots and short strips of rope?"

"It is more practical to bind someone with short strips rather than one long hank of rope. The shorter lengths can be tightened more securely. A longer rope is likely to admit slack."

Lieutenant Murray poked at the restraints around my left arm. "Any slack there, Hardeen?"

"None," I said.

"But your hands are free," he noted.

"That was so that Mr. Craig would still be able to grasp the hands of Mrs. Clairmont and Mr. Grange," Harry said. "He insisted upon it. As you can see, however, he had no movement in his hands. They had to reach over to him in order to complete the circle."

"So I see. You're telling me that Lucius Craig couldn't have been responsible for the death of Edgar Grange."

"It is absolutely impossible, Lieutenant. Had the murder

occurred in the earlier part of the evening, then I would have been the first to accuse Mr. Craig. The man is a transparent cad. But at the time of the murder he was securely tied, as you can see. We had to cut him free afterwards. He simply could not have done it. He must be eliminated from the list of suspects."

Lieutenant Murray fixed my brother with a level gaze. "You could have done it, Houdini."

Harry started. "You mean to suggest that I could have killed Mr. Grange? Preposterous!"

"No, I mean you could have escaped from the ropes, killed the lawyer, and then slipped back into your bonds. You're always telling me what a master of escape you are. You could have done it."

Harry weighed his response. "Indeed, I could have. But Houdini is without equal. There is no one else in the entire world who could have managed such a thing."

Murray tapped a pencil against his notebook. "Hardeen could have. If we leave him sitting there long enough, I bet he'll get out."

Harry's head snapped in my direction, as though he had never noticed me before. "Dash? Well, yes. I suppose Dash might be able to manage it. Perhaps not as flawlessly as I."

"A minute ago you would have had me believe that there was no one else in the entire world capable of escaping from the ropes. Now we have two men sitting in the same room. Why not three?"

"My talents are quite without parallel, Lieutenant. While it is true that my brother Dash possesses some of them to a lesser degree, that is a matter of pure heredity. It may be that he himself is not luminous, but he is a conductor of light. Some people—"

I cleared my throat. "What Harry is trying to say, Lieutenant, is that Craig's hands were bound in a manner far more stringent than the usual run of such things, as you can plainly see. Harry is the Paganini of ropes. Last night I chided him for being excessive. In the circumstances, I'm fully persuaded that Craig was completely immobile. Even if he had been able to extricate himself from the ropes, I don't see how he could possibly have managed it so that we wouldn't have noticed when the lights were restored. It's one thing to get out of restraints such as these, it's quite another to get back in." I strained at the bonds, demonstrating their unyielding strength. "As far as I'm concerned, Lucius Craig is the one man in the room that we can rule out—unless someone else was helping him."

"Like his daughter, you mean?" Lieutenant Murray shook his head. "I don't see it. You just can't have it both ways, Hardeen. On the one hand, you and your brother have gone out of your way to paint this man as a charlatan and a huckster. On the other, you'll have me believe that he'd be rendered helpless when a seasoned professional such as Houdini ties him up. I don't buy it. Not for a minute. If he's what you say he is, he'll have picked up a trick or two over the years. How old are you, Houdini? Twenty-three? Twenty-four?"

"I am of age." Harry said quietly.

"Well, Lucius Craig has a lifetime of experience over you. I don't doubt that he could teach you a thing or two about pulling the wool over a sucker's eyes."

"Possibly," Harry admitted. "But last night he'd have been obliged to teach that lesson with his hands tied."

"Have it your way," said the lieutenant. "But there's one thing I may have neglected to mention."

"What's that?" I asked.

A flicker of satisfaction passed over the lieutenant's features. "The blood," he said.

"Blood?"

"Lucius Craig had blood on the right leg of his trousers and another small smear on the silk lining of his coat. Neither mark was especially dramatic—you could have covered the pair of them with penny—but our boys noticed them last night. I find that sort of suggestive, don't you?"

I curled my fingers around the arms of the chair, wishing that

I were free so that I could begin pacing. "Very suggestive," I said.

"Can we be certain that the blood belongs to Mr. Grange?"

Lieutenant Murray scowled. "Now, how are we supposed to know that? We can't exactly ask him."

"I thought Dr. Peterson might have performed a test of some sort."

"A blood test? What do you know about blood tests, Houdini?"

"Well," said Harry, puffing his chest a bit, "I am familiar with a technique involving a chemical reagent which is precipitated by a hobgoblin—and by nothing else. It is considered superior to the old guaiacum test."

The lieutenant could scarcely have looked more surprised if my brother had begun walking on the ceiling. "Chemical reagent?" he asked. "Precipitated by a what?"

Harry glanced at his fingernails, his confidence fading. "A hobgoblin," he said.

"Harry," I said, "I believe the word you're searching for is 'haemoglobin,' and since that test has never been mentioned outside of a Sherlock Holmes story, I'm not sure that it has much bearing on the matter at hand."

"My point is perfectly valid," he insisted. "There are tests that might determine whether it is the murdered man's blood on Mr. Craig's clothing."

Lieutenant Murray shook his head. "Doc Peterson says he couldn't get enough of a sample even to try a test," he said. "Even if he had, none of those things carry any weight in court. For our purposes, all that matters is that he has blood on his clothes."

"I dare say that if you examine his wrists you will find that he has rubbed them raw," I said, glancing down at my own wrists. "That might account for it."

"It might," the lieutenant conceded, "but Doc Peterson doesn't think so. He says it looks like splashes to him. The sort of splashes that result from a cut, as opposed to a scrape."

"You'd be surprised," Harry said. "Sometimes, when I've been practicing an especially difficult escape, it appears as if I've been in a knife fight of some kind. There was one occasion, when I was trying to master the Conklin knot, that Mama nearly fainted at the sight of me."

Lieutenant Murray studied the knots around my wrists for a further moment. "I don't think so," he said. "What makes you two so eager to clear Lucius Craig, anyway?"

"The man is a scoundrel and a cad," Harry declared. "I just do not happen to think that he is a murderer."

"Well, he's the only one in the room who had blood on his clothing."

Harry considered the problem while I struggled vainly to get some slack in my bonds. "What did Mr. Craig say when you asked him about the stains?" Harry asked.

Lieutenant Murray's jaw tightened. "He says it's not blood at all. He says it's the spirit residue of the ghostly presence of Jasper Clairmont. He had a word for it. Ectoplasm."

"Ectoplasm," said Harry with a sigh. "The last refuge of the desperate spiritualist. What cannot be explained is attributed to ectoplasm."

"Does Mr. Craig have any kind of a criminal record?" I asked, trying to sound casual even as I strained against the ropes. "His early years are rather mysterious."

The lieutenant glanced at one of the papers on the séance table. "Noticed that, did you? He says he was raised in a Chinese monastery. His parents were missionaries, he claims." He drummed his fingers across the sheet of paper. "Hogwash."

"Very convenient hogwash, at that," Harry said. "It relieves him of the obligation to explain how he came to the mystic arts, and it confers a pleasing air of mystery on his persona. Our friend Harry Kellar did much the same in his own biography. Perhaps I too should adopt a colorful childhood for myself."

"Your childhood was colorful enough without embellishment, as I recall, Harry."

"Perhaps so," he answered. His eyes brightened as a new thought struck him. "Lieutenant, last night Mr. Grange seemed strongly in favor of my efforts to expose the tricks and deceits of Mr. Craig. Do you suppose that might have been a motive for his murder?"

"I don't see how, Houdini. This crime had to have been premeditated. I don't know how the killer managed to make that ghost appear, but he couldn't possibly have done it on the spur of the moment. Besides, if the motive had anything to do with your exposure of Craig's tricks, wouldn't it have made more sense to kill you?"

"An intriguing thought," Harry admitted, obviously picturing himself with a knife in his back. "I can't say I had ever considered that possibility."

"Uh, Harry." I said, having abandoned my struggle to free myself from the ropes. "Would you mind—?"

Harry ignored me. "If Craig was not afraid of being exposed, what do you suppose his motive might have been?"

"Harry. Lieutenant. Would someone—?"

"That's not too hard to figure," the lieutenant said. "Those men have all been circling the widow Clairmont like buzzards. They are determined to marry into that fortune, and our Mr. Craig seems to have decided to thin out the ranks of the competition."

"There has to be more to it than that" Harry said. "Mr. Craig seems to enjoy a rather comfortable existence without marrying his hostess."

"Perhaps he was planning his retirement."

Harry shook his head. "Not all men are suited to the joys of matrimony," Harry said, with a significant glance in my direction. "Lucius Craig simply does not seem the sort. If he were, I do not think he would have to worry himself too much over the competition. Mrs. Clairmont seems absolutely besotted with him."

"I'm not sure about that, Houdini."

"Harry, I'm really quite uncomfortable. Would you please—?"

"If you're so certain about Craig's guilt, Lieutenant, why don't you arrest him?"

"Because the minute I do, Mrs. Clairmont will hire some fancy-pants defense lawyer and get me thrown off the force. Oh, I can just hear it now. The suspect tied to a chair? A ghost with a knife in its hand? A roomful of witnesses and nobody saw a thing?" He shook his head. "She'd have my badge on a velvet pillow."

"You need to know how it was done."

"That's right, Houdini. I need to figure out how it was done."

"Gentlemen, I'm beginning to lose feeling in my hands..."

Harry gazed thoughtfully at the desk where Jasper Clairmont had died. "The lieutenant wishes to know how, and I wish to know why. A strange turnabout, is it not?"

Lieutenant Murray stepped to the door as Sergeant Flaherty appeared carrying a red-bordered messenger packet. The lieutenant tore open the flap and unfolded the single sheet inside.

"Dash," said Harry, acknowledging my predicament at last, "why are you still tied to that chair?"

"Harry, my hands are turning blue. Would you please—?"

"Well, gentlemen," said Lieutenant Murray, crossing the room, "it seems our murderer has been busy."

"What do you mean?" Harry said.

"Has someone else been killed?" I asked.

The lieutenant shook his head. "Someone tried to break into the Puck building last night. The night watchman took a cosh over the head. Whoever it was, he got away."

"The Puck Building?"

"On Lafayette Street. You'll never guess who kept his offices there."

"Don't tell me," I said.

"That's right," said the lieutenant. "The late Mr. Edgar Grange."

9

THE KALEIDOSCOPE KILLER

"I DON'T UNDERSTAND IT," HARRY SAID AS WE MADE OUR WAY across 21st Street. "Why should anyone wish to break into a dead man's offices?"

"If we knew that," I said, "we'd also know why someone wanted to kill him in the first place."

"Perhaps there was something in that office that our murderer does not wish for us to see."

"That would be my guess, Harry."

We had been at the Clairmont house for another hour or so before Lieutenant Murray declared himself finished with the interviews. We had been unable to pry any further information from him concerning the burglary at Mr. Grange's office, although we overheard Sergeant Flaherty informing him that the criminal had evidently fled without gaining entry.

"I'm sure the lieutenant will make a thorough examination of the premises," Harry said. "If there is anything to examine."

"No doubt," I agreed. "Although he didn't seem to be in a great hurry when we left him."

"No," Harry said. "He did not."

We walked on for several moments without speaking. I had not eaten since breakfast and began to feel peckish. I fished a handful of walnuts out of my pocket and offered one to Harry. He popped it into his mouth without troubling to remove the shell.

"How very delectable," he said, amid loud crunching noises. "Dash, something has just occurred to me."

"What's that, Harry?"

"Perhaps it would be to our advantage to examine Mr. Grange's offices for ourselves."

"My very thought."

He stopped walking and looked at me in surprise. "Really? I expected an argument."

"No argument."

"No? I imagined that you would say that Lieutenant Murray is one of the finest detectives in New York and that you and I are nothing but busybodies who should keep their noses out of police business."

"All of that is true, Harry. Even so, I still think we should take a look at Edgar Grange's offices."

"You do?"

"This is no ordinary crime," I said. "If it were, Lieutenant Murray would have solved it by now. So far we've had no luck figuring out how Edgar Grange was killed. If we can't figure out how, maybe we can figure out why."

"What about the lieutenant? He thinks we're chasing after ghosts."

"That's exactly what we're doing," I said.

"Splendid!" Harry cried, clapping me on the back. "We will go home and gather our dark clothing from the old Graveyard Ghouls routine! I shall fetch the dark lantern and some blacking for our faces! We shall wait for the cover of darkness and then stealthily make our approach by means of—"

"Not this time, Harry," I said. I turned and resumed walking.

"What?" he asked, falling in beside me. "But you just said that we must examine the premises! Surely this calls for the unique lock-picking talents of the Great Houdini!"

"Harry, whoever tried to break into Mr. Grange's office must be desperate. We should get down to that office building right away."

Harry whistled and rubbed his hands together. "A daylight raid! Yes, that is just the thing! I must say, Dash, this is an uncommonly bold and original plan. Ordinarily you are depressingly cautious about such things."

"Depressingly cautious? Just because I discouraged you from leaping off the Brooklyn Bridge does not make me—"

"A thousand pardons. In any event, we must plan our moves with the skill and precision of a surgeon! A rooftop approach, perhaps? Yes! The very thing! I shall gather a hank of stout rope and a pair of ankle stocks. We shall gain access from the adjacent building, then secure the rope to a—"

"Harry."

He stopped short.

"No rooftop approach, no ankle stocks. We're just going to walk in through the front door."

"How is that possible? How will we manage to get in if the killer tried and failed?"

"Simple," I said. "We'll use our ace in the hole."

"And what is that?" he asked.

I pointed over his shoulder at the familiar marquee of Ravelson's Review.

"Bess," I said.

Forty minutes later, Bess Houdini made her way along Lafayette Street with the two of us alongside, each lightly grasping one of her elbows. To the passer-by, it would have appeared that a pair of concerned young men were assisting a heavily pregnant young woman down the street, though a trained observer might have detected a certain lumpiness about the blessed protrusion—almost as if it were a wadded-up chorus girl costume.

"Dash," Bess said in a side-of-mouth whisper, "I feel perfectly ridiculous."

"Do you?" I answered cheerily. "You look positively radiant."

"This is a risky plan," Harry said worriedly. "Are you sure

we shouldn't revert to a rooftop approach?"

"I don't think Bess should be climbing ropes in her condition, do you? Just relax, Harry. This will be smooth as glass."

It is difficult to convey the effect that the sight of a pregnant woman had on the average male in those days. It was the custom at the time for a woman in the family way to remain at home through the last months of her pregnancy, hidden away from the gaze of society. "Nature's processes may be miraculous to contemplate," wrote a newspaper commentator of the day, "but they must also be counted as raw and poorly suited for public display." To judge from the reactions of the tradesmen and office workers we passed along the way, one would have thought that Bess had been carrying a keg of gunpowder with a fast-burning fuse.

"I'm not sure I can tolerate much more of this," Bess muttered as a man in a bowler hat literally jumped sideways to clear the path.

"Are you uncomfortable?" Harry asked, as though her condition were genuine. "We can turn back if you like."

"We're not turning back," I said. "We're almost there. For once, Harry, we'll follow the plan as I've laid it out."

The Puck Building, which was then the home of the humor magazine of the same name, was perhaps only ten or twelve years old at that time, and its moulded red bricks were gleaming after a light afternoon rain. A gold-leaf statue of Shakespeare's whimsical sprite peered out from the third-floor cornice at Houston as we passed, as if bestowing a mischievous benediction on our errand.

We entered the building through a revolving door at the north entrance. I lingered a moment by the glass directory board while Harry led Bess across the marble lobby. An attendant at the polished reception desk regarded us with interest. "May I be of assistance?" he asked.

"We're here to see our attorney, Mr. Hawkins," I said, coming up behind Harry and Bess.

"Do you have an appointment, sir?" he asked, pulling out a heavy leather logbook.

"No," I said amiably, "although I mentioned it to him last night at the Peacock. We'll just go on up, if you don't mind."

"I'm sorry, sir, but my orders are very clear. No one may be admitted without an appointment in the book."

"I see," I said, leaning forward in a confidential manner. "It's a bit embarrassing, I'm afraid. My brother, you see, needs to make a certain amendment to his marriage certificate. Needs to bring the date forward a bit, if you take my meaning. Wants to get it done before the blessed event. To save a bit of embarrassment later. I mentioned it to Phillip last night and he promised that it wouldn't be any bother."

The attendant winked to indicate that he, too, was a man of the world. "I understand you perfectly, sir, but I'm afraid I can't let you simply go in without an appointment, though I'd be happy to—madam? Are you all right?"

My sister-in-law had made a sudden lurching motion, and was now gripping the edge of the reception desk in an effort to steady herself. "I'm fine. Don't fuss over me, Harry. I'm quite all right." She straightened herself and turned to the desk attendant. "Young man, are you married?"

"No, ma'am."

"If you were, would you wish to see your wife standing about in this condition while your private affairs were discussed with a stranger?"

"No, ma'am, but—"

"Very well, then." Without bothering to wait for a reply, Bess swept past the desk toward the stairway, with Harry trailing behind her. I gave an apologetic shrug to the attendant and followed after them.

She waited until she had rounded a pair of stair landings and then slumped against the railing, her body shaking with laughter. "Amendment to the marriage certificate!" she cried. "Dash, that was priceless!"

"Well, the only other offices on the same floor with Mr. Grange are those of an accounting firm, and I couldn't think of what use they might be."

"I don't understand," Harry said. "What amendment? Why should we need to consult a lawyer if we intended to have a child?"

Bess dabbed her eyes with a square of linen and patted Harry's hand. "It, er, it is simply a matter of having the child added to the marriage certificate," she said gently. "Just as my name must be added to your passport before we travel abroad."

Harry pondered this information. "I don't see why this amuses you so."

Bess composed herself and continued up the stairs. "Don't give it a second thought," she said with a toss of her head. "A woman in my condition is entitled to her humors."

Harry and I followed as Bess climbed past the magazine offices to the fourth floor of the building. We pushed through a set of swinging doors into an executive suite, noting the legal offices of Mr. Phillip Hawkins to our left.

A wooden police barricade to our right advised us that the area was off limits. Beyond it we could see a glass door with the name "Edgar Grange" etched on a pebbled glass panel. Harry squeezed past the police barrier while Bess and I kept watch, pulling out his leather wallet of lockpicks as he knelt beside the door to Grange's office.

"Look at these marks and scratches!" he cried as he examined the lock. "What a barbarian!"

"The burglar tried to force the lock?" I asked.

"Worse," said Harry. "He used a crowbar. What sort of heathen uses a crowbar? A lock such as this should be treated with respect. A crowbar requires no finesse or—"

I could hear footsteps approaching from around the corner. "Someone's coming, Harry," I said.

With a show of nonchalance, he selected a coiled hook-head from his wallet and slipped it into the lock. "Then perhaps we should step inside," he said, as the mechanism gave a sharp click. Harry turned the door handle and pushed the door inward. Bess and I squeezed past the barricade and hurried through the door. Harry pulled it shut behind us, and we remained motionless until the sounds of the footfalls had faded.

We found ourselves in a well-furnished reception area, with a pair of Sheraton chairs placed before an oval clerk's desk. Oil portraits depicting sea battles were hung in ornate frames on the walls, a brass sextant and a barometric gauge sat upon a shelf behind the desk.

"Weather instruments," I said. "Jasper Clairmont had weather instruments and navigational tools in his study."

"Hardly surprising," Harry said. "The man was in the shipping business. Mr. Grange appears to have shared an interest in the sea."

"So it seems. Maybe that's how they came to be in business together." I stepped behind the desk and fingered an open appointment ledger.

"What are you doing there, Dash?" Harry asked. "That's a private—"

"Mr. Grange is dead, Harry," I reminded him. "It would be useful to know if any of our suspects have visited him in the past few days." I scanned the columns of appointment listings. "There's nothing here." I flipped back a few pages. "No, it looks as if—wait! This is interesting!"

"What's that?" Bess asked.

"There's an appointment here with Jasper Clairmont, and the notation says it has to do with filing papers at City Hall."

Bess glanced down at the line I indicated. "What's so unusual about that, Dash?"

"It's the day Jasper Clairmont died."

"Is that really so significant?" Bess ran her finger along the adjacent page. "There are no fewer than seven listings for Jasper Clairmont here."

"It may be nothing. Let's see what we can find inside."

A door behind the desk led into Mr. Grange's office. This was a much larger room, with a map table at one end and a heavy Selden desk at the other. Law books lined one entire wall of the office, their spines bound in uniform leather. A low bank of wooden file drawers ran halfway along the opposite wall, with an array of loose papers grouped into piles on top of them.

"Where do we start?" asked Bess.

"The cabinets," I said. "Harry, see what you can do about those locks."

Each cabinet was fastened by a metal rod running through security hasps that held the drawers fast. The metal rods themselves were secured with small padlocks that looped through a crossplate.

"I see no great difficulty about that," Harry said, pulling out his leather lockpick wallet again. "Let's just have a look at—oh, dear."

"What's the problem, Harry?"

"These locks. They're half-sized. The sort of thing one might find on a cash register or deposit box. The opening is too small for my picks. I require a set of jewelers' tools."

"Or a crowbar," I suggested.

"Never." He frowned over the lock for a moment. "There must be something here I can use." He glanced around the room. "What's that?" He pointed to a copper tray on Grange's desk.

"A letter opener," I said.

"Too big. What's that?" He indicated a brass cube atop the cabinets.

"An anemometer, I believe."

"A what?"

"It measures wind."

Harry picked it up to see if there were any small pieces of metal he might be able to scavenge. "No good," he said, setting it down again. "How about that thing over there?" He pointed to a wood and glass cabinet near the map table.

"I have no idea what that is," I said, lifting the cabinet lid.

"There are quite a few gears and glass tubes in here. I presume it's another navigational device, but for the life of me I can't imagine—"

"Are there any metal springs?"

"Not small enough for our purposes."

"This is intolerable!" Harry began pacing back and forth. "The Great Houdini bested by a jeweler's lock? Absurd!"

"Harry," said Bess, "might I make a suggestion?" She bent down and slipped off one of her shoes. "Would this be of any use?"

Harry's eye fell on the delicate buckle at the vamp of the shoe. "My dear, you are a genius!"

"Well, I don't know about that," Bess said mildly, "but I'm a useful person to have along on a burglary."

Harry wasn't listening. He crouched over the first of the locks and worked at it with the metal tongue of the shoe buckle. In a moment, it snapped open, and Harry pulled out the metal rod holding the drawers shut. He repeated the procedure on each of the subsequent locks, and soon we were thumbing through Mr. Grange's legal files.

"I suppose we should start with his file on Lucius Craig," Harry said.

"I don't see that he has one," I said, riffling through the headings in the drawer marked *C*. "Let's see if there's anything useful in the Clairmont file."

As it happened, there were seven bulging files devoted to Jasper Clairmont and his various concerns, and we spent the better part of two hours examining them at the map table. Most contained dry legal documents and shipping manifests, and I felt no great confidence that I would recognize anything untoward or out of place if I happened to come across it.

"This is hopeless, Dash," said Bess, paging through a fat file of correspondence between Grange and a manufacturer of builders' cranes. "We're not lawyers. We have no idea what we're after."

"There has to be something that incriminates the murderer," I said. "Why else would he have attempted to break in here?"

"Perhaps he has a tremendous curiosity about builders' cranes," Bess said.

"I think we're wasting our time," said Harry. He jumped up from the table and made his way back to the file drawers. "I'm going to look elsewhere. There must be files here for the others. Dr. Wells. Sterling Foster. Perhaps those would be more illuminating."

"Help yourself, Harry," I said, "but I already checked. No one else has a file."

"Not even Kenneth?"

"There's no separate file for him, if that's what you mean. I assume that anything relevant to his interests in the family business would be here in his father's file." I gestured at the untidy piles of paper on the table. "Somewhere. "

"I suppose so." Harry walked over to the desk and threw himself into Edgar Grange's chair. "Maybe we should have left this to Lieutenant Murray after all. It's exactly the sort of dry and methodical work at which he excels." He picked up the letter opener and twirled it across his knuckles.

"Perhaps we should check under the carpet," said Bess.

"Under the carpet?" I asked. "Why?"

"That's where. Harry keeps his drawings when he doesn't want me to see them."

"Really?" I turned back to the desk. "What sort of drawings, Harry?"

"Certain items of importance for which the world is not yet prepared," he said, his cheeks darkening.

"Nothing particularly saucy, if that's what you mean, Dash," Bess said. "The last time I checked there was a set of illustrations showing how to escape from a regulation United States postal bag."

I looked at Harry. "Why do you keep such things hidden? Are you afraid Bess is going to steal your secrets?"

"Certainly not! It's just that when I am working on a new routine I like to conceal the method from her until I have perfected the technique. That way she will be properly surprised when I perform it for the first time."

"Under the carpet, huh?"

Harry glanced at the floor. There was a round, violet-hued carpet at the center of the room. "Why not?" he asked. He walked to the middle of the room and folded back the carpet. "There is nothing here," he said dejectedly.

"Well, maybe Mr. Grange had a different hiding place," said Bess. "Try behind that seascape over there."

"No," said Harry, peering behind the painting. "There is nothing here."

"What about under the cushions of that chair?"

"Nothing. Bess, this is hopeless."

"Nonsense. Look beneath that carriage clock."

"Bess, this is a waste of—ah ha!" Harry snatched up a sheaf of papers. "I knew it!"

"What do you have there, Harry?" I asked, hurrying to his side.

"It's hard to say. It's a blueprint of some type, but I couldn't tell you what it's supposed to represent."

I looked over his shoulder. The illustration was fairly crude, showing a short tube linked to a dish that appeared to be covered with marbles. Alongside was a mosaic of spirals, zigzags, and wavy lines. The pattern was duplicated in miniature at one end of the tube.

"What the devil is that supposed to be?" I asked.

Bess studied the paper carefully. "Possibly it's a technique for escaping from a regulation United States postal bag," she said. "What's on the other pages?"

"Technical details," Harry said, "and a patent application. The tube looks to have a series of glass disks and mirrors inside. There's a great deal here about 'optical refraction.' Could it be a telescope of some kind?"

"Possibly," I said. "What's the dish of marbles for? It seems familiar somehow."

"I should think so," said Bess. "It's a kaleidoscope."

"A kaleidoscope?"

"Of course! A tube with mirrors and glass marbles at the end! You see how the marbles are arranged in a spiral pattern? What else could it be? The end rotates and the marbles catch the light to form patterns. That's what all those lines and swirls are meant to show."

"There has to be more to it than that, Bess," I said. "Why should Edgar Grange have a drawing of a child's toy hidden beneath his clock?"

"Why should Harry hide his escape plans?"

"But there's a patent application. Why would anyone file a patent application on a kaleidoscope? I find it hard to believe that someone would have tried to break into this office for the sole purpose of stealing these plans. Are you suggesting that Edgar Grange was killed over a toy? There has to be more to it than that."

"If memory serves, that's precisely what you said about Branford Wintour and that curious little automaton of his," Bess reminded me. " 'No one gets killed over a toy,' you said, 'no matter how valuable.'"

"And I was correct, as I recall. It turned out that there was a great deal more to—Harry? You've gone awfully quiet. What's the matter?"

He had been standing with the letter opener dangling from his fingers for some moments, gazing at the far wall with an expression of intense thought. "What's the matter?" he asked, turning to smile at us. "Nothing is the matter. Now that you mention it, I am quite well." He twirled the letter opener across his knuckles as though it were a magic wand. "In fact, I have solved the crime!"

"You have?" Bess asked. "You know who killed Edgar Grange?"

"I do, indeed," said Harry, smoothing the points of his bow tie. "You needn't look so downcast, Dash. I'm sure you would have figured it out eventually. You're quite clever at these things as well. But this time, I fear, the honor must go to the Great Houdini."

"Well, then," I said, "don't keep us in suspense. Who did it?"

He waved a cautionary finger in my direction. "Now, now. That would never do. A magician must wait for the proper moment before he lifts the cloth on his effect. First, we must notify the good Lieutenant Murray. I shall enjoy that. Then we must notify the suspects that they are to assemble in Mr. Clairmont's study at eight this evening." He rubbed his hands together. "This will be very gratifying."

"You want to assemble the suspects in the drawing room? You don't think that's a bit melodramatic?"

"Of course not! The only question is how I shall address them, to bring them to the very peak of anticipation." He stood up and linked his hands behind his back. "Ladies and gentlemen, tonight the Great Houdini invites you to witness his most spectacular triumph." Harry paused to consider the matter. "I suppose that might be a bit too bold, don't you think?"

"Harry," said Bess, "are you quite sure you know who the killer is? Wouldn't you like to tell us, just to be sure your theory is sound?"

"No need, my dear," Harry answered with a cheery wink. "I have reached my solution by means of the same flawless reasoning that guides my escape routines. There can be no possibility of error."

"Still," I said, "it wouldn't hurt to let us hear what—"

"Ladies and gentlemen," Harry intoned, ignoring us, "tonight the Great Houdini asks you stand in wonder as he unveils his latest miracle of pure thought." He turned to Bess. "Better?"

"You might consider toning it down a shade."

"Nonsense!" he cried. "I cannot agree with those who rank modesty among the virtues. Ladies and gentlemen, you are fortunate to be present at the very pinnacle of the Great Houdini's career in detection." He paused and stroked his chin. "Well, I suppose something will occur to me when the moment comes."

Bess cast an anxious look at me. "I can hardly wait," she said.

"And now," Harry said, "we must go home to dress."

Bess and I exchanged a look. "You're expecting everyone in formal attire?" she asked. "To hear you name Edgar Grange's killer?"

"Of course," Harry said. "It wouldn't do for me to be the only one."

"But—"

"It is essential that I wear ray stage attire. My entire plan hinges upon it."

"But Harry," I said, "you haven't told us what your plan is."

"Is it not obvious?" he cried, thrusting his finger in the air. 'Tonight is to be a very special night. It marks the return of Professor Harry Houdini, the Celebrated Psycrometic Clairvoyant, giving a spiritual séance in the open light. Weird happenings presided over by the Man Who Sees All."

With that, he turned and swept from the room.

Bess turned to me and sighed.

"Weird happenings," she said.

~ 10 ~

THE MIND-READING MACHINE

"LADIES AND GENTLEMEN," SAID HARRY, RUNNING HIS HANDS over the points of his bow tie, "I suppose you're all wondering why I've asked you here this evening."

Standing behind him at the séance table, I could not quite conceal my surprise. "That's it?" I asked, leaning over to whisper in his ear. "That's your big line?"

"It was the only thing that came to me," he murmured. "In any case, my actions will speak far more forcefully than my words."

"Let's hope so," I said, straightening up to survey the room. Glancing around, I could see that all of the others were, in fact, wondering why he had asked them there that evening. Mrs. Clairmont and Kenneth had agreed to the gathering readily enough, but Lucius Craig and Richardson Wells were decidedly cool to the idea of another gathering in the room where Edgar Grange had died. The butler, Brunson, had been pressed into service once again, and Lieutenant Murray, looking quite resplendent in the formal pigeon-breasted coat he usually wore to the opera, had reluctantly agreed to fill the chair Edgar Grange had occupied on the night in question.

"I don't see what's to be gained by holding another séance," Dr. Wells grumbled as he took his place at the table. "We've had quite enough of that nonsense in this house, if you ask me."

"Mr. Houdini assures us that he has new information," said

Lieutenant Murray, "and he insists that this information can only be appreciated in these circumstances." He fixed my brother with a significant stare. "I am very much hoping that he will not disappoint me."

Lieutenant Murray's tone made it clear that anything less than a total success would not be in Harry's best interests. The lieutenant was conducting himself with his usual decorum in the presence of Mrs. Clairmont and the others, though he had all but kicked and screamed when Harry asked him to assemble the suspects at the scene of the crime. Harry was told in no uncertain terms that the New York City Police Department was not his to command. After considerable discussion, the lieutenant had grudgingly agreed, because the prospect of seeing the suspects at the séance table suited his own agenda. I hoped, for Harry's sake, that he had something better planned for us than setting fire to the day's newspapers.

Harry spent a few further moments arranging the details before he took his place at the table. With his customary fastidiousness he pulled the sheer cloth screens into position, set the music box playing, and laid out the chalk slate at the center of the table. Only then did Harry lock and bolt the door from the inside and settle himself into the chair between Mrs. Clairmont and Lieutenant Murray.

"From the beginning, this affair has presented us with several difficult challenges, each of which led inevitably to still greater challenges," Harry said, gazing round the table with an expression of quiet confidence. "How was the crime done? Which of us could have done it? Why should anyone wish to kill Mr. Grange? And perhaps most troubling of all, why would anyone choose to do so in a room filled with people? If one wished to kill Mr. Grange, would it not make better sense to do so when one had him alone?"

"We are all acquainted with the difficulties of the case, Houdini," said Dr. Wells from his place between Brunson and Kenneth Clairmont. "We've all had our disagreements with

Edgar, but I can't believe that one of us should have gone so far as to wish him dead."

"Apparently someone did," Harry said with satisfaction, "and it is now my pleasure to demonstrate how it was done. First, it is essential that we recreate the steps leading up to the dreadful event. As you will recall, the evening began with a harmonizing of energies. This took the form of a message-reading exercise conducted by our esteemed friend Mr. Craig."

"We remember that perfectly well, Houdini," said Kenneth. "You showed us how it was done immediately afterwards. It was very instructive."

Lucius Craig spoke up instantly. "On the contrary," he said, fighting against a rising tide of emotion, "it was not instructive at all. At best it might possibly be described as amusing. As I have already endeavored to explain, however, Mr. Houdini's ability to create the appearance of a spirit effect is not the same thing as producing the effect itself. It is merely a copy of a genuine manifestation."

"Lucius is correct, of course," said Mrs. Clairmont. "Mr. Houdini is a capable performer. Nothing more."

Harry folded his hands. "That was precisely the point I had hoped to make, Mrs. Clairmont," he said, "though I am afraid that I did so in an unpardonably clumsy manner. I had sought to demonstrate that Mr. Craig's effects could be duplicated by a gifted performer such as myself. In the course of doing so, I succeeded only in wounding your feelings. For this I apologize. However, the point I was endeavoring to make is a valid one. A great man once said that when you have eliminated the impossible, whatever remains, however improbable, must be the truth."

"That's very good," said Kenneth. "Goethe?"

"Sherlock Holmes," my brother answered. "My little display was nothing more than an attempt to show that we had not entirely eliminated the impossible. I presented it purely in the interests of sportsmanship, of course."

"Of course," said Kenneth, drily.

"Houdini," said Lieutenant Murray, "what does this have to do with the murder of Edgar Grange?"

"Everything," my brother answered. "Simply put, I am not the same man I was when I first came to this house. We have all been affected by the tragedy of Mr. Grange's death, and I have had cause to reexamine my attitudes toward Mr. Craig and his mediumship. The results of my studies have been both unsettling and provocative."

"What can you mean, Houdini?" Kenneth asked. "The man is a trickster! You said so yourself!"

"A great many things were said. The time for words has ended. With the kind permission of Mr. Craig and Mrs. Clairmont, I should like to show you what I have since learned to be true."

The medium reached for his snuff bottle. "I am, of course, delighted to hear that you have moderated your tone of antipathy toward me and my beliefs," he said carefully. "If you wish it, I should be happy to assist in opening your eyes to the wonders of the spirit realm. I fail to see, however, why your spiritual salvation requires the presence of a police lieutenant."

"I hope that will become apparent soon enough," Harry said. "For the moment, with your permission, I should like to recreate the circumstances of the other night as closely as possible. In a moment, we will form a circle by grasping hands. As before, let us also be certain that our feet are touching." He turned to his right. "In fact, Lieutenant Murray, I wish you to be absolutely certain that there is no possibility that I am able to use my feet in any way. Place your foot securely on my instep. Mrs. Clairmont, please do the same. I must be held under the strictest control at all times."

Harry glanced around the table, satisfying himself that all was in readiness. "Just this once, shall we leave the lights up for our demonstration? I would hate for anyone to think that I was taking advantage of the cover of darkness to work some unseen advantage."

"The spirits are repelled by the light," said Craig stiffly. "That is the reason that I work in darkness."

"Be that as it may," said Harry, "we are all sensitive to what happened the last time the lights were turned out in this room. In view of that unfortunate occurrence, I think that we may allow some illumination. By the same token, it will not be necessary to bind me to this chair. With the lights up you will be able to see plainly that I am not using my arms in any way. Moreover, I am an acknowledged master of escape, and no mere ropes could possibly hold me a prisoner. All right, then. Might I borrow that chalk slate?"

Kenneth lifted the chalk slate from the center of the table and held it out to Harry.

"No," said my brother, holding up his palms. "I do not even wish to touch the slate. There must be no possibility of trickery of any kind. Dr. Wells, I would like for you to examine it carefully, satisfying yourself that there are no hidden flaps or other concealments."

Wells rapped at the wooden frame with his knuckles and shook the slate at his ear to listen for any loose pieces. "Perfectly ordinary," he said.

"Good," said Harry. "Now, if I might ask you to place the slate beneath the table—at my feet. Thank you. Let us now join hands, and please be certain that my feet are also under control."

Once again Lucius Craig raised his voice in protest. "You speak of the spirit circle as though it were only a means of insuring against fraud," he said, with a rising note of irritation. "We join hands at the séance table in order to pool our psychic energy, to serve as a beacon to the other world." He glanced at Mrs. Clairmont, receiving a sympathetic nod in return.

"Mr. Craig is quite right," she said in a reproving tone. "Mr. Houdini, I will not permit antagonism in this room. It disturbs the ether."

"That is not my intention," Harry said. "However, it is my nature as a performer to establish safeguards. When I am doing a card trick, for example, it is vitally important to establish that the spectator has had a free selection of cards when he makes his choice. Otherwise, the trick is ruined afterwards. The audience is likely to say, 'Oh, he made him pick the card he wanted.'"

"This is not a card trick," Craig said firmly.

"No, but our instincts are much the same. If we establish that my hands and feet are under control, there will be no one coming forward afterwards to claim that I simply cheated."

Craig did not appear satisfied with this attempt at appeasement, but he nodded brusquely and waved at Harry to continue. My brother placed his hands upon the table and indicated that the rest of us should do the same. When he spoke again, his voice was hushed and fervent, as though in a house of worship.

"My friends," he began, "you must forgive me if I falter or appear uncertain in what I am about to attempt. I do not claim to have Mr. Craig's long experience in these matters. First, I must gather my energies. Please assist me by remaining silent." With this, Harry closed his eyes and began humming in what might charitably be called a tuneless fashion. After a few moments the humming escalated. Harry's neck muscles clenched and his jaw tightened, as though some private drama were playing out behind his closed lids. Mrs. Clairmont cast an anxious glance at Dr. Wells, who merely shrugged. Abruptly, Harry brought his caterwauling to a crescendo. "I believe my inner forces are properly aligned," he declared, opening his eyes. "I am ready to begin. Mrs. Clairmont, I must ask you to place your confidence in me, to follow my commands precisely no matter how strange they might seem. Will you do this for me?"

"Your commands?" she asked uneasily.

"You have seen me do some remarkable things in this room. Tonight, we must ascend to a new plane. We are endeavoring to contact the spirit of your departed husband. I cannot attempt such a feat without your complete and unquestioning cooperation. I must ask you to join your thoughts with mine as we journey together beyond the dark veil. Will you do this?"

Mrs. Clairmont studied my brother's earnest face. "I shall try," she said, after a moment's hesitation.

Harry nodded encouragingly. "I assure you that it will be most rewarding. We must all close our eyes now. Close them tightly and keep them closed, no matter what you might hear. Listen to the sound of my voice, Mrs. Clairmont. Attempt to let your thoughts join with mine. Try to see what I see. There is much darkness and confusion, but as we grow accustomed to our new surroundings, we will begin to perceive the outlines of familiar shapes and objects. A strange and new form of light begins to shine upon us. It is as though our souls are journeying forward while our physical forms remain here, anchored to one another by the merest touch of human fingertips. Do not dare to break contact even for a moment, for it is only the integrity of our spirit circle that preserves the tether between our world and the next. Above all, your eyes must remain tightly closed."

A glance around the table showed that the others were, in fact, keeping their eyes shut as they concentrated on my brother's voice. By contrast, Harry's eyes were wide open, and he sat grinning at me with high amusement, even as his voice maintained its grave tenor.

"The light brightens as we push forward to the fateful portal," he continued, winking at me, "and we begin to apprehend movement in the distance. Could this be my spirit guide? Let us move closer. Why, yes, I seem to recognize him. It is my old—" Harry gave a sudden lurching movement that knocked the table forward several inches. The others opened their eyes in alarm and saw my brother's entire body tense and spasm in the most disconcerting fashion.

"Mr. Houdini!" called Mrs. Clairmont. "Dr. Wells! Is he unwell? Mr. Hardeen, shall we—?"

"I believe my brother has made contact with his spirit guide," I said, wishing silently that Harry were not quite so given to histrionics.

By now Harry's head had slumped forward onto the table,

although he maintained his grip on the hands of Mrs. Clairmont and Lieutenant Murray. For a moment the only sound to break the silence was my brother's heavy, ragged breathing. Then, slowly, his head rose from the table. The entire aspect of his face had changed. There was an expression of genial amusement that I had never seen before. He cleared his throat.

"*Guten Abend, meine sehr verehrten Damen und Herren,*" he said, in a voice totally unlike his own. He looked about with kindly eyes, smiling at our confusion. "Ah!" he said. "You do not understand. I speak English for you, yes? Very goot." The voice was deeper and richly accented with Germanic rhythms not unlike those of our late father. I looked at Harry in surprise. He was entirely transformed. His normally erect bearing was now slumped and weary, with the stiff, heavy movements of a much older man. "Allow me to introduce myself, please," Harry continued in the unfamiliar voice. "I am Herr Nicholas Osey, the spirit guide of your young friend, Mr. Houdini. You are confused, yes? I explain. It is not impossible—wait—a moment while I gather myself, please. The transition has required more energy than I thought."

Harry's head slumped forward and his labored breathing slowed. I looked around the table and saw that each member of the circle—including Lucius Craig—was staring at my brother with absolutely rapt attention. Harry's eyes fluttered open after a moment, and he raised his head once more. "Please forgive my momentary weakness. It requires a great deal of energy to break through the spirit veil. I am unaccustomed to it. It is only the remarkable stamina of young Mr. Houdini which enables me to make the attempt. He is quite an extraordinary young man. Destined for great things, I predict."

Harry turned to Mrs. Clairmont, as though seeing her for the first time. "You are the charming hostess of this gathering, are you not?"

Mrs. Clairmont nodded, uncertain how to respond.

"I am pleased to make your acquaintance. Your husband is a

fine fellow. He has told me much about you."

"My—my husband? Is he with you? Oh, if—"

"I fear not. He is new to our plane and not yet able to manifest himself in a form that you might comprehend. But I assure you that he is well and sends his glad wishes."

Mrs. Clairmont's hand fluttered to her throat, and almost instantly Harry's head slumped forward and the labored breathing resumed. "Th-the circle," he gasped in his familiar voice, "you must not break the circle—"

Mrs. Clairmont let out a cry and grasped Harry's hand once more. Slowly, my brother appeared to rouse himself, and the aspect of Herr Osey returned to his features.

"Forgive me," said Mrs. Clairmont. "I was momentarily overcome."

"Quite all right, dear lady," came the voice of Herr Osey. "It is not every day that such things occur, no? But I must be brief. Strong as he is, the brave young Mr. Houdini cannot stand the strain of this exertion for much longer. Even now I feel his noble life force draining away as he struggles manfully to preserve the link."

"But—but my husband!" cried Mrs. Clairmont. "Is there a message? When may I see him?"

For a moment Harry appeared to have lost consciousness. His head rolled back and a tight choking sound gurgled from his throat. With an effort, he mastered himself. "A message has been sent, dear lady. Until we meet again. *Auf Wiedersehen, meine lieben Freunde.*" With a heavy sigh, Harry slumped forward onto the table and lay still.

"Mr. Houdini? Mr. Houdini?" Mrs. Clairmont patted Harry's hand. "Are you all right, Mr. Houdini?"

With a faint groan, Harry began to stir. "What—what happened? I feel—I feel so strange."

I glanced at Lucius Craig, whose expression was one of mingled annoyance and admiration. As I watched, he appeared to reach a decision over some private matter.

"Mr. Houdini," he said heartily, "you appear to have made contact with the other side. My congratulations, sir. You have a very singular gift. With the proper training, you might well become one of the most powerful mediums of the next century."

"Do you really think so?" Harry asked, as if struggling to shake off the effects of his ordeal. "But I don't even remember what happened! Was there any message from Mr. Clairmont?"

Mrs. Clairmont clasped Harry's hand. "Your spirit guide spoke of a message, but I'm afraid it was all rather vague. It seems to have been lost in the strain of your effort."

"Was it?" Harry stood and stretched his limbs. "Such a pity. I wonder if—look!" He pointed a finger at his feet. "The spirit slate!"

Kenneth Clairmont was on his feet in an instant. He bent down and scooped up the slate, holding it aloft for all to see. A single word was scrawled upon the surface.

"'Always,'" read Kenneth. "Not much of a message."

"Hardly," agreed Dr. Wells. "It seems the sort of vague— Augusta! What's the matter?"

Mrs. Clairmont had risen from her chair and staggered away from the table. She might well have slipped to the floor if Harry had not sprung forward to catch her. "Mrs. Clairmont!" he cried with genuine concern in his voice. "Are you all right? I did not mean to—"

"I—I'm fine, thank you," she answered, as Harry and Brunson helped her to a divan by the bookcases. "Forgive me. It's just— it's just that—"

Dr. Wells stepped to the sideboard and poured a measure of brandy into a snifter. "Take a bit of this, Augusta," he said gently.

"Thank you, Richardson. I feel so foolish."

Harry appeared truly distraught. "Mrs. Clairmont, this was unforgivable of me. I am terribly sorry for your distress."

She smiled warmly at him. "But my dear Mr. Houdini, I am delighted, don't you see?" She set down the brandy snifter and began to twist at the wedding ring on her third finger. "You see?

'Always' is the word engraved on the inside of my ring! Do you realize what this means? Your message could only have come from my dear husband!"

Kenneth Clairmont looked at my brother in wonder while Dr. Wells and Sterling Foster examined the ring. Lucius Craig nodded his head sagely, as though he had somehow orchestrated the miracle.

"Extraordinary, Houdini!" cried Kenneth.

"How remarkable that Mr. Houdini should have come to us as a skeptic," said Mrs. Clairmont, replacing the ring on her finger. "It is marvelous to see the flowering of such a vigorous new medium."

"Astonishing," agreed Dr. Wells. "I was inclined to dismiss all of this business as claptrap, but in the face of this I must admit—"

Harry held up a hand for silence. "It *is* claptrap," he said quietly. "Complete and utter claptrap."

"What!"

"How do you mean?"

"It was a trick," my brother said. "I did this to show you what may be done along these lines by a clever magician. There is nothing at all supernatural in what has just transpired."

Mrs. Clairmont clutched at her ring. "But how—"

"Mr. Houdini," said Lucius Craig, seeking to regain command of the situation, "I well understand how you might hesitate to acknowledge the onset of such a tremendous and intimidating new gift. It is quite natural to feel confused and even to deny your strange powers. It was the same for me when I was a young man. I assure you, however, that under my tutelage you will—"

"It was a trick," my brother repeated, more emphatically this time.

"Then how did you do it?" Dr. Wells asked. "How could you possibly have known what was inscribed in Augusta's ring? How did the word appear on that slate?"

Harry's expression wavered. "I fear the answer does me no credit."

"Ha!" cried Lucius Craig. "He is determined to hide his gift! I tell you that this man is the most promising young medium I have come across in years! If his ability is a bit rough at this early stage, it will soon blossom into a fine and powerful talent!"

Mrs. Clairmont, having recovered her composure, stood and took my brother's hands. "Mr. Houdini, you could offer so much comfort if only you would embrace this strange and wonderful ability."

"Harry," I said, "it's time to tip the gaffe."

A pained expression crossed his face. "Mrs. Clairmont, I have taken advantage of your kindness and your trusting nature. You would do well to consider how easily I have done so." He gripped her shoulder, as if to drive the point home. "You wish to know how I was able to learn what was inscribed on your wedding ring? I assure you there was no great difficulty about this. I simply took your ring and read the inscription myself."

"Impossible!" Mrs. Clairmont cried. "My ring has never been off my—It's gone! My ring is gone!"

"Here it is," said Harry, holding up the jeweled band. "It is a simple enough maneuver. As I grasped your shoulder, you were distracted by the pressure and did not notice as I slipped the ring off your finger. Again, my apologies." He passed the ring back. "I did the same thing earlier this evening, while you were kindly showing me the portrait of your late husband downstairs. The only difficulty was in slipping it back on your finger without arousing your suspicions."

"You stole Augusta's ring?" asked Dr. Wells.

"Only to read the inscription," Harry said.

"I don't believe it! How could you have done so without—"

Harry adopted an innocent expression. "Have you seen your watch lately, Dr. Wells?"

The doctor's hand flew to the pocket of his waistcoat. "Why—it's—"

Harry held out his hand and let the watch dangle from its chain. "As I said, it's quite a simple maneuver."

Kenneth grinned broadly at the exchange. "Very clever, Houdini. It still doesn't explain everything, however. How on earth did the word 'Always' appear on that chalk slate? It's an ordinary school slate, isn't it? There's nothing tricky about it that I can see." He reached for the slate and tugged at the wooden corners.

"You can examine it as closely as you like," I said. "You'll never find the gimmick."

Kenneth looked at me. "What gimmick? It's nothing more than a piece of slate in a wooden frame. There's no room for trickery."

"That's what you're meant to think," I said, reaching for the slate. "In fact, there's an extra flap hidden there, with a hinge right down the center that you can barely make out against the black surface. It's quite hard to spot—in fact, I can't even make it out myself—but when the hidden catch is depressed, the extra flap springs across the frame. In effect, a new slate surface folds over the old one. If there's a message written on the inside of the flap, it looks as if the words have appeared from nowhere."

"I'm not sure I'm following you, Hardeen," said Kenneth.

"Here, I'll show you." I scratched at the frame with my thumbnail, looking for the latch. "Imagine that I had two identical playing cards and I wrote my name across the face of one of them. If—strange, I can't quite seem to make this work—if I dropped one card over the other without any of you seeing it, you would be convinced that my name had suddenly appeared on the playing card. It's much the same with the slate, only the mechanism is far harder to detect." I held the slate out to my brother. "Harry, I can't seem to work the flap. Would you—?"

"There's no flap, Dash."

"What?"

He shrugged his shoulders. "That's a perfectly ordinary school slate. So far as I know, Mr. Craig got it from the classroom down the street."

"Then how did the message appear?"

Harry took the slate from my hands. "Perhaps I'd better demonstrate."

My brother pulled out the chair he had been sitting in and placed it in the center of the room. He positioned two other chairs beside it, "Mrs. Clairmont, if I could ask you to sit at my right, just as you did earlier, and Dr. Wells, please take the place on my left. Thank you." Harry flipped the slate upright and wiped off the chalk message with his sleeve. "Now we shall put the slate on the floor at our feet, only this time you will be able to follow what I do, because the table is no longer blocking your view."

"I think I see," said Kenneth Clairmont. "You must have a duplicate slate beneath your jacket. You must have switched the slates while we were distracted."

"Impossible!" snorted Dr. Wells. "We'd have seen him do it! Besides, how would he manage such a thing without the use of his hands?"

"Perhaps the second slate was already on the floor, hidden beneath the carpet. He could have used his feet to nudge it into place."

Dr. Wells shook his head. "His feet were under control. Augusta and the lieutenant had their feet pressing down on his. He couldn't have moved them."

Harry smiled. "The solution will be obvious soon enough," he said. "Even my brother Dash will be able to grasp it. Let us proceed. Take control of my hands as before and place your feet firmly upon mine. Just so. Keep up the pressure. This is exactly as matters stood before, is it not? Now, watch very carefully."

I had seen my brother do some amazing things in his life by that time, but I must admit that his performance that night amazed even me. As our small party crowded around for a better view, Harry smoothly eased his right foot out of his opera pump, revealing that his silk stockings were cut away at the toe. He flexed his toes, then repeated the procedure with his left foot.

Expressions of confusion and surprise greeted this display. "I don't understand," said Kenneth. "Surely my mother and the lieutenant would have been aware of your feet slipping out of the shoes. I'm surprised those flimsy pumps didn't collapse as soon as your feet were out of them!"

"Mr. Bithworth," I said.

Harry nodded at me. "Exactly, Dash," he said.

"Jacob Bithworth," I said, with considerable wonder. "Very good, Harry. That's excellent."

"I'm afraid you've lost me," said Dr. Wells. "Who is this Bithworth, and what has he got to do with anything?"

"He's a cobbler," I said. "A friend of the family. Harry mentioned him the other night, though at the time I couldn't imagine why. That's why you disappeared so mysteriously the other day, wasn't it? You went to see Mr. Bithworth and had him put special supports in the saddle of your shoes—so they would retain their shape even though your feet were no longer in them. Mrs. Clairmont and Dr. Wells would never have felt the movement. That's why you've been walking so strangely for the past couple of days. Your feet must have been killing you."

"Indeed," said Harry. "It is also why I insisted on formal attire this evening. The discomfort was well worth it, as you can see. The supports served their purpose brilliantly. It's very useful to be on friendly terms with a cobbler, wouldn't you say, Mr. Craig?"

The medium affected not to hear.

"I'm sure I must seem very dim-witted," said Mrs. Clairmont, "but I can't see why Mr. Houdini's shoes are of such importance. And why are there holes in your stockings, Mr. Houdini? You don't mean to say—oh, good heavens!"

"I believe you have guessed the truth, Mrs. Clairmont," said Harry with a proud grin. "I wrote the message with my feet. Observe." We crowded in for a closer look as Harry flexed the toes of his right foot and used them to dip into the cuff of his left trouser leg. From the fold of fabric he withdrew a piece of ordinary chalk, grasping it between the first two toes of his right foot. With astonishing agility he then gripped the frame of the chalk slate with his left foot and held it up off the floor. In this manner, he was able to write the word "Houdini" on the slate, using the chalk gripped between his toes.

"I simply don't believe it!" cried Kenneth Clairmont. "You are as capable with your two feet as most people are with their hands!"

"Perhaps more so," Harry said. "And since my feet would have been free throughout the course of a normal séance, I would have been free to use my toes to ring a bell or pull a string or anything else that might be required to give the illusion that spirits were abroad. Is that not so, Mr. Craig?"

"See here, young man," the medium said, "if you mean to suggest that I am capable of what you've just done, you're sadly mistaken. I'm flattered that you think me capable of such acrobatics, but—"

"You can't escape me, Mr. Craig," Harry said. He stood and pointed an accusing finger at the medium. "I demand that you take off your shoes!"

"What?"

"Your shoes! Surrender them!"

"Houdini, that's enough," said Lieutenant Murray, speaking for the first time since Harry's demonstration had begun. "What difference does it make if he's a sham or not? It brings us no closer to finding the killer of Edgar Grange. I didn't come out here tonight to see you argue over parlor games."

Harry's head snapped back as if from a blow. "Can it be? Is it possible that you do not see? Lieutenant, Mr. Craig must be made to take off his shoes. It is the only way of proving my theory about the murder!"

"Your theory about the murder?" the lieutenant asked. "And what theory is that, Houdini?"

"Is it not obvious? I have demonstrated plainly how Mr. Craig was able to gain the full use of his feet without the others being aware of it."

Lieutenant Murray stared blankly.

"Harry," I said, straining to suppress a note of disbelief in my voice, "are you suggesting that Lucius Craig stabbed Edgar Grange to death while clutching the knife with his toes?"

"Of course! What other explanation could there be?"

I brought my hands to my head and slowly massaged my temples. "Let me see if I have this straight. While we were all sitting around the table, Mr. Craig slipped his foot out of his specially constructed shoes, gripped a knife firmly between his toes, and then reached around to stab Mr. Grange in the back?"

Harry's confidence appeared to flicker, but he pressed on. "Dr. Peterson said that the injury was shallow and that the killer was lucky to have inflicted a fatal wound. That would be consistent with my theory."

I pulled one of the chairs away from the table and sat down. "I don't know, Harry. If I had been seated here and Mr. Grange had been seated beside me, I would have found it somewhat daunting to twist my leg up over my head and behind the other man's back. I consider myself reasonably athletic, but that would be a little beyond me."

My brother chewed his lower lip. "Elbert Klack could have done it."

"No doubt, Harry. But Elbert Klack is a dime museum contortionist."

"Perhaps Mr. Craig is also—"

"Oh, for heaven's sake, Houdini," cried Craig, reaching down to remove his left shoe. "Here! Take the damned shoes! As you can plainly see, they are ordinary in every way. I'm pleased to say, moreover, that there are no holes in my stockings. I trust the matter ends here." The medium folded his arms and assumed a posture of wounded dignity.

Lieutenant Murray grunted. "I think we can dispense with the contortionist theory, Houdini."

Harry's lip quivered a bit. "It was a perfectly sound idea," he said.

"You think so, Houdini?" the lieutenant asked. "Did you ever stop to ask yourself why Mr. Craig should have wanted to murder Mr. Grange?"

Harry gathered some of his old resolve. "Because of the mind-reading machine."

Lieutenant Murray sighed heavily. "Mind-reading machine?"

Harry unfolded the piece of paper we had discovered in Edgar Grange's office that afternoon. "Look!" he said, spreading the paper on the table. "Do you see these symbols?" He pointed to the mosaic of spirals, zigzags, and wavy lines we had noted earlier. "These are simple geometric shapes of the type commonly used in mind-reading experiments. The subject is told to pick one of the shapes and concentrate upon it. The clairvoyant, or mind-reader, is able to discern which pattern the subject has chosen. Ordinarily it is done with a simple mirror or shiner ring. But with this device"—Harry jabbed at the illustration with his index finger—"the clairvoyant would be able to achieve his effect over a vast distance! He would not even need to be in the same room!"

"Houdini," Lieutenant Murray said, "you're not making any sense."

"Don't you see? It is a combination telescope and signalling device! Let us suppose that I asked you to be seated here at the table and choose from among several geometric patterns placed before you. Let us further suppose that I withdrew from the room while you made your selection. My actions would appear to be above suspicion, but my accomplice would be able to spy upon your choice through the telescope, then signal the correct answer to me using the mirror here at the other end! Simplicity itself!"

"Houdini—" the lieutenant began again.

"Don't you see?" Harry repeated, pointing at the bay window, "We came upon Lila Craig climbing a tree within sight of that window this very afternoon! She must have been practicing! She could easily have spied upon whatever was happening here in the study and then signalled the results to her father while he waited in a different room!"

"So let me see if I'm following you, Houdini," said the lieutenant. "You're saying that Lucius Craig has worked up this so-called mind-reading machine, the better to persuade everyone of his psychic powers. Somewhere along the line, Edgar Grange discovered the machine, so Craig was forced to kill him—which he did by wielding a knife with his foot."

Harry folded his arms. "Exactly, Lieutenant."

"Houdini, that is absolutely the most harebrained idea I've ever heard. I will personally see to it that you never again—"

We never found out what my brother would never again do. At that moment, three things happened in rapid succession. First, the lights went out. Next, Mrs. Clairmont let out a scream so powerful that it rattled the chandelier. Lastly, a glowing apparition appeared at the center of the room.

It must be admitted that this latest apparition was not nearly so frightening as its predecessor. For one thing, it was decidedly more solid, with none of the pulsing evanescence that had been so notable on the previous occasion. Additionally, it moved with a strangely earthbound clumsiness, as though perhaps the eyeholes of its sheet were misaligned, while the earlier ghost had appeared to float through the air. Still, it was the best I could do on short notice.

"Who is that?" Harry whispered, coming up beside me.

"Bess," I replied tersely. "I had Brunson sneak her into the sideboard before we got started."

"You did this without telling me? But I—"

"It never hurts to have a back-up plan." I motioned for him to be quiet.

Bess lifted her arms as she moved slowly toward us. The phosphorus-coated sheet she wore gave her an appropriate glow but restricted her movements. As she moved closer, she narrowly avoided stumbling into the spirit screens behind Lucius Craig's chair.

I had left one candle burning at the center of the séance table, and in the guttering light I could see the others held rapt by this strange, if heavy-footed, vision. Only Lieutenant Murray seemed immune to any feeling of surprise. In the dim light, he pointed to me and raised an eyebrow, an unspoken query as to whether I was responsible for the apparition. I nodded in return. He smiled slightly and turned back.

"Who dares?" Bess intoned in a marvelously throaty contralto. "Who dares summon me to this place?"

My plan was simple. Bess would wave her arms and reel off some of my surmises about the death of Edgar Grange. The idea was to rattle the man I suspected of being the murderer and provoke him to attempt to flee. Stepping back from the table, I positioned myself near the door to intercept him.

It was a good plan, and had it been allowed to continue, it might very well have worked. There was, sad to say, one thing I had not counted on. As Bess moved closer to the table, a strange pool of light rose up out of the darkness behind her.

"My God!" Harry cried, as the shimmering mass resolved itself into the silhouette of a man. "It's—"

"Yes," I said. "It's the ghost of Jasper Clairmont."

~~11~~

THE SECOND GHOST

THERE WAS NO TIME TO THINK. I WATCHED IN DISBELIEF AS the apparition grew in size, filling the room with light, a glinting dagger clutched in its hands. With its glowing eyes and translucent form, it seemed to be the very embodiment of menace, hovering uncannily in the air. I fought back a mounting sense of horror as it drew up behind Bess and raised the dagger high overhead.

"Harry!" I shouted. "Stop him!"

But my brother was already in motion. With a powerful leap he bounded onto the table and hurled himself across the darkened space. I rushed forward and snatched Bess out of harm's way even as Harry sailed past, throwing his arms wide to tackle the apparition. I watched in disbelief as my brother's arms passed through the glowing figure as though it were pure vapor. Harry gave a cry of alarm and fell heavily onto the floor in front of the bookcases.

"Someone get the lights back on!" shouted Lieutenant Murray. As the illumination was restored, the ghostly figure faded from view.

"Harry, are you all right?" I cried.

"Of course!" he answered.

"What about Bess?"

"She's fainted. The shock has been entirely—"

"I'm perfectly fine," Bess said indignantly, pulling off the clumsy sheet. "Stop fussing over me!"

Harry grabbed her hands and knelt beside her. "If that creature had hurt you, I'd have never—"

"Is she all right?" Lieutenant Murray came up behind Harry, his face taut with concern. "Mrs. Houdini?"

"I'm fine," she insisted. "What was that thing?"

"Lieutenant, there's no time for this," I said, standing up. "We have to—Craig! Where's Lucius Craig?"

The lieutenant sprang to his feet. "I'll be damned!" He pushed open the window and gave a blast on his police whistle. "I've got Flaherty outside. He won't get away."

I made for the door. "We can't wait! They'll destroy it!"

Lieutenant Murray grabbed my shoulder. "They?"

"Come on!" I bolted for the door with Harry and the lieutenant at my heels, leaving the others frozen in their places with expressions of confusion and disbelief stamped on their faces.

"Hardeen," Lieutenant Murray called after me as we reached the hall, "who or what are we after?"

"It's a generator of some sort," I said, pausing at the top of the stairs. "It's somewhere in the house. Lieutenant, search the rooms on this floor. Harry, you take the upper story. Whatever you do, don't let anyone leave!"

"Hardeen, what the—"

"Dash, how did—"

"No time!" I turned and bolted toward the stairs, with my brother and the lieutenant calling after me,

I took the main stairs four at a time, vaulting over the newel post at the bottom and landing heavily beside the door to the cellar. The door was locked. I had my picks out in a flash and matched the Orkam shaft-clasp with a number two diamond-head. The lock snapped open in seconds. I pushed the door open and hurried down the open wooden steps.

At first it appeared to be an ordinary wine cellar. In the dim light I could make out seven floor-to-ceiling racks filled with dusty bottles, along with several open shipping crates and a vast quantity of packing straw. Beyond the furnace I could see a low opening that widened into a furnace room. Ducking through the opening, I found a double-sized Everson furnace, a supply of fuel, a metal washtub and wringer, and various other household implements. In the far corner were several wooden pallets pushed together and a long deal table, the surface of which was covered with sparking guns and glass retorts and rheostats and several other types of laboratory equipment. At the center of the table sat a piece of machinery unlike anything I had ever seen. It featured a heavy, open wooden cabinet with a small glass window at one end and a malodorous glass bulb burning within. A strange metal spindle jutted up behind the bulb, topped by a metal disk punched with holes in a spiral pattern.

As I stepped closer to examine the strange device I became aware of a movement behind me. I turned and found myself face to face with the ghost of Jasper Clairmont.

The apparition appeared far more solid now and human in scale, though I barely had time to register these facts before it lunged forward, cleaving the air with its glinting dagger. I threw myself back as the blade passed, feeling the chop of wind against my face. Reeling backward, I regained my footing as the ghostly figure turned and raised the weapon once again. I avoided the swing more easily this time and managed to snatch up a metal coal shovel from the floor.

With this weapon in hand, I circled the apparition warily, looking for a chance to knock the blade out of its hands. The figure made a savage thrust at my face, but I parried and batted the knife aside with the shovel. A second thrust brought the knife slicing toward my neck. I brought the shovel up again, catching my assailant's arm with the haft. Seizing the opening, I aimed a kick at my attacker's knee. Beneath the flowing cloak of white, I heard a gratifyingly human cry of pain. The knife and the shovel clattered to the floor.

Raising my fists, I let fly with a battery of jabs to the head. These drove the figure halfway across the room amid a series of grunts and curses. A right cross to the chin sent my assailant stumbling over the metal washtub, but he recovered quickly, gripping the fallen coal shovel and slamming it full force against the side of my head.

The blow sent me flying backward. Staggered, I found myself on my knees as blood flowed freely from a gash across my forehead. I scrambled to my feet as my opponent raised the metal shovel for another swing. I barely managed to raise my arms as the weapon came crashing down. I heard a sharp crack in my forearm and felt a fiery jolt of pain. My knees buckled and I sank back to the floor.

"Your arm is broken, Hardeen," said a familiar voice. "You might as well give in."

Cradling my wounded arm, I struggled to my feet. "That device," I said, my voice coming in ragged gasps. "That device—it's some sort of ghost projector! You used it to kill Edgar Grange!"

"A ghost projector?" my assailant said, pulling the white canvas hood from his shoulders. "Not at all, Hardeen. It is something far more incredible. It's called television."

With that, Sterling Foster raised the metal shovel and brought it crashing down over my head.

I have no idea how long I was unconscious. I only know that I woke up with my head and arm throbbing with pain and found that one eye would not open. I tried to shift my weight and immediately wished I hadn't—I was bound to a chair with my hands strapped behind my back. Even the slightest movement brought spasms of agony.

"You're awake," said Sterling Foster pleasantly. "How nice. I'm not ready for you yet, however."

"Ready for me?"

"Oh, yes. I have plans." He turned and busied himself with

the strange wooden cabinet on his work table.

I glanced at the opening that led into the wine cellar and the steps beyond. My right arm was useless but I still had feeling in the left. Tentatively, I worked my fingers to test the constraints at my wrists. Rope. Heavily knotted. With two good arms, this would not have been a problem, but now?

"If you're waiting for your brother and Lieutenant Murray to come to your rescue, you needn't bother," Foster called over his shoulder. "They're still chasing after Lucius Craig. They left the premises more than half an hour ago. I popped upstairs, you see, and told them I'd seen the lot of you running off toward Park Avenue—you, Craig, that policeman out front. We won't be disturbed. Not for some time."

"I don't understand. What is this place?"

"It's my laboratory. Augusta knows all about it, of course, and it amuses her to think of her dear, sweet, drunken brother pottering around with his glass tubes and copper wires. Of course, no one imagines that I actually do any work down here. They think it's just an excuse to spend time in the wine cellar. Being a drunk can be terribly convenient at times. Terribly convenient."

He bent forward to make an adjustment to the perforated disk at the end of the spindle. "The dish with the marbles," I said. "In the drawing we found in Grange's office. They weren't marbles at all. They were holes. Holes on a metal disk."

"That's right," he said, tightening a screw on the spindle. "It's the central feature of mechanical television transmission. The beating heart, if you will."

"Television," I said. "I'm not familiar with the term."

Foster gave a laugh. "I'd be very surprised if you were. No one's heard of it apart from a few enlightened souls on the fringes of the scientific community. But soon enough this device will spread throughout the entire world."

"But I don't understand. You used your—your televisor device to make—"

"Television," he said.

"You used your television device to make the ghost appear in your brother-in-law's study? Is it a cinema projector of some kind?"

"No, not precisely. It is a mechanical scanner. It's like sending pictures over a Marconi wireless set."

"That's impossible."

"So they say." He reached for a double-headed wrench.

"I know a little about wireless radio. You couldn't possibly send a picture. It's technically impossible."

He turned away from the device. "Not at all," he said patiently. "The process uses a narrow beam of light controlled by the rotation of the scanning disk. The holes on the disk are located in a spiral so that the successive openings provide scanning of small, elementary areas of an image in a tightly measured sequence. This has the effect of breaking up an image into a rapid series of narrow lines. These are then converted into electrical impulses here in the Foster tube."

"The Foster tube?"

"Yes." He indicated the malodorous glass bulb positioned in front of the disk. "Of course, I can't claim credit for the entire system. A man named Paul Nipkow invented the scanner disk; that was years ago. I studied with him in Germany for a time. He never put his ideas into practice. Couldn't resolve the problem of synchronizing the two disks."

"Two disks?"

"One for scanning, one for receiving. The problem is that the two disks have to be spinning at exactly the same rate or the system won't work."

"I take it you've solved the problem."

"Nearly. I'd have gotten there soon enough if that skinflint brother-in-law of mine had advanced me the necessary research funds. It's quite simple really." He walked to the device and unscrewed the glass cylinder. "This is the Foster tube, a combination bulb and focusing lamp. It has a broad enough spectrum to compensate for any deviation in the synchronization of the disks, and at the same time it resolves and focuses the image in the manner of a—are you following this at all?"

"A bit." I shifted in the chair, trying to keep the movement of my arms hidden from view. "Somehow you used this apparatus to project the image of a knife-wielding ghost to your brother's study."

"Very effective, wasn't it? Unfortunately, in its present state my device is only capable of producing shadows and flickers, and even these are barely discernible much of the time. It is my primary difficulty at present. As it happens, however, these crude impressions and pulses of light are just the thing for creating the impression of a spirit visitor. What is a ghost supposed to be, anyway, but a translucent shadow? Primitive, yes. I might have improved the image somewhat, but I was reduced to using those foolish spirit curtains as a screen." He pointed to the glass window on his wooden cabinet. "When the device is perfected, the images will be properly focused onto this receiving lens."

"You projected an image of yourself onto the screens behind Craig's chair? How? The séance took place on a different level of the house! There must be a dozen walls separating the two rooms."

He smiled encouragingly, as if I were a schoolboy just beginning to grasp the fundamentals of geometry. "You are still thinking in terms of a cinema projector. This is not a cinema projector. I do not need a line of sight."

"But it must be a distance of some hundred feet!"

"Young man, when my technology is perfected, I will be able to transmit images much farther than that. Perhaps as far as a dozen miles. More, when I've solved a few technical hitches."

"But there were no wires of any kind!"

"None were needed. There was a receiving scanner hidden in the music box. I projected the image onto the screens using a conventional arrangement of mirrors and lenses hidden in the speaker trumpet."

I recalled seeing a smaller version of the disk and spindle inside the music box. "It's too fantastic," I said, shaking my head. "You couldn't possibly have managed it. You never left this room."

"There was no need."

I shook my head again. "It can't be. Edgar Grange was stabbed to death in that room. You couldn't have done that. Not with flickers and pulses of light."

"I didn't. I only televised an image of myself doing so. My accomplice did the actual stabbing."

"Your accomplice?"

"Lucius Craig, dear boy. Of course, he's of no further use to me now."

"Lucius Craig stabbed Edgar Grange? I don't see how. Not the way we had him tied."

"Yes. Your brother with his clever knots. Tell me, Mr. Hardeen, did it not strike you as at all strange that Lucius so readily volunteered to be tied up? That he knew where a length of rope might be found?"

"You're saying he wanted to be tied?"

"It was the best means of insuring that he would not be accused of doing the dreadful deed. If your brother hadn't suggested it as a safeguard against fraud, Lucius would have asked to be constrained so as to avoid following the siren call of the spirits to the other world. Like Odysseus lashing himself to the mast." Foster adjusted the flame of a Bunsen burner. "Of course, once your brother declared himself to be the world's greatest magician and escape artist, Lucius saw little difficulty in getting him to agree to the constraints."

I tugged again at the knots binding my own wrists. Every movement brought a searing flash of pain. "How did he get out of the ropes?"

Foster flicked a trip switch and watched as the metal disk began to spin. Frowning, he flicked the switch off again.

"How did he get out?" I repeated.

"He didn't. Not in the way you mean. I thought your brother might have stumbled across our little secret when he began poking around the séance table. He realized that the table had been specially constructed to Lucius's exacting standards. What he didn't fully appreciate was that the chairs had been, as well."

"A break-away armrest," I said. "I've only read about such things. The European mediums sometimes make use of them. A medium's arms can be securely bound to the armrests, but that's no hindrance, because the armrests themselves pull away cleanly from the base of the chair. When the medium is done ringing a bell or shaking a tambourine, he simply drops the armrest back into place."

"In this case the medium was able to reach across and stab a man in the back. Of course, Lucius never expected that he would be making use of the device in quite this way, but it couldn't be helped."

"But why do it in this manner? Surely there are simpler ways of killing a man."

Foster shook his head sadly. "Hardeen, you really must try to understand. Don't you see, if this had gone as I'd planned, I would have gained complete control over the Clairmont fortune! Not only would Edgar Grange have been removed, but I would have provided proof positive of Lucius Craig's so-called spirit powers! So long as Augusta believed that Lucius was bringing her in contact with Jasper, I would have been able to control her like a puppet! How do you suppose my sister would have responded if Jasper's ghost had told her to support my work? I'd have had all the money I needed."

"And Lucius Craig was willing to kill Edgar Grange for this?"

"Not precisely." Foster bent over a coil of wire. "Of course, he was only too happy to follow along with my plan at first. It would have brought him a comfortable living at Augusta's expense for as long as he cared to avail himself of it. He wanted no part of Edgar's death, however. I had to find methods of persuading him."

"Blackmail?"

"Well, yes. Obviously. Suffice it to say that his daughter is not quite what he says. He has had trouble along those lines previously and has been at some pains to erase those unfortunate memories. He was terribly eager to see that no mention of this was made to the authorities." Foster straightened up and brushed off his hands. "And now, Mr. Hardeen, I believe I'm ready for you."

I strained at my bonds. The pain nearly overcame me. "Craig wasn't the one who killed Jasper Clairmont, was he? That would have been before his time."

Foster looked at me with interest. "What makes you think that anyone killed him?" he said carefully. "My brother-in-law killed himself."

"I'm not a great believer in coincidence," I said. "According to Mr. Grange's appointment book, he had a meeting scheduled with Jasper Clairmont on the day of Clairmont's suicide. The notation made reference to filing papers at City Hall. Since there was a patent application attached to the drawing we found—"

"It wasn't fair!" Foster shouted, suddenly roused to a high state of agitation. "My brother-in-law was going to steal my invention right out from under me. Jasper had agreed to fund the research only if he retained a ninety-five percent share of the company. As though that were not sufficiently absurd, he wanted the patent made out in his name! He wouldn't have known a Nipkow disk from a wagon wheel, but he expected me to hand over all future profits to him for a few thousand dollars."

"So you killed him."

Foster studied his hands. "I did not intend it. My—my temper got away from me when he made his ridiculous demands. I threatened him. I may have struck him across the face once or twice. In any case, he felt it necessary to draw his revolver. I swear to God that I meant him no real harm. I was just angry. But at the sight of that revolver—" He paused and pressed a hand to his temple, as though the memory was causing him pain. "I pretended to calm down and eventually he set the revolver down on the desk. I took the gun and shot him at close range through the head. I was scarcely conscious of what I was doing. I seemed for a time to be under the control of a force outside of myself, as though mechanically synchronized with some distant transmitter. I could hear the others rushing toward the room and a plan came into my mind. Perhaps it was there all along. I heard my sister's voice calling to her husband from the hall, and I knew that I did not have much time. I placed the gun in his hand and tightened his fingers around it. Naturally the others assumed it was suicide."

"But the door was locked and there was no place for concealment in the room. How did you avoid discovery when they came through the door?"

"It wasn't difficult. I simply stood behind the door and hid there until they finally managed to unlock it. It swung open, and I pressed myself between the open door and the wall. Naturally they weren't concerned with checking behind the door. They rushed in and went straight to the desk. After a few seconds, while their attention was fixed on my brother-in-law's body, I simply stepped from my hiding place and rushed into the room, as if I had just arrived. I went into my drunk act. No one had any difficulty believing that I had been slow to respond to the sound of the shot." He closed his eyes and gave a shudder. "I regret killing him. It was a decision made in the heat of the moment."

"What about Edgar Grange? That was as calculated as anything one could imagine. Why did you have to kill him, too?"

"He had the plans to the Foster tube. He even had a model of the receiving unit. It would only have been a matter of time before he made the connection between my invention and the ghostly apparitions upstairs. I can't say I was sorry to see him go, in any case. He had seized control of the estate and was blocking every attempt I made to get what was owing to me. Worse, I believe that in time he would have married Augusta. That would have defeated all my plans. He had to go, and I found it pleasant that television was the instrument of his departure. The best part is, no one will ever suspect me. I wasn't even in the room when the killing occurred. Had I been present, I might well have emerged as the most likely suspect. But who would be suspicious of a man who was nowhere near the scene of the crime? Several people saw me carried from the house, but no one saw me creep back into the cellar. It enabled me to be suitably indignant afterwards. I was terribly convincing, don't you think?"

"There was something on your face," I said, trying to recall. "A dark smudge."

"Makeup. I was experimenting. The scanner is not so refined as I hope to make it. In order to register the features, they must be outlined with heavy coal and ochre. A mask was better suited to my purpose, but in some cases only the human face will do." He stepped over to a shelf near the furnace. "Which reminds me, Mr. Hardeen," he said, fingering a tube of thick greasepaint, "it's time to get you ready."

"Ready? What do you mean?"

"Just sit still. This won't take long." He crouched over me and began dabbing thick smears of makeup on my face. "Hold still! Otherwise they won't be able to make out who you are."

"Who I am? What are you talking about?"

"Dear boy, must I explain everything? I thought you were a bright young man." He sighed and smoothed a line of dark foundation cream along my jawline. "I'm planning to put you on television, Mr. Hardeen. You'll be quite a sensation, I've no doubt."

I didn't like the sound of that. I shifted in the chair and tried to continue working at the knots around my wrists. "But why?" I asked, hoping to distract him from my movements. "Is this device really so important?"

"Important? My dear fellow, the Foster tube will put Edison's lamp in the shade! My little device will consolidate the work of

Paul Nipkow and launch an entire industry! Have you any idea what sort of money this device of mine is worth? Millions!"

I glanced at the oddly shaped glass tube. "But what is it for? What does television do?"

"Can't you guess?"

I shook my head.

Foster straightened up and wiped a smear of makeup with his handkerchief. "Isn't it obvious? It's for sending navigational maps to ships at sea! That's what made it so perfect for my brother-in-law! Have you any idea how much money is lost each year due to maritime disasters? Do you know how many lives are forfeit at sea due to foul weather incidents? With the Foster television system, a ship's captain would have the very latest weather information maps broadcast directly to the bridge from the nearest observational point on shore! It will revolutionize the shipping business!"

"Weather maps?" My eyes widened with disbelief. "All this for weather maps?"

"All this for the safety of ships and seamen" he said piously. "There is a considerable difference. One day the entire world will see it that way. I will be hailed as the man who rescued sea commerce from Mother Nature."

"But you've killed two men!"

"Three men, actually." He stepped back to appraise the makeup on my face. "I'm afraid we must count you in that total. I'm sorry for this, Mr. Hardeen. I truly am." His tone was disconcertingly light, as though remarking on a sudden change of weather. I tried to match the lack of concern in his tone.

"But how do you expect to get away with killing me?" I asked. "A third body will surely bring an even more thorough investigation by the police."

"Oh, they'll never find your body," he said cheerily. "You see, I'm planning to incinerate you." He uncorked a glass retort from the work table. The smell of kerosene filled the chamber. "Your death will not be in vain, however. I'm going to set fire to you on television. There's a kind of symmetry to it, you see. First Edgar was stabbed by a vengeful spirit, now you are to be consigned to the flames of hell. I trust the display will give my sister sufficient respect for the spirit realm."

"They'll never believe it," I said.

"Perhaps not, but at least you won't be in any position to contradict me. It's a sort of distinction, I suppose, being killed on television. Ironic, really." He closed one eye and sized me up as though preparing to carve a guinea fowl. "What worries me is the mess. I'll put the remains in the furnace, of course, but the rest will be a real bother to tidy up. Can't very well have the girl do it."

I felt a sense of cold dread as he advanced on me with the kerosene bottle. "My brother will never stop looking. He'll track you down if it takes the rest of his life."

"But your brother wasn't the one to find me, was he? Your brother does not strike me as a titan of the intellectual processes. No, I think the secret is safe with us." His eyes drifted back toward the work table. "Let us see, did I remember to leave the music box running upstairs? I believe so. Now then, Mr. Hardeen..." He raised the bottle and began splashing the foul-smelling liquid onto my clothing.

It had been my plan to keep him talking long enough to allow me to escape from the wrist restraints. As it happened, I had not yet managed to do so. Perhaps if my arm had not been so badly injured I might have succeeded, but as matters stood I was as securely fastened as ever. I was entirely helpless.

Or very nearly, in any case. I waited until Foster passed in front of me, then aimed a rabbit kick at his right kneecap. He went down hard, with the white cloak billowing like a collapsing sail. I pitched forward and struggled to my feet, dragging the ladder-back chair a couple of feet until I was nearly on top of him. I put the chair down and positioned myself to send another kick at Foster's skull. His head snapped back and his eyes closed.

I hoped he would stay under long enough for me to free

myself, but I didn't have a lot of confidence in my awkward kick. I hopped over to the laboratory table and looked for some means of freeing myself. Hot waves of pain rose from my injured arm, and I had to set the chair down again before I reached the table. I could hear Foster groaning behind me and realized I didn't have much time. Then my eyes fell on the metal Nipkow disk.

I dragged myself over to the device and found the lateral trip-switch at the base. Straining forward, I gripped the lever in my teeth, flipping the crossbar over to strike the contact points. I heard a sudden crackle of electricity and the smell of burning sulphur hit my nostrils. The disk began spinning, slowly at first, then gathering speed as the sound of a high-pitched metallic whine filled the air.

I don't know precisely what I hoped to accomplish. I believe I had it in mind that I would use the edge of the whirling disk to sever my bonds, in the manner of a spinning buzz saw. In any event, I had barely managed to turn my bonds toward the disk when Sterling Foster barrelled into me from behind, sending me sprawling onto the floor in front of the laboratory table. Instinctively I tried to maneuver onto my back to ward off his next blow. Burdened as I was by the chair strapped to my back, I could only flail helplessly on my side. Foster reared back and kicked savagely, catching my injured arm and shoulder with the full force of his boot. A bolt of pain blasted through me. My eyes began to dim. I bit down hard and tried to rouse myself, knowing that if I blacked out he would finish me. As my vision cleared I saw Foster stooping to pick up his knife from the floor. Bracing myself against the laboratory table, I swept his knees with my right leg and sent him sprawling. The knife skittered toward the furnace.

I knew that I could not hold my own against him for much longer. Twisting furiously, I braced my feet against the bottom of the laboratory table. The pain burned through me. Gasping with effort, I pushed against the table with my legs, trying to make it pitch forward. Foster, meanwhile, had crawled across the floor to recover the knife. He jumped to his feet and whirled to face me, the knife in one hand and the kerosene bottle in the other. His features contorted with fury.

The table teetered for a moment on two legs and then toppled over, sending all of the laboratory equipment crashing to the floor in a clatter of broken glass and jangling metal. As the whirling disk and glass Foster tube struck the floor, the flame from a shattered Bunsen burner touched off a pool of spilled chemicals, sending jets of flame snaking across the floor in a wild pattern. At the sight of the spreading inferno, Foster darted forward to save his precious invention.

It proved to be a costly decision. As Foster bent down, snatching at his glass tube, a crackle of flame from the floor spurted up to meet the kerosene spilling from the beaker in his hand. In an instant, a brilliant orange flare shot upward, engulfing him in a cocoon of fire. Shrieking madly, he staggered backward and slapped at the spreading flames. Instinctively, I made to help him, forgetting the ropes and the chair that held me fast. A spike of pain pinned me to the ground. I watched helplessly as Foster dropped to his knees. The smell of burning flesh reached my nostrils as his screams grew louder. The acrid bite of smoke and chemicals forced my eyes closed for an instant. When I opened them, a blackened face stared back, motionless on the floor beside me.

I had little time to register this gruesome vision. Streaks of flame surrounded me, and I could do little to avoid them. A curtain of fire separated me from the opening on the other side of the room. Turning away from the spreading blaze, I pushed myself along on my side to get away from the flames. Each breath brought a searing heat into my lungs. I huddled in a far corner as best I could, my cheek pressed against the floor, my eyes swimming in the stinging heat.

I closed my eyes, knowing that it would not be long now.

★ ★ ★

That's when I felt myself lifted into the air like a sack of potatoes.

"Easy, Dash," came my brother's voice. "We'll be safe in a minute."

Cool air rushed against my face.

"How—?" But my voice failed, ravaged by smoke. I opened my eyes. Harry's hands, blackened with soot, were pulling at my bonds.

"How did we find you?"

I nodded.

"That device. Whatever it was. It came on suddenly. We could see you. Only for an instant, but it was enough."

Suddenly my hands were free, and Dr. Wells bent forward with a cooling cloth. Lieutenant Murray hovered behind him, his face white with concern.

"But—how—" my throat seemed to be embedded with shards of glass. "How did you find me in time?"

Harry's mouth tightened in a grim smile. "You have Mr. Brunson to thank for that," he said.

I turned my head to look at the elderly butler, who stood beside the lieutenant with an air of quiet pride.

"With your permission, sir, it was that chair. That chair strapped to your back. It has been missing from the dining room for some time. I've asked Mr. Foster to return it several times..."

My eyes closed under the press of a cool cloth. I could hear my brother's laughter, and then nothing at all.

~~~ 12 ~~~

THE EYE OF THE NEEDLE

"IT IS SO GOOD OF YOU TO JOIN US, MR. HARDEEN," SAID MRS. Clairmont. "I trust your injuries are nearly mended?"

I raised the plaster cast on my arm. "The doctor assures me I'll be rid of this in another week or so. Otherwise, I'm perfectly sound."

"He'll be right as rain," agreed Dr. Wells. "Quite a hardy constitution on this lad."

"I'm so pleased," said Mrs. Clairmont. "How lovely to see you again, as well, Mr. Houdini."

"The pleasure is ours," my brother replied. "May I present my wife, Bess Houdini? I don't believe the two of you were properly introduced the other evening."

"No, indeed," said Mrs. Clairmont. "It is a pleasure, Mrs. Houdini, and may I say that I greatly prefer your present attire to the glowing sheet in which I first saw you. Ah, Lieutenant Murray! How pleasant!"

"I'm pleased to see you looking so well, Mrs. Clairmont," said the lieutenant, stepping forward to take her hand. "The commissioner sends his regards."

"My health is still a bit fragile," she admitted, indicating the rolling basket chair in which she sat, "but I am grateful for the opportunity to take the air."

Several weeks had passed since the strange conclusion of the events at Gramercy Park. Much had occurred in the intervening time. Sterling Foster had been quietly interred in the family plot at Hyde Park, next to his late brother-in-law. The investigation into the murder of Edgar Grange had been quietly brought to a close by Lieutenant Murray, acting on direct orders from the commissioner.

The exact particulars had been concealed from Mrs. Clairmont, who was not present to witness the bizarre climax on that fateful evening. Her health had been thrown into a precarious state by the shock of the ghostly manifestations that night, and it was feared that the full truth would cause her permanent harm. Under the watchful eye of Richardson Wells, the matter had been entirely hushed up. To spare her the anguish of her brother's perfidy, Mrs. Clairmont had been given to understand that Sterling Foster had fallen asleep amid his test tubes and beakers on the night in question, suffering a fatal heart attack when an untended experiment caught fire. In this more palatable version of the events, Lucius Craig had been cast as the sole villain, fleeing in such haste that he had been forced to leave his daughter behind.

In fact, Sterling Foster had set the police on a false trail that evening, to allow him time to put his plan into effect. The confusion had allowed Lucius Craig to avoid capture and vanish without so much as a hint of his whereabouts, though the police had been relentless in their efforts to track him. There were scattered reports that he had been sighted in such far-flung places as California and Nova Scotia, but in each instance the local authorities came away empty-handed.

Once again, to my brother's distress, he had been denied any public credit for his part in the resolution of a murder investigation. "It's just not fair," he had groused, "I do all the detecting, and the world is denied the tale of my genius."

For my part, I had been content to emerge with my life. Only later, while relating the tale to my friend Biggs from my hospital bed, did I realize how very close I had come to sharing

Sterling Foster's fate. "I thought I'd had it," I told him. "Harry literally walked through fire to pull me to safety."

"Funny," Biggs had answered. "In his version, he's walking on water."

Biggs, too, had been bound by the conspiracy of silence, though he had borne it with better humor than my brother. It pained him to miss out on breaking a good story, but his friendship for Kenneth left him sympathetic to the motives of Dr. Wells and the commissioner of police.

It had come as something of a surprise, then, when Mrs. Clairmont wrote to ask us to meet her in Central Park on that crisp Saturday afternoon. We had found her in the shadow of the stately Belvedere Castle, busily working at a needlepoint sampler. She looked appropriately regal in a tied bonnet and high collar, with a red travelling blanket neatly tucked about her legs. Dr. Wells stood behind the wicker chair, anxiously adjusting the blanket to ward off the effects of a chill breeze sweeping across the meadow.

"I've had a letter from Kenneth this morning," Mrs. Clairmont said, waving away the doctor's ministrations. "I'm certain that he would want me to send his warmest regards to the both of you. You've heard that he has resumed his medical studies?"

I nodded. "We were delighted to hear it."

"Dr. Wells assures me that he has a promising career ahead of him."

"What about your husband's business concerns?" Harry asked. "We were given to understand that Kenneth was expected to take them up as soon as he was able."

Mrs. Clairmont smiled airily. "There are others outside of the family who may be able to carry on. I find that I am no longer so eager to retain control." She tightened her grip on the shawl about her shoulders. "I never had the chance to thank you properly for all that you've done," she said, raising her chin.

"That's not necessary," said Harry.

"I feel that it is. My brother's passing has left me quite

distraught, and I'm afraid I have become quite lax in certain matters. I could not let another day go by without expressing my gratitude. The two of you are in my thoughts every day. I can scarcely forgive myself for being so hoodwinked by Lucius Craig. If the two of you had not intervened, I might never have come to my senses."

Harry smiled and stole a glance at Lieutenant Murray. "You are exaggerating the role we played."

"I think not. And I had rather hoped that I might find some way of repaying the debt I owe you."

"It has been our pleasure," my brother said. "No other reward is needed."

"How very gallant," said Mrs. Clairmont, "but I had thought of something more tangible. It will be some time before I am able to move about in society again, but I have a number of friends who do considerable entertaining. Might I recommend your talents to some of my friends?"

"As entertainers, you mean?"

"Precisely. Kenneth tells me that you are working on a very interesting form of diversion, Mr. Houdini. What did he call you? A gustatory marvel?"

I tried to imagine a Park Avenue gathering that featured my brother dining on cutlery and burning cigars. "That act may not be quite appropriate," I said.

"Don't be so hasty, Dash," Harry said. "I have made a few refinements to the routine, to make it more agreeable to a general audience. Allow me to demonstrate."

"Harry," said Bess, "this is hardly the time or place for stone-eating."

"Perhaps not, but what I intend to do is no mere stone-eating effect. Mrs. Clairmont, I wonder if you would do me the honor of lending your assistance."

"My assistance? Of course, Mr. Houdini."

My brother stepped to her side and knelt beside the chair. "I notice that you have brought your sewing basket. If you are anything like my mother, you will have several packets of needles in there. Is this so?"

"Yes. I always keep a good supply on hand."

"Might I borrow one of those packets?"

Mrs. Clairmont appeared baffled by the request but readily agreed. After a moment's rummaging in her basket, she produced a packet of Clarkson sewing needles.

"These look ideal for my purpose," Harry said, tearing open the paper packet. He sprinkled the loose needles into his open hand and held them out for examination. "Does everyone see the needles?" he asked. "Is there anything suspicious about them?"

"Of course not," said Lieutenant Murray. "Why should there be anything suspicious about needles?"

"Why, indeed?" Without another word, Harry popped the loose needles into his mouth. Dr. Wells and Mrs. Clairmont looked on with alarm as Harry made an exaggerated chewing motion, rubbing his stomach as though he found the metal diet to be especially appetizing. Snapping and grinding noises could be plainly heard. After a moment, Harry made a large gulp of satisfaction, indicating that the needles had been swallowed.

"How very delectable—" he began.

"What have you done, lad?" cried the doctor. "Those needles will play havoc with your digestive tract!"

"Do you think so? Well, I guess we had better do something about that. First, may I ask you to take a quick look inside my mouth? As a medical man, you can offer your assurance that I have not concealed the needles beneath my tongue or something of that sort."

"Houdini, this is most irregular."

"Indulge me," my brother said with a smile.

With a sigh, Dr. Wells stepped forward and peered inside Harry's mouth. "Open wider," he said, closing one eye for a better look. "Lift your tongue. All right." He stepped back. "There's nothing hidden in there," he said firmly.

"Thank you," said Harry. "Mrs. Clairmont, if you would open your sewing basket once more, I shall trouble you for a length of cotton thread. Three feet or so should do nicely. I would also like to ask you to knot the thread in some distinctive way. You may wish to put a series of knots at regular or irregular intervals, or perhaps you might wish to tie a single knot that is doubled or tripled. I only wish to insure that you will recognize this piece of thread when you see it at the conclusion of my effect." Harry nodded approvingly as Mrs. Clairmont deftly tied off a series of six knots.

Taking the thread from Mrs. Clairmont, Harry placed one end in his mouth and began sucking it into his mouth as if it were a long noodle of some kind. Again he made exaggerated swallowing sounds and patted his stomach to indicate that he found the thread to be especially tasty. After a moment or so, he had drawn in all but the tail end of the thread, which was left dangling from his lips.

Silently thrusting his index finger into the air, Harry motioned for our strictest attention, as if our focus might have wandered during this singular display. With a count of three upon his fingers, he pinched the visible end of the thread between his thumb and index finger and slowly began to draw its length from his mouth.

After a moment, a tiny sliver of metal glinted in the afternoon sun. One of the needles Harry had swallowed could be seen dangling upon the thread. Mrs. Clairmont let out a cry of surprise. Harry merely smiled and continued tugging at the thread. A second, and then a third needle emerged from his mouth, followed by half a dozen more, all neatly threaded upon the cotton strand.

In time this trick would become a signature effect of my brother's, known throughout the world as the Needles and Thread. It became a favorite impromptu stunt, and I would see him perform it for street urchins and also for a president of the United States, but I cannot recall any occasion that produced so profound an impression as that first showing in Central Park. By the time Harry had drawn the tail end of the thread out of his mouth, our small audience—Bess and myself included— had erupted in applause and cheers. Harry's cheeks glowed as he asked Mrs. Clairmont to confirm that the needles and thread were the same that she had lent. Upon receiving her confirmation, he bowed deeply and drank in our approval.

"Could you please show me how you did that, Mr. Houdini?" came a voice from behind us.

We turned to see Lila Craig standing behind us, clutching a woolen scarf in her hands. "Oh, there you are, dear," called Mrs. Clairmont. "Thank you for fetching my wrap. I'm sure Mr. Houdini would be delighted to teach you one of his tricks, if you ask him nicely."

"Would you, Mr. Houdini?" the girl asked prettily.

"It would be my pleasure, Lila," Harry said.

"Oh, that is not her name," said Mrs. Clairmont. "That is the name Mr. Craig gave to her. Her real name is Mina. Mina Stinson."

"My friends call me Margery," the girl said.

"How do you do, Margery," said Harry, lifting his hat.

"I'm thinking of sending her to school in Boston," Mrs. Clairmont said. "I see no reason why she should suffer for Mr. Craig's crimes."

"That is most generous of you, Mrs. Clairmont," I said.

"It is nothing. I predict a bright future for this girl, wouldn't you agree, Mr. Hardeen?"

"Most certainly."

"Mrs. Clairmont is too kind," said the girl, with a becoming smile. "I hope that you and your brother will visit me in Boston one day, Mr. Hardeen."

"I'm sure we shall," I said.

"Now, then, Margery," Harry said, pulling a pack of cards from his pocket, "here is an effect that will baffle your friends and confound your enemies. Watch closely as I shuffle the deck and cut it into three piles…"

"Hardeen," said Dr. Wells, coming up beside me, "might I have a word in private?"

"Of course," I said.

"Would you join us, Lieutenant Murray?" the doctor added, leading us along one of the walkways out of Mrs. Clairmont's hearing.

We walked for a moment in silence. Behind us, we could hear Mina Stinson's laughter as Harry's card trick reached its climax. After a moment, Dr. Wells stopped and looked back at Mrs. Clairmont's basket chair. "I wanted to add my thanks to Augusta's," he began. "You and your brother have done her a great service." He folded his hands. "More than she will ever know," he added significantly.

"You're referring to Mr. Foster's death?"

"And that of her husband," he said. "It's bad enough that Sterling engineered this plot against Edgar, but to have killed his own brother-in-law—it's incredible. Augusta must never know. She's far too delicate. I cannot impress this upon you strongly enough."

"The secret is safe with us," I assured him. "We're very good with secrets."

"You can rely on Hardeen," said Lieutenant Murray. "He's as good as his word."

Dr. Wells nodded. "I'm just grateful that Augusta wasn't in the study when that—that device started working again."

"But it's lucky the rest of us were," the lieutenant said. "Incredible thing. What did Foster call it? The televisor?"

"Television " I said.

"Well, whatever it was, it's gone now," Dr. Wells said. "Sterling's plans were nothing more than thumbnail sketches. There's barely a hint of how the machine worked."

"What about the music box in Mr. Clairmont's study? Foster told me he had hidden one of his special tubes in the speaker horn."

"It's gone now," Wells said. "Lucius Craig must have taken it."

I shook my head. "The apparatus I saw in the cellar looked pretty solid," I said. "Surely some trace of the machinery has survived."

Lieutenant Murray shook his head. "The entire room was gutted by the fire. I'm telling you, Hardeen, it's a miracle that your brother managed to pull you out of there. It looked like a blast furnace when we got down there. I thought you were both finished."

I looked back toward the castle. Harry was entertaining Mina Stinson with a hand-to-hand card cascade. "I guess I'll have to owe him one," I said.

"It wouldn't do to have a lot of people coming around asking questions about the television device," Dr. Wells continued. "I've asked your brother to keep silent about that, as well. He agreed readily enough. He told me that it was a tale for which the world was not yet prepared." The doctor watched as Harry pulled a series of silver coins from Mina's ear. "Unusual man, your brother. He'll go far."

"Perhaps so," I said. "But there's one area where I will always be able to claim the advantage."

"What's that?"

I grinned and pushed my hat back on my head. "I've appeared on television."

"What did Dr. Wells want with you?" Harry asked, as we left the others to make our way home.

"He wanted to be certain that we intended to keep quiet about the matter. He was concerned about Mrs. Clairmont's health."

"Overly concerned, I would say," Harry answered.

"Surely not," said Bess. "The woman has suffered a terrible shock already. A second blow might well—"

"Mrs. Clairmont is not quite the delicate flower that she seems," Harry said. "She is a remarkable woman."

"What do you mean, Harry?"

He stopped walking and fished in his pocket. "As I was saying good-bye just now, she slipped this into my hand." He held up a piece of glass and let it glint in the fading sunlight.

"Good lord, Harry! It's the—"

"The Foster tube," he said. "So far as I know, it's the only one left."

"But that means that she knows everything!"

"So it would seem," Harry said.

I turned and looked back down the path, catching a receding glimpse of Dr. Wells pushing the basket chair toward the southern entrance of the park. "Well," I said. "I'll be a fish on a bicycle."

"Indeed," Harry said.

Bess studied the tube for a moment and then looked up at Harry. "What are you going to do with it?"

"Can't you guess?" He gripped the glass tube by its base and held it high over his head. Opening his mouth, he let it fall in.

"How very delectable," he said.

AUTHOR'S NOTE

In reading the final chapters of this book, some readers may well accuse the author of trying to pull a fast one. Houdini himself once had occasion to say, in similar circumstances, "Everything I do is accomplished by material means, humanly possible, no matter how baffling it is to the layman."

While the author has never vanished an elephant or walked through a solid brick wall, he is on firm ground when it comes to research. The strange device mentioned in the book's final pages was, in fact, conceived and patented many years before the action of this story, though many more years would pass before it emerged in a practical and commercial form.

As Houdini himself might have said, "Would I lie to you?"

the further adventures of

SHERLOCK HOLMES

THE ECTOPLASMIC MAN

Editor's Foreword

I was not the one who discovered the note from John H. Watson to Bess Houdini, but I was the first to recognise that John H. Watson was not the John Watson from Nebraska, who juggled meat hooks, but the famous *Dr* John H. Watson, biographer and companion of Sherlock Holmes.

It happened shortly after the death of Al Grasso, when we members of the New York City Society of American Magicians began sorting through the accumulated clutter in his shop, The Grasso-Hornmann Magic Company. Grasso's was – and is – New York's most peculiar landmark. It is the oldest magic store in America, and the spiritual birthplace of many of our greatest magicians. In almost any other magic store in the country you'll find the magic enclosed in glass cases. Not so at Grasso's. At Grasso's you dive into the tricks as you would a pile of leaves. It's not so much a store as a museum, a dim warehouse on the second floor of an old office building, where printed silks and tasseled wands and huge metal hoops are all jumbled together and randomly stuffed into boxes and onto shelves. The place is full of magic books and pamphlets, some of them very rare, none of them in any kind of order. In one corner is a scarred leather-top desk where Al Grasso kept his records, such as they were, and hanging above it there are more than one hundred sepia photographs of the great vaudeville magicians. And when the sun is shining in through the back window, you can catch a glimpse of some huge stage illusion among the stacks of packing crates – the corner of The Mummy's Asrah, or the golden tail of The Chinese Dragon – relics of the great full-evening magic shows of the 1920s and '30s.

It's a wonder that anybody ever found anything of use in all that dust and clutter, but every year thousands of magicians would come – beginners and professionals – and each of them would uncover the one book, trick, or memento which he had always wanted and had never been able to find.

Straightening the place out, then, even with the best of intentions was a sad, almost blasphemous task. We took our slow and deferential time about it, allowing the older members time to pause over each piece of memorabilia and tell stories of the old days. Working in this fashion, we did not begin excavating Al Grasso's desk until the third afternoon, and in the process uncovered a brittle, coffee-stained manila envelope marked "Return to Bess Houdini."

It was like hearing sleigh bells on Christmas Eve. We all knew that Al Grasso had been a close friend of Mrs Houdini. We also knew that sometime during the First World War Grasso's, then called Martinka's, had been owned by Harry Houdini. But most of us regarded Houdini as something of a mythical figure, and it just didn't seem possible that we could be holding an envelope, an envelope with coffee stains on it, meant to be given to his wife. Maybe it was something that had belonged to Houdini, we thought. Maybe it was the plans to an escape. The whole group of us, about seven that afternoon, stared at the envelope for about five minutes before someone finally dumped the contents out onto the newly cleared desktop.

The first item we examined did a lot to dispel our reverence. It was a photograph of Houdini and a friend, in which the great magician, unaware he was being photographed full length, was standing on his toes to appear taller than the other man. The Great Houdini was embarrassed about his height!

There were more pictures in the envelope, mostly of Houdini and other, shorter magicians. And there were letters to and from Houdini concerning the sale of Martinka's. And finally, there was a small piece of yellowed notepaper which had fallen to the floor and went unnoticed until Matt the Mindreader picked it up, read it, said, "Huh! The meat hook man!" and passed it to me. The note read:

12 December 1927

Dear Mrs Houdini,

   Again let me extend my warmest sympathies for the loss of your husband. I know what it is to lose a cherished spouse, and can well appreciate that the long months since his passing have done little to ease your grief. Under separate cover I am sending my chronicle of the adventure we shared in London, some twenty years ago now. Though I have no intention at present of making the facts public, I flatter myself that the account of your husband's remarkable exploits may bring some pleasure to you in these unhappy times. I remain,

Your Humble Servant,
John H. Watson

For the second time that day I felt the thrill of discovering a tangible link to one of my idols, and even more astonishingly, evidence that Sherlock Holmes and Harry Houdini had actually met! No sooner had I considered this possibility than an even more incredible one occurred to me: perhaps somewhere in the store lay an unpublished Watson manuscript!

As I recall it, I explained this possibility to my friends in my usual measured, sonorous tones. They insist I shouted like a madman. Either way, we began a frantic, reckless search for the manuscript in the darkest recesses of Grasso's. All the while I tried not to think of how slim the chances of finding it were. Even if Watson's manuscript had arrived at Martinka's, it would almost surely have been forwarded, discarded, or lost forever in the jumble that became Grasso's. But at that moment we were all too caught up in the search to worry about any of that. We must have looked like the Keystone Kops, diving into stacks of papers, dumping out cartons of documents, and rifling through the files; not missing a trick, as it were. Manuscripts were uncovered and hastily scanned, only to be revealed as treatises on dove vanishing or coin manipulation. Then, miraculously, after only twenty minutes or so, we found Dr Watson's manuscript. It had been serving as a shim under the unsteady leg of a goldfish vanish table. Ignominious as this may seem, it probably saved the manuscript from being thrown out.

The bundle was in fairly good condition, apart from the sinkhole where the table leg had rested. The first few pages were on the point of crumbling and the last few were stained with oil or grease, but all of it was legible. I know this because I immediately sat down and read straight through while my friends tried to repair the damage done by our search. If possible, Grasso's was now even more disordered than when we began cleaning it three days before, and we then abandoned all hope of restoring it to order; but I had an original, unpublished Sherlock Holmes story.

That's where my troubles really began. If discovering a Watson manuscript seemed unlikely, convincing the world of the discovery bordered on the impossible. I faced an army of disbelievers. To begin with, the sceptics said the writing was not Watson's; but surely he would not, at the age of seventy-five, have made his own longhand copies. Then there were those who doubted that he would have gone to the trouble of writing the story merely to cheer up Mrs Houdini. I can only answer that that is exactly the sort of man he was. Furthermore, in 1927 Watson had no real need of money and would have been able to pursue whatever writing appealed to him.

Though this case is unique among Holmes adventures, it was not the first time that Watson kept a completed story under wraps for reasons of discretion. His chief concern would have been to avoid embarrassing the august person involved in the episode. Whatever his reasons, Watson succumbed to viral pneumonia within two years of his note to Mrs Houdini. Surely Holmes took no interest in the project, so any hope of the story coming to light died with Watson.

No sooner were these objections answered than new ones were raised. Some people even went so far as to accuse me of having written the story myself, despite my assurances that I am an untalented boor. Then there was that contemptible faction that insists that Sherlock Holmes existed only in the mind of Sir Arthur Conan Doyle. They are a spurious lot, surely, but they comprise a large faction in the publishing industry and therefore could not be ignored. Finally, after many months of effort, I was able to convince William Morrow and Company, a sympathetic publishing house, that, however dubious the origin of the manuscript might be, it was still a damn good story. I leave it to the reader to make the final judgment. I myself have no doubts, and I assure the reader that the most fantastic assertions and events herein are the most easily verified. The episode related by Bess Houdini in Chapter Three is retold by Milbourne Christopher in his biography, *Houdini: The Untold Story*. The escape introduced by Houdini in the Epilogue became a standard feature in his stage show; and he recreated the amazing stunt described in the nineteenth chapter in the movie *The Grim Game*.

I have made a few awkward but, I hope, illuminating footnotes in those places where Watson's notorious murkiness asserts itself, but otherwise I will intrude no further on the reader's patience. Watson is in good form as always, a friend to the reader and the one fixed point in a changing age...

Daniel Stashower
New York City
February 12, 1985

Author's Foreword

In all my years with Sherlock Holmes I encountered only a handful of men whose wilfulness and ingenuity rivalled that of Holmes himself. One such man was William Gladstone, the late prime minister. Another was a gentleman in Cornwall who fashioned small weapons from dried fruit. But by far the most extraordinary of these was Harry Houdini, the renowned magician and escape artist.

Sherlock Holmes and Harry Houdini met in April of the year 1910. Holmes, drawing near to his retirement, was then at the peak of his fame. Houdini, twenty years the younger man, had not yet attained the remarkable international recognition that was soon to be his. The first meeting of these two men was by no means cordial, but while they never became intimates, there developed between them a tacit respect born of the recognition that each was the unparalleled master of his craft.

Their encounter and the remarkable events which attended it form one of the most singular cases of my friend's career. Houdini, always secretive concerning the details of his private life, forbade me to write of the matter within his lifetime. Regrettably, I am no longer bound by that constraint. Houdini is dead well before his time, and by a means which I myself might have foreseen.*

I return, then, to the year 1910. I endeavour to fix the year precisely, for I am not insensitive to the complaints of some of my readers regarding my carelessness with dates. This was the year in which George V ascended to the throne; and a time in which, though we did not know it at the time, dark reverberations throughout Europe drew us closer and closer to The Great War.

John H. Watson, MD
2 November 1926

One

❧

The Crime Of The Century

The crime of the century?" asked Sherlock Holmes, stirring at the firecoals with a metal poker. "Are you quite certain, Lestrade? After all, the century is young yet, is it not?" He turned to the inspector, whose face was still flushed with the drama of his pronouncement. "Perhaps, my friend, it would be more prudent to call it the crime of the decade, or possibly the most serious crime yet this year, but one really ought to resist such hyperbole."

"I must caution you not to make light of the situation, Mr Holmes," said Inspector Lestrade, standing at the bow window. "I did not travel all the way across town merely for your amusement. The case of which I speak has implications which even you cannot begin to grasp. In fact, I am somewhat overstepping my authority in consulting with you at all, but as I just happened to run across Watson here—"

"Indeed." Holmes replaced the poker in the fire-irons stand and turned to face us. He was wearing a sombre grey frock-coat which emphasised his great height and rigid bearing. Holmes was, as I have often recorded, a bit over six feet tall, thin almost to the point of cadaverousness, and possessed of sharp features and an aquiline nose which gave him the appearance of a hawk. Standing there with his back to the fire and his elbows resting on the mantelpiece, it was difficult to say whether he had struck a posture of ease or advertence. "I think it would be best, Lestrade, if you told your story from the beginning. You say that you suspect this young American of a great crime, is this so?"

"It is."

"And what did you say this fellow's name was?"

"Houdini."

"Yes, Houdini. Watson, will you have a look in the index?"

I selected one of the bulging commonplace books from its shelf and began paging through the entires. "H-o-u, is it? Here is the Duke of Holderness, and here – ah yes! Houdini, Harry. Born on March 24, 1874, in Budapest. This is curious, though… there is also record of his having been born on April 26 of that same year, in Appleton, Wisconsin."

"Curious indeed!"

"He is an American magician, best known for his remarkable escapes. It is said that he has never failed to free himself from any form of restraint. He is particularly fond of challenging police officials to bind him in official constraints, from which he then releases himself."

I heard a suppressed chuckle near the fireplace.

"Houdini also has an interest in the new flying machines, and has actually made several short flights himself."

Lestrade scoffed. "That's just the sort of thing I'm talking about! What kind of person is it who tampers with unnatural machinery!"

"On the contrary, Lestrade, I'd say our Mr Houdini shows a keen interest in the advance of science, as well as a highly adventurous spirit. He sounds like a most surprising individual. Is there anything else, Watson?"

"Nothing," I said, replacing the heavy volume.

"I presume then that you have something to add to Watson's description, Lestrade?"

"I do indeed, Mr Holmes," said the inspector, reaching into his breast pocket for a small notebook. "Let's see… where to begin… ah, right!" Lestrade jabbed a forefinger into the notebook. "On the day before yesterday, this fellow turns up at the Yard and demands to be locked up in one of our cells! Well, I've been on the force near thirty years now and this is the first time anyone ever volunteered to be locked up. So we looked him over pretty carefully, and he says, 'I want to be locked up so

I can escape!' We all got a good laugh out of that, I can tell you. But this young fellow wouldn't give up! He insisted that he'd done the same thing in Germany and France, and he brought out the newspaper clippings to prove it!" Lestrade slapped his notebook against his open palm.

"Well, Mr Holmes, it's one thing to break out of those tin boxes they have over there, but our British gaols are the finest in the world. If this little American thought he was just going to walk in and walk out, quick as you please, we were only too happy to oblige him. So we took him into the ground floor cell block and put him in a free cage. Frankly, I thought he'd back away when he saw the lock on the door, but he didn't, so we locked him up tight. I promised to come back for him in a few hours, when he'd had enough."

Holmes looked over at the inspector. "And then?"

Lestrade clasped his hands behind his back and looked out of the window. "Thirty minutes later we received a telephone call in the C.I.D. office. It was Houdini. He said he'd made it back to his hotel alright and he just wanted us to know he'd left a surprise in the cell block. Naturally we didn't believe it, but when we got in there we saw that not only had he broken out, but he'd also switched around every prisoner in the entire wing! Seventeen prisoners and not one of them was in his right cell! We had quite a job just – Mr Holmes! I fail to see what is so amusing in all this!"

"Quite so, Lestrade," said Holmes with a short cough, "forgive me. But still, I don't see that your problem is as grave as you suppose. I'm sure it's simply a question of improving the design of your goal. Perhaps Mr Houdini could be persuaded to cooperate—"

"My God, Mr Holmes!" Lestrade cried impatiently. "Do you really think me such a fool as all that? The cells are nothing! That was only the beginning! But if he can get in and out of our gaol cells he can get in and out of anything! Anything at all! Some of the men even suspect… well, they suspect…" He paused and looked down at his notebook.

"Yes?"

"It's nothing."

"There, Lestrade, you were on the point of saying something."

Lestrade cast a wary eye at Holmes and then at me. "I don't believe any of it, mind you, but some of the men say that Houdini is a… a spirit medium."

"Oh, come!"

Lestrade held out his palms in a gesture of disavowal. "It's not my theory, I assure you, but it has to be taken into account. I've done a bit of research on this fellow and the results are very surprising. Very surprising indeed. Just consider the facts for a moment, Mr Holmes, and see what you make of them. Every night, on stages all over the world, Houdini allows himself to be tied up, wrapped in chains, nailed into packing crates, and I don't know what all, and he always gets free! Now what does that suggest to you?"

"Great skill and technical proficiency?"

"Perhaps, but don't you find it in the least strange that he never fails? Not once? Can you say the same?" Here Lestrade was referring, rather indelicately I thought, to the theft of the black pearl of the Borgias, an affair which even Holmes had been unable to penetrate. Though he would soon recover the pearl in a case I have recorded elsewhere,* the matter weighed heavily on him at present. I realised then how great was Lestrade's sensitivity over the issue at hand, for he was never one to open old wounds.

Holmes reached into the scuttle and threw a lump of sea coal onto the hearth. "Occasionally my methods fail me," he observed quietly, "but then, I receive no assistance from the other world."

Lestrade looked away quickly. "I didn't mean to give offence, Mr Holmes, I'm simply asking you to keep an open mind to this thing, as I've done." He flipped through the pages in his book. "Now, there's a group in America that calls itself the Society for Psychic Research. These aren't witch-doctors in this group, they're scientists and doctors, reasonable sorts like you and me. This society swears up and down that Houdini achieves his effects through psychic means. They say no other explanation is possible."

"And what of Houdini himself? Does he claim to traffic with the spirits?"

"No, he's denied it repeatedly. But don't you see? Even that fits the theory. If he were using special psychic powers to make a living as a magician, he'd have to conceal his gifts in order to protect his livelihood!" Lestrade gave a nervous laugh. "I know that what I'm saying sounds incredible, but two days ago this fellow walked out of one of our tightest cells without turning a hair. No one has ever done it before, and frankly I doubt if anyone will ever do it again. A thing like that sets me thinking maybe we are dealing with... well, with the unknown. Now I'm not saying I hold with all of this psychic claptrap, but after Houdini was at the Yard I went down to the Savoy to see one of these performances of his. What do you suppose I saw?"

"Do tell."

"It was astonishing. I've never seen anything like it. During the course of his magic show, Houdini had his workmen construct a solid brick wall on the stage behind him. There was no trickery about it, I'm certain. The wall was put together brick by brick; it was absolutely solid. And he had it positioned so that he couldn't get around it in any way, but somehow he managed to travel from one side to the other, right before my eyes! Right through the wall! Now how could he possibly have done that?"

"He was assisted by elves?"

"According to the Society for Psychic Research, Houdini can only do this trick by reducing his entire body to ectoplasm."

"Ectoplasm?"

"It's the substance of spirit emanations. What ghosts are made of. I know that sounds ridiculous, but how else could a man pass through a solid substance? At least at Scotland Yard there was a door in the cell, but this was a solid brick wall. So naturally when the theft occurred—"

"Theft?" Holmes was instantly alert. "Would this theft be the crime of the century you mentioned earlier?"

"The same. I can't give you the details just yet because the matter is highly confidential and involves certain highly placed individuals. But I'm convinced that the crime can only have been committed by someone who can walk through walls. Mind you, I'm not saying he actually does walk through walls, but he certainly manages to convey that impression. So if you would just come down to the Savoy with me and have a look—"

"Lestrade, this crime—"

The inspector held up his hands. "I'm sorry, I've told you all I can.

You are not an official detective, Mr Holmes, and this matter is absolutely confidential."

"Then I'm afraid I can't help you."

"What—"

Holmes threw another lump of coal onto the fire. "I am clearly out of my depth, Lestrade. Men made of ectoplasm, thefts of such high confidentiality." He shook his head. "No, no. It's too much for me. Watson, would you care to take a stroll in the botanical gardens?"

Lestrade's mouth fell open. "But – but you don't understand! All I'm asking is that you come down to the theatre with me and see this Houdini for yourself! Now where's the harm in that? It's not so much to ask, is it?"

"I'm afraid it is, inspector," Holmes said evenly. "You are asking me to enter into a criminal investigation with no knowledge of the actual crime. You are asking me to entertain a theory which accommodates men who walk through walls. I am not an official detective, as you have so conscientiously reminded me, but neither am I a haruspex. Should you need my services in matters pertaining to the corporeal, my door will be open. Until then, good day."

Lestrade let out a long sigh and moved towards the door. "It's just as well, I suppose," he said, taking down his hat and ulster. "We were given specific orders not to consult you on this case. I just thought—"

"Orders?" Holmes whirled about, his features drawn tight. "Orders from whom?"

"Why, the government, of course!"

Holmes stiffened. "What branch?"

"The message came from Whitehall. It was unsigned."

A high colour crept into the gaunt cheeks of Sherlock Holmes. "Lestrade," he said, his voice rigid with emotion, "either you are the most devious man at the Yard or you are an unpardonable lummox."

"What—?" The inspector stammered, but Holmes was already gone, running down the steps to Baker Street, blowing two shrill blasts on his cab-whistle.

ABOUT THE AUTHOR

Daniel Stashower is a novelist and magician. His works include: *Elephants in the Distance*, *The Beautiful Cigar Girl*, the Sherlock Holmes novel, *The Ectoplasmic Man* and the Edgar-Award winning Sir Arthur Conan Doyle biography, *Teller of Tales*. He is also the co-editor of two Sherlock Holmes anthologies, *The Ghosts of Baker Street* and *Sherlock Holmes in America*, and the annotated collection *Arthur Conan Doyle: A Life in Letters*.

THE SEVENTH BULLET
by Daniel D. Victor

THE WHITECHAPEL HORRORS
by Edward B. Hanna

DR. JEKYLL AND MR. HOLMES
by Loren D. Estleman

THE ANGEL OF THE OPERA
By Sam Siciliano

THE GIANT RAT OF SUMATRA
by Richard L. Boyer

THE PEERLESS PEER
by Philip José Farmer

THE STAR OF INDIA
by Carole Buggé

THE TITANIC TRAGEDY
by Willaim Seil

THE WEB WEAVER
By Sam Siciliano